RACHEL SINCLAIR

PRESUMED GUILTY

BOOKS

By Rachel Sinclair

Southern California Legal Thrillers

Presumed Guilty

Justice Delayed

Insanity Defense

Wrongful Conviction

The Trial

Vinci Books

vinci-books.com

Published by Vinci Books Ltd in 2025

1

Chapter One

AVERY COLLINS

Present Day

I WOKE WITH A START, as I always seemed to do nowadays. Most of the time, I woke up screaming or with the feeling of being suffocated. This time, I simply woke to the sound of my pounding heart. I looked around the room, which, as usual, had every light on, for I no longer could sleep in the dark.

At first, I thought I was back there – the place where my nightmares weren't nightmares at all, but, rather, were the moments of my waking existence. The prison cell where I spent 7 long years on a hard cot, eating disgusting food, showering in front of a bunch of other women and only seeing the daylight during the one hour a day I was allowed into the prison yard.

I soon realized I wasn't in my prison cell. I was in my bedroom, safe in my $10,000 California King. Snuggled beneath soft sheets, my head on a specialty orthopedic pillow that gave firm support to my neck and spine while I slept. I was very careful about my bed and my bedding because I was determined that, if I ever made it out of that Joliet, Missouri prison, where I slept on a rock-hard cot with thin sheets and a limp pillow for 2,756 nights, I'd treat myself to the very best that sleep technology had to offer. My settlement with the State of Missouri for wrongful imprisonment, which netted me a cool $10 million, definitely went a long way towards my realization of that particular dream.

I looked at the ceiling, seeing it was 3 AM. I was wide awake, and if history was any guide, awake I would stay. I sighed, seeing my boxer pup, Lola, snoring beside me while her sister and littermate, Harlow, lay sawing logs at the foot of the enormous mattress. They wouldn't get out of the warm bed for anything or anybody. I knew that, so I didn't even try to wake them.

I put my feet on the hardwood floor and went to the balcony attached to my bedroom. My *Harvard Class of 2020* mug was still on the small table, still filled with the nasty herbal tea I always took before bed because I couldn't sleep without it. A joint was stubbed out in the marble-blue ashtray, no doubt a leftover from my brother, Aidan, and some of his surfer friends who always seemed to be hanging around my house.

Aidan was 25 and in his last year of law school at the University of San Diego in the Linda Vista area. USD was a private Catholic college, which was ironic, as Aidan was anything but religious. He really only wanted to go to that school because it was the only decent law school in the area. When I graduated from Harvard Law and came out here to start my new life, Aidan was determined to live with me. This meant his choices of law schools were limited to the schools in the area. He thought for sure UCSD would have a law school, which would've been his first choice, but they didn't, so USD it was. He didn't mind it. The law school was secular, so his atheistic brain wasn't offended by having to be subjected to a constant barrage of, as he put it, "Jesusy bullshit."

I closed my eyes, smelling the scent of the ocean and listening to the waves crashing in. Lola the boxer nudged the French door open with her nose and came out to sit next to me. She lay down next to my chair and promptly fell asleep.

I looked at my phone, wondering if my former cell-mate Regina was awake. She probably was. Like me, she had problems sleeping. The poor woman was suffering from severe PTSD from her years on the streets, working as a sex worker, and she never felt safe, even in her own home.

She was currently working for me as an investigator, which was the perfect job for her, as she knew the language of the streets. Criminals were the same all over, and Regina understood them, much better than I did.

I picked up the phone to call her, seeing the clock read 4:11. She picked up right away.

"Yeah, girl, what's up?" she asked me. Her voice didn't have sleep in it, so my instinct was right. She was probably sitting on her own balcony, wondering when she would start hallucinating a domineering buddy like Tyler Durdan in *Fight Club*, a figment of the narrator's imagination brought to life by sleep deprivation.

"Will it ever get better?" I asked her, knowing she would know just what I was trying to say. We were cell-mates for the better part of three years, so we had long since developed a short-hand in our communication.

"No, dude, it's not," she said. "It's not, so don't even

think it's gonna get better. Life's a bitch, and then you die, man. Life's a bitch, and then you die."

She started coughing, the rasp blaring through the phone.

"How's your quitting smoking coming along?" I asked her, knowing the answer before she even said a word.

"Tomorrow, I quit," she said, and I could tell she was taking a drag even as she said those words.

"It *is* tomorrow," I said, looking at the clock again. 4:17.

"Shut up," she said, and I could imagine her deep green eyes rolling in exasperation.

"So what are you doing up at this hour?" I asked her.

"Talking to you, or did you forget you called me?"

It was my turn to roll my eyes. "I mean, I could tell you were already awake when I called."

"How could you tell that?"

"You didn't sound like you were asleep."

"What does a person sound like on the phone when they're asleep? I mean, do sleeping people talk on the phone these days? I wasn't aware of that."

I sighed. "You know what I mean."

"Yeah, I was just giving you shit. I was dying my hair when you called, actually. You're going to love it. Bright blue streaks. It's really kinda lit AF if you want to know the truth about it."

I imagined her jet-black hair with bright blue streaks and realized that if anybody would pull it off, it would be Regina. The woman was gorgeous, plain and simple. In prison, of course, she didn't wear makeup, but she didn't need to. Her skin was flawless and olive. Her hair was thick and dark, her eyes bright green, her cheekbones sharp enough to cut glass. Her body was curvy, but, in her case, "curvy" was not a euphemism for "fat," as so many women used the term. One of her arms was basically a tattoo sleeve, which didn't put off most men and plenty of women because it just made her seem hotter. Indeed, she was the woman most straight women pegged as their "one lesbian fantasy girl" - the one woman they would screw if they got permission from their husbands.

"I'd imagine your hair is. Lit, I mean," I said.

"Not just lit, but lit AF. Get it right." I could hear the laughter in her voice, so I didn't take offense to her words. "Anyhow, you called me for a reason, so out with it."

I drew a breath and shook my head, realizing I really didn't know exactly why I called her. "I don't really know. I guess I needed to hear a friendly voice. I knew you probably would be awake, as you're the only person I know who would possibly be up at this hour."

"I'm a vampire. What can I say," she said and then coughed again.

"That shit will kill you, you know."

"So will your bottle of Jack, but you don't hear me nagging at you about it. Besides, I got the patch. I just haven't put it on yet. Maybe if I take a long plane trip some-where, I'll wear that patch because I've talked to guys who've had a nicotine fit on the way to Singapore, and, trust me, that shit ain't pretty. But I don't plan on flying to Singa-pore anytime soon, so I guess you won't get your wish."

I pet Lola's head as she groaned in her sleep. Lola apparently had as many nightmares as I did. She was always whining, moaning and twitching as she slumbered next to her sister and me in our enormous bed. I specifically got the California King because I wanted my two girls sleeping next to me. Since they were both Boxer dogs and not exactly small, the bed had to be pretty huge for all of us to sleep in it comfortably.

I looked at the ocean and noticed that it was finally starting to get light out. The sand was beginning to get a pinkish tinge to it, and I could smell the strong scent of the strings of seaweed that washed up on the beach.

"Well, I called you in the middle of the night, so I guess I need to say something profound to make it worth your while," I said.

"Yeah, don't worry about that," she said. "If you had something real to say, you probably would've already said it. You just wanted to shoot the breeze with me because that's what you're used to."

That was true enough. My chronic insomnia began when I was in prison. It was hard to sleep when people all over were screaming and crying, and the temperature was near freezing or sometimes just too hot. It was also hard to sleep when you were obsessed about what went so terribly wrong. Regina didn't sleep much, either, so she and I would end up talking long into the night.

Now I had my freedom and was living in paradise and I still couldn't sleep. My therapist told me my insomnia came from buried rage about what had happened to me. My fury stemmed from the fact that my prosecutor hid DNA evidence that completely exonerated me. He also hid the fact that my friend was raped before she was murdered. Obviously, I would've been found not guilty if these facts would've been made known.

I took a deep breath. "You still there?" I asked her.

"Yeah, still here. Admiring my handiwork. I think you're gonna love it."

I looked around, saw it was now 5:01, and realized that Aidan would be getting up soon enough. He had an early morning gig at Starbucks, and I knew I would probably have to rouse him out of bed so he didn't lose his job.

While my brother looked like a typical surfer slacker – longish brown and sun-bleached hair, tanned skin, fit body – he definitely had the mentality of somebody on the move. Like me, he always blew the roof off any IQ test. He always got straight As, all through college and now law school, even though he didn't study nearly as much as other straight-A students did.

But he did tend to burn the candle at both ends. Case in point was last night, as he had several of his buddies over to smoke some weed, drink some beer, build a fire in my fire pit, and just watch the waves crashing on the shore. They were awake until 2 AM. This was actually comforting for me because there was nothing worse than tossing and turning for hours on end and knowing that nobody was around to hear you.

"Listen, I gotta go," I told Regina. "I think my brother needs to be roused out of bed so he's not late for work."

"You're not your brother's babysitter," Regina scolded. "He's a grown-ass man. He can get his own butt out of bed."

"Yeah, I know, but-"

"Whatever. Listen, I'll be seeing you later on today. Word on the street is you're getting a doozy of a case. Your ass will be in the fire if you take this one."

I didn't quite know what she meant. I did take many of my cases *pro bono* if I truly believed in the person. That was the advantage of my large settlement – I had enough money to tide me over for the rest of my life. I didn't have to work for money, so I often took cases as passion projects.

"What do you mean?"

"You'll find out what I mean. Trust me, you're going to get it good and hard with this case, without KY jelly. But only if you decide to take it."

I didn't even want to ask. "Will you please stop being so opaque and just tell me what's going on and how you know about whatever this is and I don't?"

"Dude, I got my sources. If I told you who they are, I'd have to kill you, and, well, been there, done that, not doing it again. Later." At that, she hung up.

I clicked the phone, patted Lola's head and saw that Harlow had finally decided to join us on the balcony. I didn't have time to think about what Regina was just implying about some juicy case I would have dumped on my lap.

I padded down the hallway to Aidan's room and heard his snoring. "Aidan," I said, nudging him. "Don't you have to be at your job in about an hour?" He usually worked the 6 AM-9AM shift, which worked well with his school schedule.

He opened one eye and squinted. "Who let the hamster sleep in my mouth?" he asked as he opened and closed his mouth and stuck out his tongue. "Water. I need water." At that, he got up and headed out the door of his bedroom and padded to the kitchen. He stuck his entire head into the sink and put the hose nozzle directly into his mouth. Then he put that same nozzle over his head, soaking his brown hair. "Much better," he said.

I tried my hardest not to give my usual big-sister lecture about how hard it is on a person's body to drink and smoke pot all night, then get up just a few hours later for work, then go to school and try to stay awake during lecture and try to answer questions. Like all law schools, USD used the 'Socratic Method', in which every student could be conceivably put in the hot seat about the reading assignment for the day. Granted, since Aidan was a third year, this method was much less intense than it was in the first year when the teachers were consciously trying to thin the herd. However, I knew he still had to know his reading assignments for class.

"Well, you better get into the shower quick and get your ass on that bike." Aidan had both a motorcycle, which he drove to his school, and a bicycle, which he rode to work. Since the Starbucks where he worked was only 2 miles from our condo, he usually could get out the door with only 10 minutes to spare and still make it on time to make his fancy lattes.

He saluted me, smiled and ran down the hall. I soon heard the shower going.

I fed the dogs, showered in my own bathroom, got dressed and packed three hard-boiled eggs, a handful of walnuts and a small almond milk into a small bag and got the dogs ready to go to their daycare. I got the harnesses on my dogs, and they eagerly leaped into my Tesla SUV, which was parked in the underground parking lot beneath my condo. I could hear them whining and panting in the back as I drove the 10 miles in God-awful traffic to my office.

Chapter Two

ONCE I DROPPED off the dogs and got to my office, I realized what Regina was talking about.

On my desk was a large manila envelope which looked like it contained a file. On it was a note from Steve Rattner, a good friend who was in the trenches doing criminal defense.

I read the note.

Have a look at this case if you don't mind. I ran into this client's cell-mate when I was in jail, and she's looking for counsel. She doesn't have a dime to her name, and doesn't want to take her chances with appointed counsel. She's facing the death penalty, so I don't blame her. I immediately thought of you because you're the only person I know who would take a case like this without pay. I hope you can take her on. Thank you.

I tore open the envelope and immediately saw what Regina was apparently talking about when she said my ass would be in the fire with this new case.

There was a case that had absolutely blown up in the media. A wealthy family who lived in one of those $15 million mansions on Coronado had recently reported their daughter, Aria, missing. It turned out Aria was not exactly missing, but was dead – she was found in the guest house, having been strangled with a hemp rope.

The live-in maid, Esme, short for Esmeralda, was charged with her murder. Esme lived in the guest house, in which Aria's $10 million rare pink diamond necklace was found. The theory was that Esme stole this jewelry, and when Aria confronted her about the theft, Esme murdered Aria.

I stared at the letter from Steve in disbelief. I knew why he'd thought of me for this case. He was right – there weren't many attorneys who would take an enormous death penalty case *pro bono*. Plus, I'd tried death penalty cases before. I was associate counsel on one six months prior, so I was the second chair. We lost that case, and our client was currently on death row, filing one appeal after another. I'd also tried quite a few murder cases in my short legal career. When I was at Harvard, I'd worked in the Capital Punishment Clinic, helping to represent clients facing the death penalty in Alabama.

I knew I could handle a large case like this, especially if I could rope somebody into second chair. But I was slightly nervous about *just how* high-profile this particular case was. Aria Whitmore's case was on the front page of just about every magazine on the newsstand. Aria's beautiful face and silky blonde hair stared out from the most recent *People* magazine. That publication featured a six-page spread on her life and death. There was also a small story about Esme. Aria also graced the covers of the lesser tabloids in the supermarket. These magazines were much more lurid than *People* and much sleazier in their reporting as well.

And, of course, this case was blowing up on TikTok. Endless videos were going viral with one amateur sleuth after another giving their theories on the case. Misinformation was rampant on X, Meta and Instagram, too.

What made me even more apprehensive about this one was how the case was portrayed in the media. The anti-immigrant forces in this country had seized on Esme's case and were beating the war drums about it. Esme was tailor-made for their cause. Aria Whitmore was not only wealthy but was also a piano prodigy and very talented in music composition. She was beautiful, popular and was, by all accounts, a generous and kind person.

I dialed Steve. He picked up on the third ring.

"Hey, kid," he said to me affectionately. Steve was a 60ish man, having been in criminal defense for the past 35 years. He was one of the first members of the San Diego bar who took me under his wing when I was a baby lawyer and trying to find my way around the system. I met him at an ABA reception for a retiring Superior Court judge and liked him immediately.

"Hey yourself," I said. "Listen, I wanted to talk to you about the case you…" I wanted to use the words *dumped on me* but decided to be a bit more circumspect. "Gave me."

"Yeah, and you're welcome. This will make your career there, kid, believe me. You want this case."

"Steve, I appreciate your confidence in me, but-"

"But what? Listen, I know you. This is the case for you. I've seen you in action. There ain't nobody who cares about clients more than you do. This woman has no lawyer. She can't afford one. You're her only hope here."

I rolled my eyes. "With a case like this, I'm quite sure

there are plenty of other attorneys who would be salivating to take her on, whether or not she has the money to pay for her case. There are plenty of show-boat lawyers who have to know a case like this would make their career. It's a chance for some show-off to get his mug in front of every camera in the country. It's really a false choice to say it's either me or some rando appointed counsel."

"True enough, kid, but here's the thing. This woman doesn't deserve some jackass who's only on her case because he wants the publicity. Those publicity whores really don't care if they win or lose as long as they're playing the game. And that's all her case would be to them – a game. She deserves somebody with a passion for justice, and that's you. So, yes, it is only a choice between you and a rando who would be appointed by the State of California. Sorry to have to dump this on you, but I have faith you'll do a fantastic job."

I twirled my dark hair around my finger as I spoke to him. *Looks like my insomnia issue isn't going to be getting any better anytime soon.* "So, I take it you think this woman didn't do it?" I asked him.

"I don't know if she did or didn't. Haven't spoken to her, only to her cellmate. Her cellmate thinks she's being railroaded, though, I know."

"Does she speak English?" I asked him.

"Yeah, she speaks English. She's been here for six years and speaks the language perfectly."

I didn't really know what else to say. I wouldn't turn down the case before I even met the woman.

"Okay. I'll go down and see her. If she hasn't already been assigned an attorney from the State of California, I'll think about representing her. I just hope I don't regret this.

I've never done a case with such a bright light shining on me."

"You can handle the bright light," Steve said. "Trust me on this. You walked down a prison sentence. You can handle anything. Listen, I have to go. The court beckons me."

I hung up the phone and sighed. I called Regina first thing. "Well, you were right," I told her. "My ass is in the fire."

"Told you," she said, laughing.

"How did you know?"

"You're going to be pissed at me, but I went down and saw her cellmate. I'm doing work on Amelia Reid's case. When I found out Amelia was cellmates with Esme, I told her about you, and how you were the shit, so Amelia talked to her lawyer, Steve, and I guess Steve dumped the case on you."

"Oh, that's just great. I guess you have your own ulterior motive for my taking this case, then?"

"You got that right. I've been dying to take a bite out of this case ever since I found out about it. A young girl with a platinum stick up her butt bites it in her own mansion? That shit's solid gold. Those Coronado rich-fuck treasure trolls with their first-world problems and their yachts can kiss my candy ass as far as I'm concerned."

"So, why exactly do you want to take this case?"

"Because, dude, here's the thing. This chick didn't do it. It's the stupidest set of facts imaginable. I mean, come on now, this lowly maid will get access to a $10 million bling? Really? You mean that chick just had that shit lying around on top of her chest of drawers? She don't have that shit in a safe somewhere?" Regina snorted on the phone. "Sounds like a set-up to me. Chick is being railroaded, plain and simple. I think one of the other bougie richasses did her and made it look like Esme did it."

"Oh? You already have it figured out, do you?"

"Bet your ass. I mean, I don't know who did her in, but, trust me, it was somebody in that Aria chick's world. You can't let that woman get her ass railroaded into the chair."

"Well, they don't have the chair in California. They have lethal injection."

"Even worse. You ever go and see one of those executions? I have. It's not pretty and it's not fun."

That was news to me. I didn't know Regina had seen an execution. "You went to an execution?" I asked her.

"Yeah," she said matter-of-factly. "My father was shot in cold blood by this tweaking guy named Danny Bowles. Bowles was high on PCP or some shit and killed my dad while he was changing a tire on the side of the road. Bowles was put to death for it and I watched him die. I went into that chamber thinking that prick could burn to death for all I care. I left it feeling sick to my stomach and thinking that the state killing people is the most barbaric thing in the world. Trust me, you don't want your client dying because some wealthy jerk-off needed a scapegoat for killing that poor girl."

I cocked my head. "Regina, how is it you never told me about your dad and how he died?" Regina had always talked about her father with a great deal of affection, and I knew he died, but I didn't know the story of just how he died.

Not until now, anyhow.

"Guess it never came up. Listen, I was raw about that for years. Messed up in the head. My old lady, she treated me like dog shit after my father died. That's why I ended up running away and getting with that worthless Michael. I just figured my dad was dead, my mom didn't want me, Michael did, and that was that. I don't know why we never discussed this before. It was just hard for me to talk about, I guess." I could hear she was on the verge of getting choked up on the other end, so I decided it was best to drop it.

Regina, for all her bravado, really was a marshmallow inside. I'd learned that early on – her tough-girl act was just that. An act. If she didn't feel like talking about it with me before, it was her right.

"Well, I guess I need to at least see this woman before I turn her down. See her, hear her story, gauge whether or not I think she did it."

"Hey, listen, even if she did it, so what? You in the habit of only taking innocent clients these days? I mean, I never got the memo you ain't taking guilty people anymore, Avery."

Truer words were never spoken. Most of my clients were guilty as the day was long. I still took them, though, because I really did believe that everybody had a right to counsel. It was a right guaranteed by the Sixth Amendment of the Constitution. However, if my client was clearly guilty, I simply tried to get the best deal I could. I didn't feel comfortable trying cases where my client did it. Not just because I didn't like to lose, which was true enough, but also because I didn't want to win these cases. I didn't want to be the one responsible for a murderer or rapist going free.

Besides, my life's passion was the unjustly accused. When I was the one on trial for my life, nobody was there for me. My court-appointed attorney, Gloria Flores, was overworked, underpaid and didn't even want to try my case. She made that clear from the start. She came at me with one plea offer after another. At one point, she threatened to withdraw from my case if I didn't do what she said and take an offer for 30 years in prison, plead to Man One. She thought that was the best offer she could get. When I said I wanted to take my chances, she threw my file across the room and flatly proclaimed she couldn't work with me.

I didn't care. I knew the truth, and that was that I was innocent. I also knew she'd been assigned my case, so I knew for a fact she couldn't withdraw from it. I knew enough in talking to some of the women in the jail to understand that court-appointed attorneys were always going to threaten to walk, but they couldn't. They were stuck with us no matter what.

Of course, at trial, I got the book thrown at me. Life in prison without the possibility of parole. After the jury found me guilty, Gloria had a *told you so* smirk on her face. I wanted to slap that smug smile right off of her, and it was tempting to do just that. I would've even risked a contempt of court charge to attack her in the courtroom. But the bailiff put the handcuffs on me before I could even think about spitting in her eye.

"Of course I don't just take innocent clients. It's just that I won't go to trial with a guilty one. If I think that Esme did it, I either won't take her as a client, or I'll tell her my only role will be to get a decent plea agreement. That's all."

I heard Regina snort on the phone. "A lawyer with principles. What is the world coming to? Anyhow, what time you going to see her? I'd like to come with you and take notes. I guess I'll be doing the investigation for you."

"Of course. Goes without saying." Regina liked me because she knew I had deep pockets and always paid on time. Besides, I was the one who got her started in her private eye practice. When I got out of prison and was awarded my money from the state of Missouri for false imprisonment, then went to college and law school, I started my practice out here. When she called to tell me she, too, was released from prison, I immediately hired her to do my investigations. I knew she would have an issue with finding decent employment. After all, her previous jobs consisted of being a stripper and a prostitute. Plus, she was a felon, even without her overturned murder charge. When she was 18, she'd been down both for felony drug charges and for possessing a weapon while out on parole.

Regina was only 33, the same age as me, yet it seemed she'd lived several lifetimes. I never regretted giving her a chance to do PI work because it turned out she had a real knack for it. She was smart as a whip, spoke the language of the street, and was extremely thorough.

"Well, then, I better go down and see her, too, don'tcha think?" Regina asked. "You aren't the only one who needs to get a feel for this chick and hear her story. See how her face is when she talks about what happened. Look at her body language. Besides, I'm like a built-in lie detector machine. Nobody gets past my bullshit-meter."

I looked at the clock and then looked at my schedule for that day. It was packed with hearings and client intake interviews, and it looked like the only time I could fit Esme into my schedule was 6 PM. "Hate to tell you, Regina, but today's schedule is packed tighter than a Jetblue puddlejumper. I have to make it this evening at 6."

"Cool. You know I don't have nothing going on at night these days. I'll buy you dinner afterward, how about that? What's a good place downtown by the jail?"

"Oh, I don't know. The Old Spaghetti Factory. But you don't have to buy me dinner."

"I know I don't, but that's not the point. I want to pick your brain after we meet this chick, and I know I don't want to go to your hoity-toity condo to do it. Why do you like living around there with all those bougie richie-riches, anyhow?"

Coronado was known for its wealth, that was for sure. I remembered coming to town and seeing that a 1940s-era 600 square foot home was selling for $2.2 million. It was then that I understood that the real value in the houses on Coronado wasn't in the homes themselves but the land the houses sat upon.

My condo was worth some $3 million, even though it was only a two-bedroom. I wanted it, though, because it was close to the water. Other beaches around town didn't have condos right on the ocean. Mission Beach had enormous homes by the ocean. Ocean Beach didn't have condos or homes right on the ocean, and neither did Pacific Beach. La Jolla had some, but not as nice as the one I chose in Coronado.

"I just needed to be by the water," I said. "That's really all." Sometimes I regretted living there because my condo abutted a very public beach, one that got really crowded, starting in the summertime, and people tended to get really loud. But mostly, it was comforting to live in such close proximity to the vastness of the Pacific Ocean.

"Okay. Well, listen, chica, I gotta go. I've got to shake down a couple of goombahs in Imperial Beach for somebody. I'll be meeting you at 6 at the jail, huh?"

"Right. Six at the jail."

"Gotcha."

Chapter Three

I GOT to the jail right at 6 PM. I waited for Regina to show up, which she did, about ten minutes late.

"Sorry, boss," she said in a tone that was slightly out-of-breath. "I got stuck talking to some gang-bangers over on Market Street. Looks like I'm going to TJ tomorrow to talk to some dudes. Good thing I got my passport updated, huh?" TJ was local slang for Tijuana, the Mexican town right on the other side of the border from San Diego.

The passport thing was the one reason why I hadn't yet been down to Mexico – I'd never bothered to get a passport. You can go to Mexico without a passport, but good luck trying to get back out.

"Not a prob," I said. "I see you have your tape recorder. Looks like you're ready to go."

"Oh, God yes," she said, rubbing her hands together. "Never been more ready for a case in my life."

I looked at her hair, which showed some bright blue streaks running through her dark hair. "You were right," I said, looking at the streaks. "Those highlights really are lit."

"Lit AF," she said, nodding. "Get it right."

"Whatever," I said with a smile. Regina was gorgeous, bright blue streaks or not. "Okay, let's see the guards and our new prospective client, shall we?"

I showed my bar card to the guard, told her who I was seeing, and she nodded and called on the phone. Then she pressed a button, motioning to us, and we went through the door that led to the elevator. Esme was on the fifth floor, although she was apparently being held in protective custody, necessitated by her notoriety. Apparently, there were threats against her from some of the women who were virulently anti-immigrant. One of the women brought a knife into the lunchroom. She slashed Esme's arm and threatened that much more was coming. Turned out the woman was married to a white supremacist and was a standing member of the Federation for American Immigration Reform. FAIR was a group with the singular mission of limiting immigration to the United States. The founder of FAIR, John Taunton, had expressed a desire for America to remain majority white.

———

AFTER ABOUT A HALF-HOUR, Esme appeared in the room. She was shackled, both her hands and legs, and was dressed in an orange jumpsuit that hung on her tiny frame. Her skin was light and freckled, her blue eyes inquisitive and intelligent. Her blonde hair was thick and coarse and hung down to her shoulders. When she saw the two of us, she smiled, her teeth straight and white. She nodded her head slightly to the two of us.

I stood up when she walked in, and the guard went back to his station. "Ms. Gutierrez," I said, "good to meet you."

"You must be the lawyer Steve was telling me about," she said. "I hope you can take me on because you're my last hope, amiga. You don't want to talk to me and I'm stuck with whatever lawyer the state of California wants to throw at me. This is my life we're talking about. They want to put a needle in my arm. I didn't do it, Ms. Collins. I loved Aria. Loved her like a sister. I would've never hurt her."

She looked over at Regina, examining the blue streaks in her hair with a smile on her face. "Cute," she said to her. She self-consciously put her shackled hands to her own hair. "Wish I could do something like that with mine. Never had the cojones to, though, you know? And the Whitmores, they probably wouldn't have ever let me do something like that, anyhow. Their fancy friends might've talked about the blue-haired maid." Then she rolled her eyes. "Lord knows we can't have that."

"Oh, I'm very sorry I didn't introduce you. This is Regina Baldwin. She's my private investigator. She'll be working your case."

"Hello," she said to Regina. "What is it you say? The more the merrier?" She smiled. "If Ms. Baldwin helps you win, Ms. Collins, I'm all for her helping out with the case."

"And Regina will be recording this conversation if you don't mind," I said.

"Of course, I figured somebody would be."

I took a deep breath and brought out my list of questions.

"I understand you've been working as the Whitmore's live-in maid for the past six years. Do I have that right?"

She shook her head and started to mumble in Spanish.

I didn't quite understand her, but Regina spoke and understood Spanish. She explained that it was a necessity living out in Imperial Beach, which was the closest beach to the Mexican border. Most of her neighbors spoke Spanish. I was impressed she could pick up a different language so rapidly, but she told me that was just her. She was able to pick up languages really easily, and it had always been so.

I looked over at Regina, who was still studying Esme intently.

"I'm so sorry, but I don't understand Spanish," I said to Esme. "Could you please speak English?"

Regina just looked at me. "She was just blowing off steam," she said. "Mostly, I just heard a lot of curse words."

"Yes, sorry," Esme said to me. "Sometimes, when I think of those people, I just get so angry I could scream. What I said just now I can't repeat in English."

"I see," I said. I had no idea why Esme had that reaction, but I had to admit it intrigued me.

Regina leaned over to me. "She was cussing a blue streak just now about the family she was living with. Guess the good family Whitmore ain't exactly the pillars of the community they're pretending to be. Guess they really are a bunch of greedy bastards who treat their hired help like crap." Then she looked over at Esme. "But I guess the term hired help really doesn't apply here, does it? I think the term domestic slave is probably the more appropriate term in this case."

Esme nodded. "You got it, muchacha," she said to Regina. "I got to this country with nothing. Less than nothing. My family – murdered. My home – burned to the ground. The things I went through to get here, you don't want to know. It might ruin your view of the world and how people are treated."

Esme continued. "I got here with just the clothes on my back. Worse than that, I arrived here with a child in my belly. I was raped by an old man by the name of Humberto

Gonzalez and all of his friends. I had no idea who was the papa of this baby. I had no idea what I was supposed to do in this country. I had some skills – my family had a small farm. I knew about agriculture. But I asked around, some of the muchachos I met on the bus and just around, and they told me they're working for $6 an hour, back-breaking work. I knew it would be the same for me. How could I support a child on that kind of wage? There wasn't anything else I could really do, either."

I felt my sense of injustice burning brightly within me as Esme spoke. $6 an hour for back-breaking work in the hot sun? That was much less than minimum wage, which was over $16 an hour in the state of California. The only reason these migrants accepted that low of a wage was they didn't have a choice. They were just happy to have a job.

Esme continued. "I met a man while I was in line at an employment agency. José Garcia. We talked, and he told me about Colleen Whitmore. He said he heard along the line she was looking for a live-in housekeeper and lived in a big house in Coronado. I thought that nothing could be better for me. At that time, I was living in the United States without any kind of documentation. I was in line to get a hearing in the immigration court, but I didn't have the right papers for an actual job. I went right to Colleen's home and knocked on the door. She answered it, wanted to know why I was there. I told her I heard she was looking for a housekeeper."

Something about that story wasn't ringing true for me. "I don't understand. You just show up at her door, and she hired you? She didn't have an actual process for inter-viewing and trying to find just the right person?"

Esme shook her head. "Yeah, that's what happened. Turns out the Whitmores were looking for a certain type of girl if you know what I mean." She looked over at Regina, who looked back at her knowingly.

I thought I knew what she was getting at, but I had to pin her down. "No, I don't know what you mean."

"They wanted a woman to have children for them. They were looking for a woman who was light-skinned and light-eyed and who was desperate and couldn't object to anything they wanted that woman to do. I fit what they were looking for perfectly."

I looked over at Regina, who was looking revolted. It was hard to shock her, but I thought I saw just that on her face – shock. Disgust. "You mean that old geezer knocked you up?" Regina asked Esme. "Did you actually have to make it with him?"

"Mm-hmm chica," Esme said with a disgusted look on her face. "I did. Nasty old beast. I had to have an abortion when I went to work for them, of course. My mama would tell me I would go to hell for killing my child, but I felt only relief when I went in to have it done. Colleen told me, right before I had my abortion, what they really wanted from me."

"You mean they weren't upfront and honest with you from the start?" I asked her.

"No, muchacha. When I showed up at her door, she told me she wanted me to be their housekeeper. She didn't tell me she needed me as a surrogate."

Regina was shaking her head. "Man. That's all kinds of messed up. That's some kind of weird *Handmaid's Tale* shit right there."

"Right?" Esme agreed, shaking her head. "That's what they ended up wanting from me, but they didn't tell me that until I accepted the job."

I looked at the file. "Let's see...Jacob Whitmore is 75.

Colleen Whitmore is 35. That must mean Aria's mother was somebody other than Colleen. Do you know anything about that? Who her birth mother was?"

Esme shook her head. "No, nobody ever told me about that. All I know is that, after I took that job and got settled into the house doing the usual kind of housework – cooking, dusting, toilets, windows, laundry, mopping, picking stuff up at the dry cleaner, dishes, the usual – Colleen came to me, crying. She told me she couldn't have kids. She told me she'd just married Jacob and he needed an heir to pass on his fortune. I asked her about Aria, what about her? She was his heir. But she said he specifically wanted a son to run his empire. She told me Aria had no interest in the business. Aria wanted to become a classical pianist and didn't have the desire to run the hotels. Also, Aria didn't have any kind of business skills. She was always the kind of person to sit in trees. She was a writer, a musician, a composer, a ballerina. An artist. But a businesswoman? No way."

"I see," I said.

Regina rolled her eyes. "Typical patriarchal crap. 'Needs a son to pass on the business,'" she said dismissively. "What kind of 19th Century bullshit is that?"

Esme shrugged. "That's just how he thought, I guess. He just needed a son who was like him. Cold, ruthless, greedy. Colleen told me that the only thing Jacob cared about was having a son who could be forced from a young age to learn everything he could about Jacob's business. I guess Jacob believed that any daughter who came into the world would be just like Aria – emotional, artistic and useless in the business world."

"I guess that makes sense," I said. That was a red flag, the fact that Jacob wanted a son so badly, but I didn't quite know where it all fit into this whole scenario. "So, what happened after Colleen came to you in tears?"

"She told me she needed me to have Jacob's child. I told her no. I wouldn't do that because I was already pregnant with my own child. I didn't want that child, but I wouldn't have an abortion. I didn't even know how that would work, anyhow. What would her friends say about me, the maid, having her husband's child?" She shook her head. "I didn't know what would come. I really thought the Whitmores were decent people. I had no idea."

"What do you mean?" I asked her. "What did they do?"

"Colleen immediately told me I had to go along with everything they asked of me. If I didn't, they would go to ICE and turn me in. I told them I was waiting for my asylum application to be approved, so I couldn't be deported. She told me her husband had influence with my immigration judge. If I didn't go along with their plan, her husband would tell that judge to deny my application. On the other hand, if I went along with their plan, her husband would tell him to approve it."

"Was that true? Jacob had influence with the immigration judge?" I asked.

"Yes, it turned out that was true. I called José, the man who referred me to the Whitmores, and asked him about that. He told me he'd heard around that Jacob was responsible for three different people getting deported in this area. These people worked in Jacob's hotels. They'd do something he didn't like, and he'd fix things with that judge to make sure their asylum applications were denied. José told me this was just a rumor but I shouldn't take my chances."

"So, you went along with the plan?"

"I didn't feel I had a choice. My asylum application would be hard to win as it was. Those gang members killed my entire family, but I didn't have proof of nothing. The United States government wouldn't be able to verify anything I said. I knew I'd be sent back, even if Mr. Whitmore didn't influence my judge. If Mr. Whitmore could tell that judge I should stay and be given protected status, but only if I went along with his plan, I would go along with his plan."

"What happened next?" I asked her.

"Colleen told me I had to have an abortion, which I did, then went to confession about it and did my Hail Marys. Then I had to have sex with Mr. Whitmore. I was shocked. I thought they would take me to a clinic and have the whole thing done in a test tube, like they do. Or use a turkey baster – I've heard of lesbians using that. I didn't think that actually having sex with Jacob would be involved, but when I found out that it was, I said no."

"And after you said no?" I asked.

"Colleen said that it had to be that way. She didn't say why. She told me I had to do it. I had no other choice. Then I kept saying no, and, one day, some ICE agents showed up at the door to come and get me. Handcuffed me, took me to a detention center. I told them I'd applied for asylum and I was waiting for my court date, but that fell on deaf ears. I couldn't afford an attorney to get me out of there, either. They told me they could deport me for working for the Whitmores without a work permit." Then she started to speak Spanish again, shaking her head.

"You got that right," Regina said to her, nodding along as Esme continued to speak Spanish at a rapid rate. "Our governmental policy is all kinds of wacked out."

"What is she saying?" I asked Regina.

"She's talking about how stupid it is you can't work until your asylum application has been pending for 150 days. Yet people in this country get all up in the migrants' grills about going on public assistance. What are they supposed to do if they can't legally work for 150 days after they get here?" Regina shook her head. "Stupid."

Esme nodded. "Sorry, Ms. Collins, but sometimes I get so damned mad at this country."

"That's okay. I agree completely. So, the ICE agent came and took you into custody. And then what happened?"

"They started a removal case against me. I didn't know what to do. They were right. I was violating the law when I went to work for the Whitmores. I was working without a permit. I was terrified of going back to El Salvador. All I knew was that the people who killed my family would kill me. Those Mara Saltruchas, they don't forget. I was marked for death in El Salvador. And I'd gone through too much to get to this country. Too much."

She started to cry. "I was raped repeatedly on the way to this country. Beaten. I lost 30 pounds during the six months it took to get to this country because I was starving all the time. I weighed 90 lbs when I got to the border. That was why the farmer kidnapped me – he caught me eating his potatoes and corn. Said he would turn me into the authorities, who would send me back, for stealing from him. I begged him not to, and he said he wouldn't if I spent one week with him on his farm. Then he raped me every night and had his amigos come over and rape me too. I didn't protest. Didn't say a word, because I was so scared he would call the policia. He was through with me after a week, gracias a Dios, and I continued on my way. But there were other times I was beaten and raped. I feared for my life every minute of every day. I had a traveling companion, two of them. One of them was killed on the train on the way up here. We had to ride on the top of the train. We call it The

Beast. She fell off the train and was decapitated. Her limbs were severed. Her body was left where it was for the animals to feed on. My other companion, she made it to the border with me. Her name is Camila Juarez."

"And what did she do when you were abducted by the farmer?" I asked her.

"She took the same punishment as me. She wasn't caught eating the potatoes and corn, but she was eating them, too. They just didn't catch her. I tried to save her, tried to tell them she didn't eat the vegetables, but they didn't care. Nasty old goats."

"Are you still in contact with her?" I asked.

Esme shook her head. "No. She wasn't as lucky as me. Her asylum application was denied, and she was sent back to El Salvador. I heard she was murdered by the Mara the day she got back." Esme started to cry again. "So, when ICE detained me and started the proceedings to deport me, I was desperate enough to do anything at all to stay in this country. Colleen came to see me at the detention place about two weeks after I got there. She told me Jacob would pull strings to get me out of the detention place and off the deportation schedule. She told me that all I had to do was have sex with him until I got pregnant with his child. She also told me she'd called the ICE agents when I refused to have sex with Jacob."

Regina looked like she was about to hurl when she heard what Esme was saying. Thankfully, she didn't have a comment.

"So, what happened?" I asked her.

"I told Colleen I'd do anything. Three days later, I was getting out of the detention center, the removal proceeding was dropped, and I was back with the Whitmores. But they gave me Quaaludes before I had to have sex with Jacob, so the whole thing wasn't that bad." Then she shuddered. "I just never thought I would have to do something like that in my life. I felt so dirty. I was 18 when I left my home country. I'd never seen a man in the flesh. My life in El Salvador was peaceful. We farmed, raised chickens. Our family was close. I didn't know that my father was involved with the rival gang, the 18th Street. I had no idea. I should've known, though, because both of those gangs rule El Salvador. There is not a person in that country who is not touched by one or the other. My life changed when my family was murdered. My four brothers and sisters, my parents, my mama's parents, all shot in the head and left in the house for the maggots to eat them."

My heart went out to Esme. She'd gone through so much. Now, this. "Did you get pregnant with Jacob's child?"

"Not right away, but eventually, I did. But it was a girl. They found that out while I was pregnant, and the baby was aborted. That happened three more times before I finally got pregnant with a boy."

"Did Colleen try to pass off the child as her own?"

"Yes," Esme said. "That was always the plan. That was why they were looking for somebody who looks like me – light-skinned, light eyes. The Whitmores wanted the coloring of the baby to look right. Colleen has brown hair, light skin and blue eyes. Jacob has grey hair, but he was a blue-eyed blonde when he was younger. As I grew bigger, the Whitmores hid me away when their friends would come over. They used another girl to serve them their food when people were over, and Colleen got a special pregnancy pillow to make it look like she was getting bigger. She had all kinds of baby showers, five of them. I had the baby at home, they named him Jacob Jr., and he's 5 years old right now."

I'd read about Jacob Jr. in the file. He was simply called Jake. There was no indication of anything amiss about his birth. Nothing in the file about his being adopted. Perhaps there was not a notation in the file because it wasn't relevant. "So, Jacob Jr. was born 5 years ago. What happened after that?"

Esme shrugged. "Nothing. I mean, I didn't have to give birth to anymore of Jacob's children, if that's what you're asking. They kept me on, though, even though they never paid me." She shook her head. "They got another woman to start giving them children. Calista. An immigrant from Syria."

"Wait," Regina said. "You weren't even being paid? I mean, even after you gave that old coot his kid, you still had to do all the housework around the house and the cooking and errand running, right? Those greedy old goats never gave you a dime for all that work?"

Esme just shrugged. "I didn't mind not being paid. They fed me pretty well and gave me a place to stay. That was all I've ever asked for – a place to stay and food in my stomach. They gave me both, plus they took me out to the movies once in a great while. I didn't mind working for them after I gave Jacob what he really wanted. It was better than being deported, believe me."

"And were you threatened with deportation even after you were given asylum?" I asked her.

"All the time. The immigration judge didn't hear my case for the first six months, so they threatened me that whole time. Even after the judge approved my asylum application, the Whitmores told me they could have me deported by planting drugs on me and calling the police. I didn't doubt they would do that, so I did everything they asked me to do."

Regina shook her head. "Still. That whole thing is way messed up, dude. That's like next-level messed up if you want to know the truth."

Esme nodded her head. "I know. But I got along well with Aria. She was only 15 when I took the job with the Whitmores, so I saw her grow from a teenager to an adult. She bonded with me, you know? She didn't have a mother, really. Colleen wasn't very motherly. She treated Aria like a stranger, you know? Aria's real mother wasn't around. I don't really know what happened to her. Maybe she died. Maybe they got divorced. I don't really know, and Aria didn't, either. Or maybe she did, but she didn't want to talk about her."

"So she bonded with you as a mother figure, then?" I asked.

"Yes. I thought of her more like a younger sister because I wasn't much older than her. She was 15 when I came into the family. I was only 18. I had sisters around her age in El Salvador." Esme looked sad when she said that. "So, I was only 18, but she needed a mother figure, and I was the one around the house doing all the things mothers do. The cooking and cleaning and that sort of thing. She saw me as her mother."

She tapped her fingers on the table, which wasn't easy to do with her handcuffs, and then she lightly banged the cuffs on the wood. She started to cry again. "I'm sorry," she said, "but just thinking about poor Aria lying dead in that guest house... Dios Mio, she didn't deserve that. She was young, so young, and so talented. She was a good person, you know? Even though Colleen ignored her, and so did her father – after Jake was born, Jacob only paid attention to him – Aria always stayed sweet. She never complained about anything. I know she was hurting. She had to be. Her father and her stepmother pretended she didn't exist. But she always did her thing. She practiced her piano all the time, even though Jacob and Colleen never came into the room to hear her play, and they never went to her recitals. She was working on composing music, composing a symphony, and Jacob and Colleen weren't even aware of what she was working on. She got into Juilliard without their help, with a full-ride scholarship."

"Tell me how you found out Aria was dead," I said.

Esme got a faraway look like she was looking right at Regina and me and not seeing either one of us. "I went out to the beach that morning. It was a cool morning, as it is in the wintertime around here. There had been a storm, so the waves were 10 feet high, and the sky was grey. The Whitmore's house is right close to the water, there's only a street and a sidewalk between the house and the beach, so I liked to go there before I started my workday.

I was out on the beach about 6 in the morning, just picking up seashells and looking for sand dollars – I collect sand dollars – and listening to the seagulls cry. Some people were running on the beach, some people were walking their dogs. I always report to work at 7 in the morning to make breakfast for Jacob and Colleen and help Jake get ready for school.

I headed back into the house at around 6:45 so I could take a shower before work. I got into my house, the guest house where I stayed, and I found her there. Strangled, lying on the floor. Her tongue was sticking out, and her eyes were open. She had a rope around her neck."

Esme shook her head and then looked down at the table. "Poor ninita Aria. She didn't deserve what happened to her."

"And what happened after you found her?" I asked Esme.

"I called the police," she said. "I called the police, and then I went to tell Jacob and Colleen about it. But I called the police first."

"And that necklace was found in your sock drawer," I said. "How did that get in that drawer?"

"I don't know, chica. I wish I knew how it got there. But I don't know. I didn't even know Aria had something that expensive, you know? I didn't steal it. I don't know where she even kept it."

I was starting to get the picture about this family she lived with. It wasn't a pretty picture, either.

"When you were on the beach that morning, did you see anybody you knew? Did you say hello to anybody at all?" I asked her.

She shook her head. "No. I just saw people walking about, walking their dogs, jogging. People starting to line up on the street next to the beach. But I didn't know any of the people I saw."

"So there was nobody who would've been able to give you an alibi, then?" I asked her.

"No. I thought about that when they arrested me. I tried to think if I saw anybody I knew that morning, but I didn't."

I looked over at Regina. "Do you have any questions for her?" I asked her.

"No," she said. "But I'm sure I'll come up with a bunch of them after I start my investigation on this mother." She patted Esme's shoulder lightly. "You're an amazing woman," she said. "All the crap thrown at you, and you're still standing. You're still on this side of the dirt. I've got to hand it to you."

Esme smiled at Regina. "You too, right? You've gone through some things, too, haven't you?"

"You don't know the half of it, sister," she said. "I'll be back, sooner rather than later. I have to ask around, see if there's anybody who might know something about what happened to this girl. You never know. Sometimes rich girls like that who don't have parental supervision end up knowing people on the street. They get their drugs from the same people the trailer-trash people get them from. Not that this Aria was into drugs, but I'm going to rule that out before I do anything else."

"So, does this mean you'll take my case?" Esme asked me hopefully.

"Yes. I will." I took a deep breath. "I'll take it *pro bono*. I can afford to do that. But it's conditional, of course. If I find out you've lied to me about anything, I'm off your case. No questions asked."

"I'm not lying about nothing," she said. "I only wish I was. I wish that none of this was true. But I can't say that because it's all true. Every word of it."

I looked at my watch and saw it was 8 PM. "Well, Regina, what do you say you and I grab something to eat, and we can start work on this thing tomorrow."

"Sounds good." She nodded at Esme. "Peace," she said.

I motioned to the guard, who came out to get Esme. "Do you think I can bond out?" she asked me.

"I doubt I can get a bond you can afford. Plus, I don't think you'll have a place to stay even if you do bond out. You obviously cannot go back to your house. That's a crime scene. I can try, but you're going to have to come up with quite a bit of money to get out."

Esme looked resigned. "Well, it was worth a shot. I'll be seeing you sometime soon, hopefully."

"You will see us soon," I promised.

At that, Esme was taken back to her cell by the guard. She hung her head and shuffled her shackled feet, and looked back at Regina and me one more time.

When I left the jail, I immediately went to the courthouse to put in my Entry of Appearance on her case. I was committed now. No going back.

I didn't know what to think about it all. I only knew I was about to embark on a case that would change my entire life.

Hopefully, my life would change for the better.

But that wasn't a guarantee.

Chapter Four

GRAYSON

GRAYSON JACKSON WAS a corpulent man who loved his bacon, wine and donuts. As far as he was concerned, these, along with french fries, should be the four basic food groups. The other food groups, the real ones, were so boring, in his opinion. He had no use for fruits and vegetables, although he did love his meat, dairy and breads.

And so it was that he was eating some bacon donuts, which were the specialty of a donut shop around the corner from his recording studio in Sarasota, Florida, and drinking an entire bottle of wine, while he got ready to take his place behind the microphone for his 3 hour show. Grayson Davis was considered to be a rising star in the satellite radio talk show world due to his willingness to say anything at all. No conspiracy theory was too far-fetched for him and, as far as he was concerned, the only good liberal was a dead one.

While he enjoyed whipping up his listeners into a frenzy by informing them that the jack-booted thugs from the FBI were going door to door, kicking in doors and seizing guns, in violation of the Constitution, and that the MS-13 had infiltrated every police force in the United States, he worried he was going to lose his grip on his audience. The things he said to his listeners were generally things he had made up in his head, although most of them already had some kind of a basis in a conspiracy theory already making the rounds on the Internet. He just took the nugget of truth and embellished on it, making it more outlandish. He was very careful not to actually impugn an individual person, though, because he didn't want a lawsuit. It was much easier to just use broad terms like "deep state," and "antifa" and other words his listeners responded to with vile and venom.

His job, as he saw it, was to make sure the people who listened to his radio show were afraid of just about everything. He knew that fear led to anger, which led to his listeners coming on his show to vent their spleen. When people were afraid of vaccines or illegal immigrants or losing their gun rights, then they were emotional and likely to spread the word amongst their friends about what was going on.

He found out about the case of Esme Gutierrez and knew that he had to exploit it for everything it represented. Not that he was the only one leading off every broadcast with her story. It was just that he was the only one willing to dive into her case in-depth and make shit up about it along the way. While he usually was afraid of telling outright lies about individuals, with Esme, he decided to take off the gloves. This was a refugee, working as a maid for a rich family in California, not making diddly-squat in wages. There was no way she would have the money to hire an attorney to come after him, so he knew that he could say anything at all about her and get away with it.

And her case was the perfect one for what he wanted to

do. He had struggled to put a face to his constant rants about the invasion happening right on our shores. America was settled by European Christians. They were the ones who came over to this country all those years ago and used their blood, sweat and tears to tame the wilderness and establish a working society. They had to battle hunger and freezing cold and savages around every turn. They died young from disease and malnourishment and hypothermia. 100 people came over on The Mayflower, and half of them were dead by the end of the first year.

Then the pioneers were the ones who settled the west. They, too, experienced all manner of sacrifices on the Oregon Trail. They drowned in swollen rivers, were crushed by covered wagons, eaten by animals and attacked by Indians. They died when cholera and small pox spread throughout an entire wagon camp. It was said that a person could go from healthy to dead in a half day when cholera struck. They buried their dead right in the middle of the trail, then carried on their way.

The Donner party, perhaps the most famous of the American pioneers, were trapped by snow in the mountains. Help did not reach them for four months, long after their food supply had run out. They were forced to eat one another to survive.

These people were the ones who settled America. They made it what it was today. They suffered unspeakable tragedies, and, without them, we wouldn't have a country. So it chapped Grayson's hide that these interlopers wanted to come into this country without putting in any effort at all. This wasn't their country. It was settled by white people, plain and simple, so how dare these people expect to just come to this country and have their broods of children, all the while not learning the language and using welfare that was paid for by hard-working Americans? They just expected to come to this country and be educated at the taxpayer's expense, taking food out of the mouths of working-class citizens and taking jobs away from native-born Americans.

What Grayson wanted was pretty simple, really. He wanted this country to belong to the people who put the work into making it what it was. The land of the free, the home of the brave. As far as he was concerned, only those people who could trace their ancestry back to those great pioneers and Pilgrims should be allowed to remain in this country. To him, that meant that anybody from Asia or South America or Latin America didn't belong in this country. Neither did the Muslims. They not only didn't help found this country, but they worshiped a violent God that made them want to kill all Christians. Every last one them needed to leave this country yesterday. That the Islamic religion was one of peace and so were the vast majorities of Muslims were facts that Grayson refused to acknowledge.

Grayson begrudgingly admitted that African-Americans belonged here, just because they were brought here involuntarily. There wasn't really much that he could say about their existence in this country, although he didn't like them, either. They were all the same, the blacks – they all lived in poverty, no baby daddy around because they were all in prison, all their mamas were on welfare, every last one of them. They were all useless, a stain on this country and a drag on the economy. Like the brown people, the blacks were a net negative in this country because they never had jobs and the taxpayers had to subsidize them.

Yet he couldn't begrudge their presence in the country. He wished that his ancestors could have foreseen what kind of problems they would bring to this country and just let them stay in Africa where they all belonged.

That African slaves were truly responsible for making this country great, as they toiled for their masters for zero pay and worked hard to feed the people in the country and helped build the towns and cities with their labor, did not cross his mind. He never acknowledged their contributions to what built this country, because, in his mind, it was only the European's ingenuity and physical labor that really counted. Neither did he acknowledge the contributions that African-Americans had made to this country, and that a great percentage of African-Americans were professionals. Doctors, lawyers, CEOs, professionals at all levels. They were just as hard-working and intelligent as anybody else, but, to Grayson, they were all on welfare and gang-banging.

Nor did Grayson really examine the role that later Europeans played in the building of the country. The Irish and the Italians, among others, weren't really among the early settlers. They didn't give their blood, sweat and tears to the settlement of the country. They came in large numbers at around the same time as the Chinese, around the turn of the 20th Century, long after the country had been made liveable by the early colonists, but Grayson really didn't think about that one. All that he knew was that the Irish and the Italians were white. Well, the Irish were, anyhow, and the Italians didn't tend to have skin as brown as those coming from south of the border, so they automatically got a pass.

Grayson never really thought about the reasons why brown people, including people from south of the border and people from the Middle East, might want to come to this country. That they were fleeing oppression and violence and extreme poverty and were coming to this country for a better life didn't factor into how he felt about them. The irony that many people from the Middle East and south of the border were coming to this country for the very reason the early Pilgrims came here – because their home country had become inhospitable – never dawned on him. All that he could see was that they were dirty, they had way too many children, they didn't work, they lived off white people's dimes and and they couldn't speak the language.

Never mind that none of these things were true and there were more white people who had kids out of wedlock and were on welfare than any other race. He never saw that institutional racism was responsible for much of the lack of upward mobility in minority races – the crumbling infrastructure in their failing schools, the overcrowded class-rooms, the burned-out teachers barely scraping by, and the lack of nutritious food in the minority schools were all factors that contributed to the oppression of the poor.

No. None of these things crossed his mind. He was a white supremacist, and was proud of it, and he used his three hours per day on the air to spread his beliefs while basking in the hosanna's from the people who called into his show.

Esme Gutierrez was like a gift from the heavens from him. He talked about illegal immigration daily until he was blue in the face. Even he was tired of hearing himself complaining day after day about building the wall and about how all illegal immigrants needed to be rounded up and deported. Now. That included their children, even if they were brought over here when they were young.

But there wasn't really much he could say about legal immigration. Oh, he tried to get the masses whipped up about chain migration, where the brown people managed to get their mothers, fathers, grandparents, aunts, uncles and cousins over here once they got here. But he didn't have the same passion about the legal immigrants about the illegal ones, because it was the government's fault that these people were here in this country. There wasn't much that could be done about policy.

That was before Esme's case, though. He suddenly realized that the reason why his arguments against legal immigration never got much traction was because there wasn't any one incident that captured the public's imagination. He lived for the mass shootings that were carried out by Muslim men, because it made his argument for deporting all Muslims that much stronger. When illegal immigrants murder innocent young women, as what had happened Mollie Tibbetts, it was great for him to whip his listeners into an absolute panic. He was very successful in taking the anecdotal case and make it stand in for every member of the particular group. One illegal immigrant murders an innocent girl, and that meant that illegal immigrants, in general, were dangerous rapists and murderers.

So far, though, he wasn't able to make a refugee the face of the brown menace. Esme changed all of that. That woman murdered an innocent young lady of means, the daughter of a billionaire, who had her entire life in front of her. Aria Whitmore was a senior at Juilliard, studying classical piano. She was a woman who everyone was watching, because she not only was a prodigy on the piano, but she also was a genius when it came to music composition. She was working on a symphony when she was murdered in cold blood. The world was deprived of her genius. Who knows what she would have went on to do with her talent? The truly talented composers of today were the ones who ended up working on movie scores. If Beethoven or Mozart were alive today, that's what they would be doing –

composing music for movies. That's probably what Aria would have ended up doing, and she probably would have ended up winning several Oscars along the way.

She never got the chance to realize her potential. Esme Gutierrez took that away from her. Cut down at the age of 21. Aria was beautiful, talented, and from a good family. She didn't deserve to be strangled in her parent's guest house. Worse, Esme killed her just because she was greedy. She wanted to take something that didn't belong to her, namely Aria's fine diamond necklace that was valued at over $10,000,000. That's what was found in Esme's sock drawer when the police went to the scene of the crime. Aria's necklace. It was very valuable because it was created with a very rare pink diamond, and it was almost 5 carats. It was a gift to Aria from her father when she graduated from high school and was accepted to Juilliard.

Grayson took his blood pressure, as he always did before he got on the air. He knew that, once he got going, ranting and screaming into the microphone, his blood pressure tended to soar. He had to make sure that it wasn't already high before he took his place and started taking calls. That was difficult for him, though – just thinking about what that goddamn worthless spic Esme Gutierrez did to that beautiful girl Aria was enough to get his blood boiling. He took a deep breath, saw that his blood pressure was 150/100 – it was high, as usual, but not life-threateningly high, so he felt safe to go on the air. He looked at his producer who was standing behind the glass, about to motion to him that he was soon going to be live.

He put on his headset, saw the light flash and started to talk.

Chapter Five

THE HOMELESS WOMAN

THE WOMAN SHUFFLED her feet while she stood by the side of the road with a specially-made sign. "Will work for food" was way too played in her mind. She went with refreshing honesty, hoping that people might give her money if she came right out with it. Her sign said, "I need money for alcohol and cigarettes. I won't even try to lie." She needed money not for food but for alcohol. Cigarettes. The things that made life on the streets worth living.

She remembered one sign, on the Fourth of July, when she went to the beach to spend the day with her kids. The sign said *Help me get high on the Fourth of July*. It was held up by a long-haired hippy-type, and the sign disgusted her. Why didn't that man just get a job? Did he have to advertise he was one of the dregs of society and he was proud of spending his life toking it up instead of working?

That was then. That was some 15 years ago. A lot had changed since then, to say the very least.

At that time, she had it all. A daughter, a son, an adoring husband. However, he wasn't really adoring. He only pretended he was, but when it came right down to it, he was in love with the idea of her. The perfect idea of the pretty blonde housewife who spent her days getting perfect manicures and pedicures in perfect little day spas, drinking a perfect glass of wine while closing her eyes and imagining her perfect home in the perfect neighborhood. Then she would meet with her friends in an exclusive restaurant on one of the beaches in La Jolla or Del Mar, maybe Coronado, the "better" beaches with the "better" people and the "better" food. She wouldn't be caught dead in a place near Mission Beach or Ocean Beach or Pacific Beach because that was where the riff-raff went. The people who didn't have the money to spend $50 on a lunch consisting of a rare cut of prime rib and a glass of wine or three.

That was what her husband loved. He loved that she was fit. She did a Pilates class three days a week and alternated that with a personal trainer who charged her $500 per session. When she had her son and her daughter, three years apart, she bounced back from her pregnancies each time and fit into her size 3 pants within a matter of days after she pushed those kids out. She limited herself to 1500 calories per day during her pregnancies and only gained 15 lbs with both her daughter and her son, so she returned to her skinny self in no time.

Now, she didn't even like to look in the mirror. She was only 42, but she knew she looked much older than that. During the rare times she scraped up enough money to treat herself to a Chinese buffet, she was always asked if she needed a senior discount. At first, she was outraged by that presumption. So outraged, in fact, she complained to the manager and loudly shouted she would never come back. In the back of her mind, though, she knew she would be back. She was as addicted to greasy egg rolls and orange chicken as she was to Jack Daniels and Marlboro Reds. Plus, she could get a meal that would tide her over for days when she went to the Chinese buffet. This was important because there were many days when she just didn't eat because she couldn't afford to.

She stood on the street corner, holding up her sign that honestly said she needed money to get cigarettes and alcohol. People actually did give her money. They would slow down, handing her the dollar bill or the occasional five through their window, and nobody actually propositioned her to do something more for that money.

That was another way she knew how unattractive she was - nobody propositioned her. Once so smooth and pale, her skin was now just a mess of wrinkles that were the color of griege. Griege was a combination of beige and grey, and that was the color of her skin. Her body, once muscular, flexible and strong from her daily workouts, was now just skin and bones. Her blue eyes, once so clear and bright, were now bloodshot and hollow. Once so silky, thick and strong, her blonde hair was a mousy brown and was patchy at best. She had bald spots all over her head. She used to cover up the bald spots with a knit cap, but on days like today, when it was over 100 degrees, she couldn't stand that. When she was high on heroin, she would dress up in a coat and hat, no matter the weather, because she was always freezing when she was on that junk. But she hadn't been able to afford a fix in a long time, so she hadn't been taking to wearing a hat, coat and gloves in 100-degree weather for a while.

She always worked a certain corner in Point Loma because the people in this area had money to spend, and she was less likely to be told to move along than in other rich areas, such as La Jolla or Del Mar. Of course, she eventually was told to move along, but she just went to a different street corner until she was kicked out again.

That was her game, going from one street corner to the next, always staying one step ahead of the police, before catching the bus downtown to join the rest of the homeless population who lined the sidewalks, sleeping in sleeping bags, many of them with a dog by their side.

She could never get a bed in a shelter because she didn't have kids, which meant she was put in the back of the line, and she never seemed to manage to get to the shelter on time to get a bed. The beds went too quickly. Occasionally, she got lucky, but she was now used to sleeping on the streets, so it wasn't that bad anymore. Nobody bothered her, and, like everyone else around her, she was tucked into her sleeping bag by 7 in the evening. She usually slept through the night in a drunken stupor.

She coughed, putting her hand to her mouth, and saw a spot of blood on her hand. She didn't know what that meant, but she knew it wasn't good. She was sure that it had something to do with the packs and packs of cigarettes she smoked every day. She used to go to the Public Library to hang out because San Diego had a brand-new one that was state of the art and huge, so she could find a cubby-hole corner and hide. But she'd have a nicotine fit after only a half-hour, so she would try to light up inconspicuously. Some busy body would always turn her into the library cops, so she was asked to leave. This happened several times, so she was banned from the place for six months. She couldn't even walk in there now without being asked to turn right back around. Now, she preferred to stay outside so she could smoke non-stop.

FINALLY, it was sundown, and she decided to try her luck on the beach. She would go down and listen to the waves crash while trying to get close to whoever might happen to be making a bonfire and put her sleeping bag down. Sometimes she got lucky, and nobody asked her to leave, so she was able to listen to the crashing waves all night long. Most of the time, though, she was kicked out sometime around 2 AM, at which point she found a bus and went to her usual place downtown.

She got on the bus with her sleeping bag under her arm, well aware of how she looked and smelled – it was tough trying to find a restroom she could use anywhere in the city, so she usually did her business in an available bush. This meant that more than a few drops of urine ended up on her pants and underwear.

She sat down, putting her head against the window. She closed her eyes, not wanting to think about how she ended up here, in this situation.

She tried to block out the voices in her head that told her to kill virgins and drink their blood or that told her aliens had planted a probe in her brain that transmitted United States government secrets. She tried not to see the colorful monsters that boarded the bus after her, with their skins the color of the rainbow, their eyes bloodshot and bugging out of their head, their mouths a mawing gape of teeth that threatened to eat her alive. She only saw these things and thought these thoughts at night, when she was through with her work and knew she would be completely alone.

She shook her head rapidly, trying to get the intrusive thoughts and visions out of her head.

But it was no use.

Chapter Six

AVERY

"SO, what did you think about Esme's story?" I asked Regina over a dirty martini and rare steak enjoyed at the Stake Chophouse and Bar, one of my favorite places by my condo. Stake was a modern steakhouse, with a bit of a retro feeling to it, with the wood-paneled walls and leather bucket seats, combining that with distinctly modern touches such as stone backsplashes, lighted murals and a large wine rack in one corner of the room.

Regina shrugged. "She didn't do it, that much I know. Who did it, I don't know, but I know that girl is innocent."

"What makes you so sure?" I had an idea that Esme was innocent, but I wanted to pick Regina's brain to find out what made her so positive.

"I told you, I got a finely tuned bullshit meter, and it wasn't getting set off when I talked to her," Regina said. "That's really all. I didn't get hairs standing up on my arms when she spoke. Good enough for me."

I sighed. I knew we had a long investigation ahead of us, too long, and I really had no idea where to focus for this one. The obvious place was on the creepy father and equally creepy stepmother. As Regina said, that was some weird shit, what those people were doing with Esme. It was bad enough they needed her to be a baby incubator, but what was up with making her actually have sex with Jacob Whitmore? Couldn't they have artificially inseminated her? They certainly had the money to do it that way. The only thing I could think of was that Jacob and Colleen had some kind of fetish that involved Jacob sleeping with the hired help. I'd heard of that kind of thing in reverse – that couples got off on the wife sleeping with a random guy while the husband watched. It was called "cuckolding," but it was usually the wife having sex with a guy, not the other way around.

"You said you would start by asking around on the street if somebody knew something," I said. "What makes you think a girl like Aria would've known somebody on the street?" I asked her.

Regina shrugged. "It makes sense. A rich girl who's ignored by her parents, got money to burn and no doubt feeling depressed and rejected. Wouldn't be surprised if she turned to drugs in that kind of situation. Trust me, girls like Aria are ripe for the picking with the drug dealers around town. And she wouldn't have to get her hands dirty by actually going to the dealer herself. She could use a stooge to get her the junk. But I wouldn't be surprised if she actually did see the dealers herself, just because she was bored and looking for adventure. That's the kind of thing I could see someone like her doing. I could even see her banging a dealer just for kicks." Regina cut into her prime rib, dipped it into the horseradish sauce once and then into the au jus, and pointed her fork at me before putting the piece of meat into her mouth. "You gotta think outside the box."

I nodded. "Just don't spin your wheels. I'd like to start my part of the investigation with Jacob and Colleen." I smiled at Regina. "No offense, but-"

She nodded. "I know, I know. I'm a little too rough for little rich shits like Jacob and Colleen. You don't even have to tell me that. Which is bullshit because you don't see me reverse cuckolding. I mean, that's just all kinds of wrong, if you ask me. I don't care what you want to do in your bedroom, but to coerce an innocent woman into your sick games..." She shook her head. "Have sex with my shriveled prune of a husband or go back to El Salvador and get murdered. What kind of crap is that?"

"I agree," I said. "I also want to know about her mother. What happened to her? Why didn't Aria know what happened to her? Don't you think that's just a bit weird that everything seemed to be such a secret about her?"

Regina shrugged. "Not really. Probably the rich bastard got rid of her, not killed her or nothing like that, but paid her ass off to go away when Aria was young. Then, when Aria got a little older, old enough to ask questions, he just told her some kind of crap story. 'Your mother didn't want you, so she went to Europe, never to return. So sorry, could you please pass the butter?' Happens all the time."

"I still want to find out about the mother," I said. "I want to cover every base around the Whitmores, their associates and friends. I have a feeling there's something there. You go ahead and do your street investigation. Hopefully, you'll turn up something along the way. I'll stay close to the family and hope to get some leads there. Maybe between the two of us, we can come up with a reasonable theory."

Regina nodded. "I hope so because what's going on out there in the media is just crap. You should try to get a change of venue because every single hearing with this woman has resulted in hundreds of protestors lining the street in front of the courthouse. I've seen the news coverage on her hearings, her bond review, her arraignment and all that. There's usually some douche with a bullhorn standing on the top of the steps telling the cheering morons that all Central American refugees were criminals coming over here to murder our rich young beautiful women and Esme was just the start. They held hearings in Congress today on capping the number of refugees that can come to this country to, like, 1,000 a year or some shit. Saw the coverage on C-Span because I was bored and curious. They had a picture of Aria blown up on some easel while some loud-mouth was carrying on about how we would lose our country if we keep letting these people in to rape and murder us white folk." She shook her head. "When did we get like this and how?"

"I wish I knew," I said. I hadn't paid too much attention to the media circus surrounding this case. I tried to limit my exposure to what was being said because I didn't want it influencing me. I knew I was as susceptible to rhetoric as anybody else. If I listened to what was being said about my client, I might start to believe it. I couldn't have that, so I tuned out all the noise. And that was all it was – noise. None of it had any basis in reality. Or, maybe, there was a kernel of truth somewhere buried in all the lies, and that was what made the lies more believable.

There was a faction in this country that believed that immigrants were the cause of most of our problems. Esme was apparently caught in the cross-fire of this undeclared war on immigrants. Her case was too on the nose for there not to be a big deal made about it. The victim was too perfect, Esme was too powerless, and the mood in this country was too hot. Just as she'd been made a villain by the anti-immigrant right, she was a martyr and a cause célèbre for the other side. Each side was just as passionate as the other, and, in the meantime, there was Esme, caught in the middle of the warring factions.

It was too much to bear for any woman.

Chapter Seven

I GOT HOME THAT NIGHT, just wanting to get into the tub with a glass of wine or three. Just light some candles, get a good book and soak. I had some lavender bath crystals that relaxed me more than anything else ever did.

But that was not to be. Harlow and Lola greeted me the second I walked in, and Aidan was sitting on the couch, surfing through Netflix.

"The dogs been outside?" I asked him. Aidan had picked the dogs up from their doggie daycare after his last class at 3:30. That was the arrangement we had, but he also was to put the dogs out periodically until I got home to do it myself.

He shook his head. "Nah. Listen, I've had a shit day at school and work, and all I want to do is veg out in front of a good movie." He continued to surf the site, clicking through one picture after another.

I took a deep breath. "Aidan, I thought we had an understanding." Our understanding was that Aidan would help me around the house, including cooking for me, walking the dogs and cleaning up. I took one look around, at the half-eaten pizza in the box, the clothes strewn around the floor, and the dirty dishes, and I lost it.

"Get up. Off your ass." I picked up his jacket, which was covering the back of the sofa, and threw it at him. I picked up his shoes, which were on the dining room table, and hurled those at him, too, for good measure.

"What's your problem?" he asked as a shoe flew at his face. He covered himself and ducked before the other shoe could make a similar trajectory.

"Why are you losing your shit right now?"

"Why? Why? Because, you lazy POS, I've let you live here, and you've done jack for me. These dogs have to be walked before I get home. And I expect the dishes to be done, your crap to be picked up and the bathrooms to be cleaned. I don't think that's asking a lot, considering you're staying here for free."

Aidan just shook his head. "You better not throw me out of here. You might need me."

"Why would I need you?" I asked him. "What do you bring to the table?"

He got up off the couch and flexed his muscle and pointed to it. "This. This is what I bring to the table. That and the fact I'm proficient in MMA. I can take anybody, anytime, anywhere."

"Yeah. So?" What was he getting at?

"Well, sis, in case you haven't been paying attention, which you clearly haven't, you are public enemy numero uno these days." He brought his laptop over to me. "I got on your personal email when I found out you have the Esme Gutierrez case. I think you need to read some of the messages you're getting. It's some pretty jacked-up shit if you ask me. If I were you, I'd get a gun."

I shook my head. "What are you talking about? Listen, I can't deal with this right now. Lola and Harlow need to go out. How would you like to hold your pee for hours on end?"

He waved his hand at me. "I took them out an hour ago. Chill, baby, just chill."

"What do you mean, you took them out? You told me you didn't."

Aidan shrugged his shoulders. "I like seeing you lose your shit. What can I say? But I took them out. I'm not that cruel."

I sighed and closed my eyes. My brother was standing on my last nerve, to say the very least.

"You sure the dogs have gone out?"

"Positive. While I was out there, by the way, I ran into a bunch of people with cameras and microphones and shit. You must not have seen them because you came up through the garage, but they're out there."

I went out onto the balcony and looked down. Sure enough, there was a crowd of people standing on the boardwalk, some of them with bullhorns in their hands. I also saw some satellite trucks that apparently had just arrived. They were parked out on the street.

"What the hell?" I asked.

"They're trying to talk to the neighbors and anybody coming out about what they know about you. They asked me a bunch of questions, I guess because somebody tipped them off I'm your brother, but I told them all to F off." He smiled broadly. He loved this type of thing. Ate it up. Being in the middle of the action was right where he wanted to be. "Anyhow, sis, I think you need to look at your emails. You're not going to like what you see."

I hadn't looked at my personal emails for a while, I had

to admit. I typically only looked at my personal email account every third day because it was 99% spam anyhow. I always meant to unsubscribe to stuff and mark other things as spam. I either never got around to it, or I didn't do it because I thought that maybe someday, somehow, these email messages might come in handy. Maybe one day I would go ahead and print out a discount coupon for Macy's, so I better not mark it as spam. That was silly, though, because I hardly ever shopped in a regular store. I mainly did like most everybody else – I bought everything on Amazon.

With a sigh, I put out my arms. "Go ahead, show me my emails. I have to admit, you got me curious."

"You're not going to be curious when you read these emails, sis," he said. "You're gonna be pissed. And maybe scared, although you're a badass and ain't nobody scaring you."

I sat down with my laptop on my kitchen table and saw that my email inbox was flooded. "What the hell?" I asked, seeing that most of the messages were not from companies and the usual suspects. These were email addresses I'd never seen before. And they had hateful and unsubtle message lines such as *to the whore representing Esme*, and *I hope you die*.

Subtle, these messages were. Real subtle.

I opened one message after another, seeing that most of them were threatening in nature. One of the emails threatened that if I stayed on Esme's case I would be "gutted like a pig." Another said I deserved to get the needle along with my client. Quite a few accused me of destroying this country by defending Esme and people like her.

One of the more coherent emails began innocuous enough. Argumentative, but innocuous.

Dear Ms. Collins,
I'm writing this email because I'm concerned you don't know what you are getting into by representing Esme Gutierrez. I don't think you know exactly how the country feels about her. I realize that Ms. Gutierrez is entitled to representation, even though she's not a US citizen. I've read about you, and I know you enjoy taking on cases that are long-shots. Underdogs. I know you were wrongfully imprisoned in your youth, and that's why you have a passion for taking on cases that are hard to win.

I shrugged as I started to read this email. After reading hundreds of messages filled with people misspelling simple words like "kill," and messages that talked about my "loosing my head," in reference to their fantasy about my being beheaded like Marie Antoinette – I mean, come on, it's *losing* my head not *loosing* it, get it right – a coherent and reasonably intelligible email like this one was a refreshing change.

Which was why the second part of his email was that much more chilling.

Ms. Collins, I don't want to be rude, but if you continue on this case, you will die. That is a fact. You are representing a cold-blooded murderer, one that should not even be in this country to begin with. Nobody asked her to come to this country. She killed a beautiful and talented woman, and if you walk her, you have signed your death warrant. Believe this. I know many people who believe like I do, and they all agree with me – both you and your client should be shot.

I hope you treat this message fairly and in the spirit to which it was intended. Withdraw from her case or suffer the consequences.

Sincerely,
X

Oh, boy. I looked up at Aidan when I finished reading my death threats and hate mail.

"How did these clowns get my email address, I wonder?"

"Duh. Did you use your personal email address when you signed up for Facebook?" he asked.

"Yeah. So?"

"So? After all the data breaches places like Facebook have seen and with all the privacy issues that site is having, and you think your personal information isn't going to get out there? All it takes is for a few hackers to get your email address and post it online and consider yourself Doxed, my friend. Doxed. I've been doing a few Google searches, and your personal information is all over the Internet by now."

I took a deep breath and went out onto the balcony. By now, there were quite a few protestors that started to line the boardwalk, signs in hand.

"This won't stand," I said. "These are private condos. They're trespassing."

"Well, actually, the boardwalk isn't private property. It belongs to the city of Coronado. Those people are well within their rights to be there. Now, if they make themselves a nuisance, they might be sternly talked to by the beach cops who run around on those Segways. But they have a First Amendment right of assembly, they're peaceful so far, and..."

"And they're blocking the egress of the people on the boardwalk," I said. "Surely there's something that can be done about them."

"I'm afraid there's not," he said. "I've been studying my Con Law for the bar, so I know from where I speak."

I looked up at the ceiling, trying to remember Con Law myself. I studied that stuff, too, for my own Bar Exam, but it seemed so long ago. It wasn't, really, it was only 4 years ago that I was studying for the bar, but it seemed like a lifetime ago.

I was doubtful that crowd of people couldn't be shooed off, so I did a quick Google search, which brought me to the ACLU site, which clearly stated that protestors had an absolute right to use a public sidewalk. They didn't even need a permit.

I took a deep breath. "Okay, smartypants, you win. They can stay down there. At least, until one of them gets out of hand." I felt my cheeks flush, and I put my hands on my face. My skin was burning hot. "Oh, God, I didn't expect this."

Aidan had a smirk on his face I wanted to slap right off. "What were you expecting if you got on this case, sis? Everybody's been just waiting to see who would represent her after the state decided to go for the death penalty on the case. You won that lottery. Now you get the prize."

I heard the shouting beginning from down below, thinking I didn't want this particular prize.

"You mean they can't be asked to leave even though they're disturbing the peace?" I asked Aidan. "Come on, there must be something that can be done about this. And something that can be done about all these death threats. I mean, seriously. I'm just trying to do my job."

"I'm sure the cops were called and they'll probably just be told to tone it down. It's 10 o'clock, and people are trying to get some shut-eye. But they can't be asked to leave if they're quiet."

As if on cue, the crowd below quieted down. But they were still down there, holding up their signs. I was stunned to see that quite a few of these signs had my picture blown up on them, with a circle and line through it.

"I don't like this." I took a deep breath. "Somebody could get hurt in all this."

"Well, my MMA skills will come in handy, then," he said, flexing his muscle again. I had to admit that my brother was really buff, thank God. He worked out just about every day and kept in shape by riding his bike and running on the beach just about every evening.

"Thanks," I said. "Maybe we should get a gun."

"Probably wouldn't hurt," he said. "Anyhow, I have to do some studying before I hit the hay. Got a hot date this weekend, so studying will be out for the next few days. See ya." At that, he went into his bedroom, leaving me to watch the protestors warily down below.

I sat there and watched the crowd until they finally disbanded at 2 AM, while drinking some hot tea and petting Harlow and Lola, who were out on the balcony with me. I was probably anthropomorphizing them, but it seemed like they were just as worried as I was. Their little ears were perked up, and they kept whining softly while pacing around the floor of the balcony.

I went down to the boardwalk after I thought it was safe and walked them so they could do their business before we all tried to get to sleep.

That was a mistake.

"You," a 50ish man in a baseball hat said to me as I walked Lola and Harlow. "You're the bitch who's going to be getting that illegal piece of shit off for murder!" He pointed at me, and five people surrounded me almost immediately. They apparently were stragglers from the earlier protest. They were all men, all about the same age as the first guy, and they all stood close to me and yelled obscenities. They were careful not to touch me, though, because I could have anybody who laid a hand on me arrested for battery.

A beach cop on his Segway came up to the group immediately. "Move along," he said, getting off his Segway and brandishing a club.

The men obeyed, dispersing onto the beach while giving the cop the stink-eye.

"Thank you," I said to the cop.

He nodded but said nothing and continued on his way.

I was shaking as I walked the dogs. As usual, they sniffed around for several minutes before finally getting down to business, and I cursed both of them silently. It was irritating on a regular evening, the way they had to find just the right patch of grass to pee on. I thought they did it on purpose because they wanted to stay out as long as possible. Tonight, though, it was scary to stand outside with the dogs. I half expected some guy to come along and force me into his truck.

Every noise I heard made me jump out of my skin.

Lola and Harlow finally did their business, and I ran back into the condo building, punching the elevator button with shaking hands.

I got into my condo and jumped into my bed, putting the covers over my head.

What did I get myself into?

Chapter Eight

GRAYSON

GRAYSON JACKSON WAS in a particularly agitated mood. He usually was, but he really was on this particular day. He had read online something that disturbed him greatly. He frequented the site called 8Chan. That site was talking about the Esme Gutierrez case, and there was a rumor posted on that site that Esme was actually part of an underground network of people who were plotting to take over the United States. It was not a coincidence that she chose to go to work for one of the most prominent men in America. One of the wealthiest men in America. Jacob was known to be somebody who was sympathetic to the cause.

Then again, according to Grayson, everybody was sympathetic to the cause. He could think of no rational person in America who would not agree with him on the subject of immigrants. To him, it was as plain as the nose on his face. He and his kind belonged here, they and their kind did not. Simple as that.

He was going to have to step up his harassment of Avery Collins. He was one who had gathered together the people to protest outside of her window. That was the only thing he could think to do to have some power over what was happening in this case. It wasn't like he could go down to the jail and organize protests there. That would not have any kind of effect. Esme Gutierrez would not even know about the protests. And it wasn't like him making his voice heard would change anything at all about this case.

But if he could use his influence and pressure to harass Avery enough, then there was a possibility that Avery would withdraw from the case. That would be the best-case scenario, because, presumably, Esme would have to go with a court-appointed attorney at that point. And he knew something about court-appointed attorneys – they tended to not give it their all. A court-appointed attorney would no doubt see Esme as just one of many cases that person would be trying. They would be distracted, probably wanting to plead it out. They probably wouldn't have the kind of resources Avery had at her fingertips to do investigations and follow every lead.

There would also be the possibility, of course, that if Avery withdrew from the case that another attorney, a private attorney, would take the case on. After all, this case was generating a lot of publicity. Some showboating attorney would take it just to get his mug on television. Of that, Grayson had no doubt. If that was the case, then he would rinse and repeat. Whoever decided to take this case was going to get harassed. Because if there was one thing he knew, it was that Esme was guilty, and she needed to go back to where she came from. Better yet, since she was guilty, she should be on the gurney. With a needle in her arm. That would be the only way his agenda would be achieved. If every immigrant who came to this country saw what happened to Esme, then they would know better than to kill one of our own.

And so it was that he used another on-air four hours to whip up hysteria against her. But, instead of merely whipping up hysteria about Esme, he decided that he would spend much of his time on the air fanning the flames against Avery. He was going to have to show that Avery was a whore, a hired gun who would go to the highest bidder. She wasn't a whore in the sexual sense, at least not that he knew about. But she was certainly a whore who took cases she shouldn't. He didn't know if she was simply doing it for publicity, or for some other reason, he couldn't think of anything else, but whatever reason she took it, it was the wrong one.

He turned to the microphone to begin his show. "And now folks, I'd like to talk about the person who is trying her hardest to make sure a murderer like Esme Gutierrez walks free. Avery Collins is Esme Gutierrez' lawyer. And if there's one thing I can tell you about her, it's that she is somebody who should not be practicing law. She was behind bars for seven years for killing her best friend. A jury of 12 people found her guilty of that crime. She was convicted, and sent away, for the rest of her life. But now she's out. She shouldn't be out. She should not be allowed anywhere near a court room unless she's going to a court room to answer for her own sins. If Esme goes free, then blood is on her hands. We can't let that happen.

We can't let this invasion continue, and it will, unless it is stopped right now. If Esme gets away with it, then everybody will know that this is the kind of country we have. You can just come in here and murder in cold blood, and nothing will happen to you. That's the kind of message that will be sent if Avery Collins is successful in defending this woman. That's why I wanted to spend this time today talking about Avery. I want to make sure everybody knows exactly what this woman is about, and how she will stop at nothing to make sure that guilty people walk free. Avery Collins is what is wrong with this country. She's the reason we aren't safe to walk the streets around our own homes. It's because of her and women like her. So now, everybody who's listening to this program, hear me when I say this. Avery Collins must be stopped."

Grayson knew that a good percentage of his listeners weren't aware that every accused is entitled to an attorney. So he knew that he could get away with making people think that if Avery Collins was destroyed in some way, that would mean Esme would be left with no representation at all. And if she didn't have representation, she would lose at trial for sure. Grayson was counting on the ignorance of many of his callers because he wanted them to think if they harassed Avery enough that she would withdraw and Esme would lose.

One caller after another called up to talk about the case, focusing on Avery's role. Many of them knew her back story, and they agreed with Grayson. A jury of her peers had found her guilty of murdering her best friend, and that's all they needed to know. Most of them didn't know the reason why she was out of prison. Most of them had no idea she was set free because someone from the Innocence Project had taken an interest in her case and made sure she got out. Most of them just assumed she had gotten out after seven years because that was common knowledge as to how long a murderer served time in prison. All murderers got out after seven years, according to a lot of people who called the show.

Bob Winslow, from Dearborn Michigan, was a good

example of the kind of calls he got that day. "I wanted to talk to you about how life in prison anymore pretty much means seven years. You know that's the average length of time a murderer serves in prison. And then they're just going to get out and do whatever they're going to do. They're going to get out and kill again, and then go back into prison and serve another seven years. Just keep on doing that. Every seven years, they commit another murder, and then get out again. That's what happened with that Avery Collins. She was sentenced to life in prison, which is where she belonged for the rest of her life, then she got paroled after seven years. Free as a bird just to do whatever. And you know that's the reason she's defending other murderers. She's trying to stick it to all of us. She's basically sticking out her tongue at us, laughing at us, because she got out, and she's gonna make sure all other murderers get out too. You're right, she must be stopped."

Grayson was a fairly educated man, so he knew better than anybody that the myth that murderers only served seven years in prison, was just that – a myth. There was no state in the union where a prisoner with a life sentence got out after only seven years. He didn't know when or where that story got started, but it was a useful one for him. That myth gave him a way to bash on the criminal justice system, and show how law-abiding citizens were taken advantage of by those liberals who just wanted criminals to be out on the streets as soon as they got into prison. Those damn bleeding heart liberals were the reason our society was as bad as it was. All they wanted to do was make sure nobody served time in prison, and that everybody just got a slap on the wrist. Avery Collins managed to check both of those boxes - she was an example of the criminal justice system gone awry, and she was a bleeding heart who wanted to make sure other people did not serve time in prison either.

He was surprised by just how passionate the people were who called into the show that day. They, too, saw Avery as a symbol for all that had gone wrong in society. Just like Esme had become the face of immigrants everywhere, and how violent they were, Avery had become the face of the bleeding heart who got out of prison after murdering somebody after only seven years.

By the end of his show, he knew he had whipped up enough people into a frenzy that Avery would be in danger.

And that was exactly what he was aiming for.

Chapter Nine

THE NEXT DAY, I got into my office suite and saw a guy sitting in the waiting area. I figured he was waiting for one of the other attorneys in the suite, but, when he saw me, he immediately smiled and stood up.

He was definitely handsome. That is, if you like perfection. Perfect teeth, straight nose, chiseled chin and cheekbones, eyes that were a bright combination of blue and green and were fringed with thick dark eyelashes. His sandy hair was cut short, but not too short, as his bangs were slightly long and swooped to one side. His suit was impeccably tailored to his 6 foot plus frame, and his shoes were wing-tipped, leather and buffed to an impossible sheen. In his perfectly manicured hand was a briefcase, and on that wrist was a Rolex watch.

I raised an eyebrow. This guy looked monied.

"You serving me with papers for something?" I asked him. I knew I didn't have any clients coming in, but he seemed to be waiting for me, so that was the only thing I could think of - this guy was some kind of process server. I didn't know who might be suing me, but I guessed there was somebody who might have an imaginary malpractice case against me.

He chuckled. "No, I'm not a process server." He held out his hand. "Christian Davis. Damned glad to meet you."

I looked over at the receptionist who was watching Christian with stars in her eyes. Christian saw me make eye contact with Sarah, the receptionist for our suite, and smiled. "I didn't have an appointment. I took a chance to come down here and meet with you." I noticed he had dimples when he smiled. "I knew you come into the office early, so I knew I could catch you before you really get going."

I was wary about people knowing too much about me, especially after my close calls from the night before with the mob on the boardwalk.

"How did you know I come into the office early?" I asked him.

He cocked his head. "I follow you on Facebook. You make early posts from your office all the time, so I figured that it was a safe bet you'd be here at this time."

That was a bad habit of mine, one I would quit doing *tout de suite*. I did post on Facebook from my office. I was one of those annoying people who liked to show off different pictures I bought from art fairs or some of the cute little figurines I nabbed for my office shelves. I realized that many of those postings were at 6 AM, which was when I usually got into the office in the morning.

"And why do you follow me on Facebook?" Who was this guy? Was he a creeper or a stalker? God knew he was a good-looking creeper or stalker, if that was what he was, but so was Ted Bundy.

"I found out you're on the Esme Gutierrez case, so I

looked you up on Facebook. I would've called you to make an appointment, but you probably would've just thought I was a weirdo."

"And just showing up here will make me think you're less of a weirdo?" I asked him with a shake of my head.

"Well, I guess I thought I could charm you in person," he said, "more so than over the phone."

"Huh. Because you're such a pretty boy? I'm quite sure you're used to women dropping their panties the second you walk through the door, but if you thought that would happen here, think again. I'm not in the mood." After the scene last night, I wasn't in the mood for much.

His smile never lost his face. "Touché. Listen, if I could just have five minutes of your time, I'll explain why I'm here."

"You sound like a door-to-door salesman," I said. "Leave a brochure of whatever you're selling, I'll be in touch."

"Actually, I'm not wanting to sell you on anything. Except myself. I want to sell you on myself."

"Excuse me?" I asked him. "What do you mean, you're selling yourself?" Was he a male prostitute? That was a new one, selling sex door to door. New one on me, anyhow, but maybe it was a thing.

At any rate, that was the last thing I needed at that moment. Pretty boy or no.

"Just five minutes," he said, putting his thumb and forefinger together to show he was only asking for a little thing. "And you can throw me out of your office if you don't like what I have to say."

I looked over at Sarah, who was studiously pretending not to hear anything that was being said between this Greek God and me, but I could tell she was hanging on every word. She was clearly as curious as I was about what this whole thing was about.

I motioned him to follow me. "My office is back here," I said, "but I'm leaving the door open. And I'm warning you, I have a gun." I didn't have a gun, of course, at least not yet. But I had the sneaking suspicion I would have to get one after last night.

He followed me into my office and sat down in front of my desk. "Nice office," he said, looking around. "That a Klimt print?" he asked, pointing to a painting I had on one of my walls that was, indeed, a copy of a Gustav Klimt painting. "He's one of my favorite artists."

"Yeah," I said, nodding my head. "Good eye. Now, down to business. Who are you and why are you here?"

"A direct woman," he said approvingly. "I love it. Well, I'm here because I want in."

"Into what?" I asked him.

"I want in on the Esme Gutierrez case," he said. "You don't have a second chair lined up yet, do you?"

"Ah, I see. So, like a circling vulture, you stalked the Esme Gutierrez case and just waited to pounce on whoever was suckered into taking it?" I leaned back, observing him. "Gotta give you an A for effort there, but-"

"Listen, I'm an attorney down at Gordon and Rees," he said, referring to one of the largest law firms in the San Diego area, "and I'm going out of my mind working for them. 80 hours a week, grinding away, and never seeing a courtroom. I'm on the partnership track, but, quite frankly, if I make partner, I don't think I'm going to see my fortieth birthday. I mean, I'm making 250K a year, but my billable hour requirement is just insane." He took out his resume. "You went to Harvard. I went to Yale. Class of 2020, just like you."

"Wait," I said, looking at his resume. It showed he was specializing in intellectual property law at Gordon and Rees, and that his career, thus far, consisted of legal research, document preparation and review and lots of deposition and settlement work. He hadn't yet had any trial experience, so I was wondering why he thought he was right for the job.

I did need a second chair, that was indisputable, but I was thinking I needed to find somebody who I knew well in the criminal bar. Somebody who knew what he was doing. I certainly wasn't looking for a big firm muckety-muck who had never been inside the San Diego Superior courthouse.

"Why do you think you're qualified to second-chair a case like this?"

"I know this is a death penalty case. And I know that the stakes are high. Incredibly high."

"You might say that," I said. "I lose this case, and my client gets a needle in her arm. Not to mention the fact that her life is probably in danger as we speak. The passions on this case are sky-high, I don't think I need to tell you. So, yes, the stakes are very high. Too high to hire an inexperienced second-chair to help out with this."

"I understand, and I knew you would say that," he said. Then he straightened his back and looked me in the eye. "Look, I'm going to tell you something, and, trust me, I'm taking a gamble in saying this to you. You could call the California Bar and turn me in. But I think I might have some skills that could come in handy to you in this case."

"Oh, great," I said. "Sounds like you're about to tell me you skirt ethics or something."

"I'm a computer hacker," he blurted out. "And I'm very good at it."

"Okay," I said. "And-" I wasn't quite sure what him

being a good computer hacker had to do with the price of tea in China.

"And, believe me, my computer hacking skills will come in handy. It always does. You don't even know right now what kind of records you're going to have to get illicitly." He nodded his head. "Plus, I'd imagine you're getting some pretty choice emails lately. You've been doxed, big time, and everyone knows everything about you."

I rolled my eyes. "So my brother tells me. I haven't Googled my name online, though, because I don't want to know what's being said about me."

"Trust me, you probably don't want to know, but you probably should. There're stories about you on the dark web, and they're not exactly flattering. I realize you served a 7 year prison sentence for something you didn't do, but, according to the people on the internet, you bribed your way out of prison and you really did kill your best friend, Becky Whitfield. Just about everyone agrees you should still be in prison, including the family of Becky Whitfield. They've been chiming in with postings of their own. It's ugly out there."

I took a deep breath and looked at my balcony. I had some red geraniums growing there in a pot, and looking at them always comforted me. But nothing could comfort me when I heard what Christian had to say about what was being said about me. I didn't like people talking about me, just like anybody else. I didn't like hate emails, either. A certain amount of hate emails went along with this job, because every time I walked a defendant, I got a slew of emails accusing me of being an accessory to murder and the like. But I'd never gotten death threats and I'd never gotten the vitriol that was flooding my email inbox even as we spoke. And just knowing that literally the whole world knew about my going to prison…there were no words for how humiliated I felt.

I looked at Christian and saw an expression on his face that enraged me. It was a cross between a pitiful *poor you* look and a half smile, and I immediately thought he was actually enjoying himself. He was digging the knife in and twisting it around and was getting some kind of sadistic pleasure out of my agony.

"Out," I said to him, pointing to the door. "I don't need your help, thank you very much. There are plenty of attorneys out there with death penalty experience who can help me in this case. I need somebody with relevant experience." I took a deep breath and counted to ten, then shut my eyes. "Thank you very much for thinking of me, but I'm afraid I'm going to have to reject your offer."

He nodded his head. "Okay, I thought it was worth a try." He brought out two of his business cards. "But if you change your mind-"

"I won't, but thanks," I said. "Sarah will show you out."

He turned around and walked out of my office without another word.

And the second he left, I lost it. All the pain, all the rage I'd felt ever since Becky was found dead came to the surface. I doubled over on the floor, holding my belly while I screamed impotently against…something. The nameless person who killed her. My public defender who didn't give a crap about me. The prosecutor who intentionally withheld exculpatory evidence. The people who were still convicting me, who never forgave me even though there was nothing to forgive. I knew I'd never escape my hell, because there would always be thousands, maybe even millions, of people who would still think I was guilty.

It was like the congressman Gary Condit. He was

suspected of killing his intern, Chandra Levy, with whom he was having an affair. He lost his career over it, even though somebody else was eventually convicted for the intern's murder. People still thought him to be a murderer, even to this day. It didn't help that the person convicted for poor Chandra's murder eventually was freed because somebody lied on the stand.

The only way that it would stop would be if I could track down Becky's murderer. I'd never even bothered to try to find her murderer all these years, because I wanted to move on with my life. I didn't want to reopen that particularly painful wound. But I knew I would have to. If I ever wanted to walk around in public without feeling that people were pointing and staring, I would have to try to figure it out. It was a cold case at the moment, but cold cases were meant to be reopened. And if I could just find some clues, then maybe, just maybe, I could convince the cops to give the case a second look.

And maybe I could actually sleep at night.

Chapter Ten

THAT NIGHT, I got home and found that Aidan wasn't around. That was fine. It was Friday evening, and he had mentioned something about having a hot date. If it was a really hot date, he might not return until the next day. I decided to take advantage of the relative quiet of the evening and really dig in deep into Esme's case. The answer to what had happened was right there in that file. I was convinced of it.

I prepared a motion to inspect the crime scene, and made a note to myself I needed to set up interviews with Colleen and Jacob. With any luck, they would speak to me willingly. If they didn't, I would have to subpoena them for trial, but I didn't want to be feeling around in the dark like that. Because of the California rules regarding depositions, I wouldn't be able to depose them before trial, which would mean I would be asking them questions on the stand I didn't know the answer to. That was always a bad idea, because you never knew what they would say. Sometimes it worked out. Sometimes it didn't. When it didn't work, it was usually devastating to the case.

There were a few protestors out on the boardwalk again, but they weren't shouting like they were the previous evening. I figured that the beach cop was down there keeping the peace. But they were there with their signs, including signs that had pictures of me with the circle and line through my face.

I didn't want to look at my emails again. I figured that what I didn't know wouldn't hurt me.

How wrong I was.

Chapter Eleven

I ACTUALLY GOT to sleep that night. It was a dreamless sleep, but I shut my eyes and actually went unconscious, so I counted that as a win. I listened to the snoring of my two precious pups, and the sounds of their snores actually came into my unconscious brain.

So did the sound of their frantic barking.

I opened my eyes and saw a figure was in my bedroom. "Aidan, what are you doing here?" I asked the figure, and then looked at the clock. 2 AM. "How was your date?"

Then I saw it. A knife. That was when I noticed that the figure's face was covered completely with some kind of ski mask. The figure had on a hoody that covered his or her head as well.

Harlow and Lola weren't barking anymore, and I immediately thought the worst. Then I noticed they were on the bed with me, both of them alert, but not barking. They looked cowed, frightened, as if they, too, knew the meaning of a sharp knife in an intruder's hand.

"What do you want?" I asked the figure, thinking I was really going to have to get that gun.

The figure didn't say a word, but handed me a piece of paper with writing on it.

It simply said "Get off her case or you will die."

Then the figure came over to me and put the knife against my throat.

That was it for Harlow and Lola. They weren't going to let this figure slash my throat. His or her back was turned away from them, and they both lunged at him. The figure fell back against the nightstand, and I quickly thought it was my chance to get the better of the person. But I was entangled in my covers, and, before I could disentangle myself, the figure had gotten up off the floor and had ran out of the room. Harlow and Lola chased after it, barking and lunging, and, before I knew what was happening, the figure had disappeared out my front door.

I ran after the intruder when I finally got out of my covers, but the figure apparently had gotten lucky and had gotten the elevator as soon as he or she arrived in the hallway. Figures. The elevator wasn't the fastest one in the world, and if that person got the elevator, then I wouldn't be as lucky for at least a few more minutes.

I went down the stairs, taking them two at a time, but I knew I wouldn't be catching the phantom. I had to try, though, so I ran down the 10 flights of stairs and got into the parking lot. I looked around and saw nobody. I looked through every bush and under every car, and then ventured out onto the boardwalk. Nobody was around from the earlier protest, thank God, but there were still a few people milling about.

It was Friday night at the Coronado beach. My condo was right next to the historic Hotel Del Coronado, a very popular hotel that always had a lively night scene. People were on the boardwalk – a couple was walking along, holding hands, and a group of drunk 20-something guys were stumbling along. A guy on a large tricycle was pedaling by, blasting music out of a boombox on the back of the trike. A couple of women on scooters whizzed by, and then another group of drunkards consisting of 3 men and 2 women passed me on my right.

I didn't see any kind of figure in a ski mask and hoody, though.

I went up and down the boardwalk for the next hour, and went down to the actual beach to see if the intruder had ended up closer to the water. I saw nothing that resembled the figure that was in my bedroom that night.

I finally gave up and went back to my condo.

And I did something that was really rude, but seemingly necessary at that moment. I felt I didn't have a choice, because I couldn't just find a hotel room in the middle of the night, at least not one that would take two large dogs.

I picked up one of Christian's business cards, which were on my table, and called him. I noticed that the other business card was gone, though I didn't pay attention to that fact. I was just focused on getting ahold of him.

"Hello," he said. "Christian Davis."

"Christian, hello, this is, uh," I said, just realizing that it was just past 3 AM. Crap! How rude was I, calling this guy in the middle of the night after throwing him out of my office? "This is, uh-"

"Avery Collins?" he asked me. "And, no, I'm not a total stalker. I don't have your cell phone number, but I'm taking a wild guess. Am I right?"

"Yes," I said hesitantly. "I'm really sorry to bother you at this late hour, but-"

"Okay," he said.

"I know that this will sound really bad. Presumptuous. Downright crappy after the way I treated you today in my office, but…" I took a deep breath. "Something happened tonight that really freaked me out, and I could use some, uh, somebody here with me."

I squeezed my eyes shut, wondering why I called Christian before I even bothered to call the police. I didn't want to even think about what that meant.

"What happened?" he asked.

"A person came into my bedroom. A masked intruder with a hoody. It could've been a man or a woman, I really don't know. He or she, I don't even know anything about this person. I-"

"Where do you live?" he asked me.

"Coronado. In a condo complex right next to the Del. I'm so sorry, you are-"

"Downtown. You're pretty close. There's no traffic on the street right now. I'll be there in fifteen. In the meantime, call the cops."

"I will. Thank you, and I'm so sorry to be bothering you. My brother, he's usually around, but he's gone tonight."

"Hot date?" Christian asked, amusement evident in his voice.

"Something like that."

"I'll see you in a bit. What's your address and condo number?"

I gave it to him, and he hung up.

Then I called the cops.

Chapter Twelve

IN FIFTEEN MINUTES, both Christian and the Coronado police were at my door. Lola and Harlow, wary from what had happened earlier, barked their heads off at everybody, so I had to put them both in their kennels. They continued to whine from inside their little cages, but it couldn't be helped. I hadn't yet trained them to be good when I really needed them to.

The cops took my statement, and Christian waited patiently in one of my leather chairs that was next to the balcony sliding doors. He looked as handsome as he did the day before, even though he was dressed much more casually than he was earlier. He was in a pair of distressed blue jeans and a black sweater that was loose, but still showed off his rippling muscles. He watched me and the cops talking with interest, seemingly soaking in everything.

"Do you need any kind of additional protection, Ms. Collins?" one of the officers asked. His name tag said that his name was Gunther Mulroney. He was a tall man with ascetic features – sunken cheeks, a long beak-like nose and eyes that were slightly too close together. With him was a woman whose name was Frances Johnson, a slight blonde woman who kept talking into an intercom on her shoulder.

I shook my head, and looked over at Christian. It occurred to me that the stress of the past few days had finally caught up to me, and my brain started to feel fuzzy. Like I couldn't think straight.

"I don't know," I said uncertainly. "Do you, do you…"

"Well, we certainly are aware that there's been a great deal of activity in this area these past few evenings. There have been reports of peace disturbances on the boardwalk, with protestors carrying signs and chanting. The case you've been involved with has attracted a great deal of publicity. We could give you some names of some private bodyguards who might-"

I shook my head again. "No, that's okay. That's fine. I don't want a bodyguard. I mean, this is a two-bedroom condo, and my brother stays here, too. He's usually around, but he wasn't tonight. But he usually is, so-"

"It's up to you," Officer Mulroney said. "Obviously. I just wanted to let you know that's an option, and I can give you some recommendations if you need them."

"Thank you," I said, looking over at Christian, who was still watching the scene unfolding, not saying a word. "But I think I'll have to pass on that for now." I nodded my head. "For now," I repeated.

The officers didn't try to press me further on this, but they both patted my shoulder before they left. "We'll do our best to catch the perpetrator, but you didn't give us much to go on."

"I know, and I'm sorry about that."

"Not your fault," Officer Johnson said. "But I would suggest you get a silent alarm system that will notify the police about any intruder. That and a remote doorbell that watches for anybody who comes to your front door and notifies you if somebody is trying to get in." She gave me some information about the best remote doorbell and burglar alarm systems, and then she and Officer Mulroney both left with a tip of their hat to Christian and me.

When they left, I looked over at Christian. "Thank you for coming. I don't know why I called you, except I needed a man around."

"Oh?" he said with his usual amused expression. "You must've been desperate to have called me. I figured I would've never heard from you again after today's scene, but I have to admit I was happy you called. Even if it was 3 AM."

"I'm so sorry about that," I said. "I was panicked and I really wasn't thinking about what the time was. Then I looked at the clock when I was talking to you, and I was all like 'crap.'"

"Well, I was asleep when you called, I won't lie," he said. "But I actually had an early night last night. I got home at 9 and kinda crashed. So I got 6 hours of sleep by the time you called, which is actually what I usually get anyhow, so…"

"Wait, you got home at 9? On a Friday night?"

"Yeah. I told you, I work 80-90 hours a week. I try to take Sundays off, because everybody needs at least one day off, so I pretty much work 14-15 hour days. I don't get a lot of sleep in the best of times, so six hours is just about right."

I stood up and sat back down. "I feel awful. You have to go into work today, too, don't you?"

"I'm supposed to, or at least work from home. But yeah, I usually head into the office at 6ish on Saturdays. Get home around 9, but Sundays are mine."

I looked at my watch. "So, you're going to be heading into the office in about an hour then?" For some reason, the thought of him leaving me there alone gave me a slight feeling of panic. Maybe I did need an alarm system and remote doorbell and bodyguard and gun. All things I never imagined needing in my life, but now seemed like necessities.

"Yeah, about then," he said. "Unless you hire me. Then I'll tell my job to pound sand. I mean, I gotta give them two weeks notice and all, but I'm going to stop busting my ass for them. I'm telling you, my old man died at the age of 50. Worked his whole life, two or three jobs, so he probably put in as many hours as I put in, but barely made enough to provide for us. He died without ever getting to know his kids that well because he was always gone. I don't want that fate for me. And I really want to get into a line of work where I can make a difference to somebody. An individual, not a faceless and cold corporation who really doesn't need my help. That's why I went to law school – to fight the good fight. Fight The Man, instead of working for him."

I took a deep breath. "Do you want something to drink?" I asked him. "I know it's only five in the morning, but I could really use a Bloody Mary."

"Well, I'd join you, but I really have to get home and change for work. And my job generally frowns on me coming in sloshed." He stood up and held out his hand.

"Okay," I said, squeezing my eyes shut tight. "I'll hire you as my second chair. I mean, I'll of course have to rent out another office in my suite, but that's not a problem. It's a pretty big suite, and there's a couple of empty offices for rent. And, of course, if you come and work with me, I'll probably just treat you like an associate. That means I'll have to go to you for help with other cases, too. But feel free to also eat what you kill. If you rainmake, you can go ahead and work your own cases without worrying about me."

I was making up terms as I went along. I'd never hired an associate before, so I really didn't know what kind of terms I needed to extend to him. "As a matter of fact, let's just do this. You can work for me on this one case, and I'll pay you, um, $250 per hour." I knew that was a bargain-basement rate for him, as he probably billed at a rate of $1,000 per hour or more with his firm. Then again, he was making 250K and working around 4,000 hours per year. That worked out to around $60 an hour for him at his current job.

Once I figured that out, I felt more confident in my offer. "$250 per billable hour on this case, and, other than this case, you can feel free to find your own cases and work them. But I'll get you an office, though, in my suite."

Christian was watching me with a smile on his face. He held out his hand again, and I shook it. "Okay, then, we'll figure it all out later. For now, I'll take you up on that Bloody Mary. I mean, I don't have a reason to start drinking this early in the morning, but I certainly don't want you drinking alone, and, Avery, you've earned this drink." He went over to the balcony and looked down at the boardwalk below. "Looks like you're getting some company down there."

"Already?" I asked. "Man."

I went into the kitchen and got out my tomato juice. I added some Grey Goose vodka, my favorite type, some hot sauce, salt and black pepper, and went out to meet Christian on the balcony.

He took the drink. "Thanks," he said, taking a sip. "Damned good. You could be a bartender with this drink."

"Yeah? Actually, being a bartender is sounding pretty good to me right now. It sounds like a helluva better job than my actual one. I'm pretty sure that most bartenders don't get death threats and picketed."

"No, probably not. I mean, sometimes you get a crappy drink, but I wouldn't imagine somebody would threaten their lives over it," he said. "So, I guess I won't go into work today. I'll just go in tomorrow, and today will be my day off. I'll put in my notice on Monday, and then I'll start working for you after I officially quit. But, for today, it's time to kick back a little. Get to know my new boss. Somehow, I don't think you're going to be slave-driving me the way my old one will be, but, then again, maybe you will."

"This isn't going to be an easy case to win," I said. "I mean, I don't know, because I haven't yet started a real investigation, but, just on its face, it's not so great." I took a sip of my drink, savoring the spice and coolness. I loved the way that the smooth vodka hit the back of my throat. "Grey Goose," I said. "For liquor-store vodka, you really can't beat it."

He nodded his head. "Now, tell me what you need for me to do." He raised an eyebrow.

"I will. But first, I want to apologize to you about my behavior in my office." I looked at the waves that were crashing on the shore, while trying to avoid looking more directly below me at the boardwalk, where protestors were starting to congregate. "I've never gotten over Becky's death," I said. "We grew up together. I knew her in kindergarten, and we were best friends from that point on. I would've never hurt her. I don't know who did. I have my ideas about it, but nothing concrete."

Christian was looking at me, his eyes showing empathy. "What ideas do you have about who killed her?" he asked.

"Well, I think it was somebody powerful. Rich. Somebody who had pull with the prosecutor's office, because they withheld evidence from my public defender. DNA evidence, and evidence that Becky was raped." I took a sip of my Bloody Mary, not even caring that the sun hadn't even come up. I wasn't exactly used to drinking before sunrise, but it wasn't unheard of, either. "Then again, my public defender was so awful, anything would've gotten by her. I don't think she asked for discovery even once before my trial. The public defender's office had investigators, but I don't think the investigators worked much on my case. It was almost as if she was in on the game as well. All I know is that the only thing she ever did was pressure me into taking one plea deal after another."

"Sounds like a perfect storm," Christian said. "A corrupt prosecutor, a lazy public defender."

"Well, lazy wasn't exactly the right word," I said. "Gloria was overworked. She had a ton of cases on her desk, and she'd been working for the public defender's office for 10 years. I think that burnout was the name of her game. I think she just had so many trials that autumn she couldn't handle them all. Usually cases don't go to trial, but, if I can remember rightly, three of hers did in the span of two months. All of them first degree murders. That would be hard for anybody to handle."

"So you don't really blame her?"

"I blame everybody. The system – nobody should have to try three murder cases in two months. The prosecutor's office, obviously, because they were the ones who withheld evidence. And the actual murderer, whoever he or she is. That person not only got away with killing my best friend, but also got away with putting me away for the murder of my friend. I spent the first year of my prison sentence crying over Becky's death. I wasn't even angry yet about what had happened to me. Then the last six years were spent in a state of impotent rage."

"And what is your state now?" Christian asked, shaking the ice in his glass. His glass was empty except for the ice, so I took it and went to the kitchen and poured him another one and one for myself as well.

"What is my state now," I said, giving him his glass of Bloody Mary. "Well, I really don't know. I know I enjoy representing people I believe are innocent. People who are getting screwed by the system. That gives me satisfaction and happiness. But I don't sleep very well at night. I find myself wanting to run over pedestrians in the street who are walking against the light. Wouldn't mind sending the ghost of Ted Bundy after people who leave their shopping carts in parking stalls. I mean, what's up with that? What I'm trying to say is that little things in life, the first-world problem stuff, sometimes gets to me more than it should. So, I guess I haven't really dealt with everything just yet. But I'm trying."

"Which is why you're on Esme's case," he said. "Because you think she's getting a raw deal."

"A raw deal is right. That is, if she's actually innocent. I haven't yet determined that. I have a hunch she is, but I have to do some digging around before I can feel confident she didn't do it."

"And if she did do it?" he asked. "What then?"

"I'd have to plead her out, of course. Anyhow, I have a status conference on this case. I got the notice in the mail. Since I'm her new attorney, the judge wants to see me and the prosecutor to find out where we are and what discovery needs to be exchanged. I'm not going to try for a bond reduction for her, because it's pointless. She doesn't have the money to get out of jail, and, even if she got out of jail, she wouldn't have a place to stay. Her only home is a crime scene. She wouldn't be allowed to return."

"What's her bond now?" he asked.

"It's $10 million," I said. "I could try to get it reduced to $5 million or something, but it's pretty much pointless to get it down to even that. Even a bondsman would have to charge her $500,000 in that case, because that would be 10%. For a woman like that, the bond might as well be a billion dollars."

Christian stood up and went to look down at the ground below. "Beautiful view," he said. "You like living out here?" The sun was just now coming up, illuminating the beach and the tops of the waves that looked like glistening jewels, and the protestors down below.

It was a Saturday morning, and, apparently, there were hundreds of people in the city with nothing better to do than harass me.

"I love living out here," I said. "It's calming to sit on the balcony and listen to the water. It's comforting hearing people on the beach at all hours of the night. When you can't sleep, anyhow, you want to hear other people. It reminds you that the world hasn't stopped. I love the old hotel across the street. It's a treasure. Did you know they filmed *Some Like It Hot* over there? And on that beach?"

"I did," he said. "That's part of San Diego lore, you know. That and the fact they filmed part of *Top Gun* at that Kansas City Barbecue Place."

I smiled. "I'm from Kansas City. They're famous for their barbecue."

"And does that place measure up?"

"Oh, yeah. It does. It does Kansas City justice."

"Good to know."

I stood up. "Well, if you'd like to get started with Esme's case, we can get going right now. I'll start the clock if you like." I gestured over to the enormous file that was sitting on my dining room table. "What do you say?"

"Let's go."

Chapter Thirteen

REGINA

REGINA DROVE down to Barrio Logan, which was where she had several contacts she could talk to about the Esme Gutierrez case. She not only wanted to get some word on Aria Whitmore, to see if maybe she knew anybody on the street – she had a hunch there was more to Aria's story than what anybody saw – but she also wanted to get some word on Esme herself.

Esme had presented herself as a complete innocent, but Regina knew better. That girl was tough. She had to be tough to survive what she did – the sexual assault, the witnessing people getting decapitated on the tracks, the forced abortions, the beatings. Regina had a good feeling there was more than one person around the Barrio who would know something about both women.

She started with Juan Castro. Juan was a Mexican immigrant who owned a garage right across the street from Chicano Park, a park that was located beneath the Coronado Bridge in the heart of Barrio Logan. He was a straight businessman, was not involved in any kind of drug dealing or

95

gang-banging, but he knew just about everybody around. It was a combination of his being friendly and owning a business where plenty of gossip floated around about the goings-on in the neighborhood, that made him such a good contact for her.

She had a dozen donuts in her hand, a kind of bribe for giving her information she might need. Truth be told, he would talk to her even if she didn't give him donuts, because he liked her and always was eager to help. But Regina was a firm believer that her contacts should be paid, even if they were only paid in donuts. And these donuts were the best in town – they were made by little Mexican ladies and sold on the street.

He saw her coming up the walkway, and he smiled. He had a dirty rag in his hands, and his hands were dirty as well, but he went up to her and gave her a big hug. "Amiga," he said to Regina. "Long time, no see, huh? Where've you been keeping yourself?"

"Working a lot," Regina said. "And it hasn't been that long. I think we just talked a couple of weeks ago."

"Well, it seems like forever when I don't see your smiling face. And your delicious donuts." He took the box of donuts and put them over on a metal desk on the side of the garage. The metal desk had stacks of important-looking papers on it, and he put the donuts on top of these papers. He took one of the donuts out and bit into it. "Raspberry jelly, my favorite," he said, the raspberry filling spilling out onto his chin. "Want one?"

She went over to the donuts and picked one up and bit into it. It was a chocolate éclair. The chocolate icing was rich, buttery and sweet, while the insides had the perfect amount of sweet goo. The donuts were hot when she got them, and they were still somewhat warm.

"Thanks," she said.

"No, thank you," he said, leaning on a metal chair. "Now, what can I do for you?" His brown eyes danced with warmth, his thousand-watt smile on display. Juan was an attractive guy, and if he didn't have a wife and three kids at home, Regina might've looked at him as a possible romantic interest. Not she was in the market for a romantic interest – her feelings about men were still raw after the Michael incident – but if she were, she would've definitely thought of Juan in that way.

She brought out a picture of Aria Whitmore. "Do you know who this is?" she asked him.

"Yeah," he said, looking at the picture. "That's that chica who got strangled in her own guest home, isn't she?" He nodded. "I knew her. Not well, but I met her a few times. Sad about her, though. Too young for what happened to her."

Regina's heart skipped a beat, and she knew that her hunch was probably right. There was just something about Aria's background that made her think that Aria had more going on than what people had thought.

"Tell me what you knew about her."

Juan shrugged. "She went with Julian Rodriguez for a little while. I remember because she came in here with him a time or two when he was bringing in his cars to be serviced. He has a classic '57 Chevy, worth more than his entire house by a long shot." Then he screwed up his face. "Scratch that. I keep forgetting that houses out here start at 600 grand. Put it this way, if Julian lived in TJ, that car would be definitely worth more than a house out there. I loved to work on it, and it always needed a lot of fine-tuning. Oil changes, spark plugs, tire rotations, things like that. Not that he drove that car all the time, but when he did drive it a lot, he was bringing it into me to service it."

"And you saw Aria with him a few times?"

"Yeah," he said, nodding. "Nice girl, really. Lived over in Coronado, so not too far from here. Not too far miles-wise, but an entire world away at the same time. But she saw him during her summer breaks. I guess she was studying at Juilliard. That's what Julian told me. Told me she was studying to be a classical pianist and also studying to be the next Hans Zimmer. But the female version, of course." He got a faraway look as he got another donut out of the box and bit into it. "Come to think of it, there aren't too many female composers around, are there? I can't remember the last woman who won an Oscar for best original score. Huh."

That thought hadn't occurred to Regina, either, but, now that he mentioned it, it did seem weird.

"Well, maybe Aria was looking to break the glass ceiling on that," she said. "But what did you know about her?"

"Not much, just that Julian was proud of her. He told us he was just friends with her, though. I don't know, none of us could imagine the two of them together, but they seemed to like each other."

"Why couldn't you imagine her with him?"

"Well, Julian, he…has problems. I mean, he's had big problems. Just a little bit loco in the head, but nothing bad. I mean, I don't think he's a serial killer in his spare time or nothing like that, but he's had his issues."

"What kind of issues? I mean, what do you mean by loco, exactly?" Regina asked.

"Loco, crazy. Hearing voices and shit like that. I mean, not all the time or nothing, but he's had his episodes where he's heard people telling him what to do.

People on the radio and television, giving him instructions. Only to him. I think he's been in the nut house a time or two, but that's just a rumor. I don't like to repeat these kinds of things, but, yeah, I think he's been in the funny farm."

"Hm," Regina said. "Julian use any drugs?"

"No, not that I've heard. I mean, I think he takes drugs, but the kind his doctor gives him and stuff like that. I don't know, I don't think he has schizophrenia exactly, but maybe something else. What's that thing called when you get all hyper and wacko for a little while, and then you get all sad and depressed for a little while? Manic depression or something like that?"

"Yeah, manic depression," Regina said. "But I think it's called something else right now. Bi-polar disorder or something of the sort. Did he tell you that's what he had?"

"Well, no, but I do know that sometimes he came in here, talking a mile a minute, man. Talking all kinds of shit, too, like he'd talk about running for congress or something like that. Would talk about how he was working with Aria on a symphony, he was really the genius of the two of them. Stuff like that. Then, other times, he would come in and be all…" Juan slumped his shoulders and frowned, his brown eyes looking like a sad puppy, to show how Julian acted when he would come in depressed. "You know, I'd ask him how he was, and he wouldn't say nothing. He'd be all sad and everything, he wouldn't look me in the eye, and he wouldn't say nothing. I asked his sister about all that, name's Veronica, she told me Julian had that manic depression and he just started taking drugs for it. But I think he's been in the nut house for it, too."

Regina found this all terribly interesting, and knew that this conversation with Juan would prove significant. She just didn't know how significant it would be, only that it would bear fruit.

"And Aria hung out with this Julian dude, then?"

"Yeah, but, like I said, Julian said he was just friends with her. I didn't know why a rich gringa like that would be palling around with Julian, but, well…" He shook his head. "Weirder things have happened, I suppose."

"Did Aria ever say anything to you that you can remember?"

Juan looked into the distance and squinted his eyes, as if he was trying to think of something. Then he shook his head. "No, I really don't remember her saying anything to me that stood out. She was kinda quiet, kinda shy. She was a tiny little chica, very little and skinny and she always looked like she was kinda not wanting to be there. I don't really know how to explain it except she seemed to like Julian, but maybe she didn't like getting dragged around town with him. I don't know."

"What else can you tell me about her?" Regina asked.

Juan shrugged. "Nothing else, but I'll be sure and give you a call if I think of something."

"Thanks. I'd like to talk to Julian, so, if you could give me his phone number, that would be great."

"Sure, just hang out here for a second, and I'll get that for you." He went over to a metal filing cabinet, then came over with a file in his hand. "Here it is," he said, "619-555-0719."

"Thanks for that," Regina said.

"De nada. Well, I really have to get back to work, so…"

"Of course, and thanks for your time," Regina said.

"Another donut for the road?" Juan said, holding out the box.

"You got it," Regina said, taking a bear claw out. "Man, these donuts are the best."

"My mama made them better," Juan said with a smile. "But that was because I ate them fresh from the deep fryer. Anyhow, you take care, Regina, and I'm always around if you need to know anything else."

At that, a guy was coming in and bringing in a car to work on, and Juan greeted him while Regina left. She knew she would have to talk to this Julian character as soon as possible. He was the one who actually knew Aria, so he might have a few answers about her.

Chapter Fourteen

THE HOMELESS WOMAN

THE WOMAN COUGHED while she lay in her sleeping bag. She managed to sleep in a tent in the Presidio Park, because she found an abandoned campsite in a different area of that park, and she took everything she found there. In the abandoned camp was a roll of toilet paper, a half-eaten bag of chips and a new sleeping bag. She couldn't believe her luck when she came across this treasure-trove one day when she was looking for a place to sleep for the night.

She didn't think she would get lucky enough to actually stay in the park for more than one night, so she planned on moving on that same day. The tent actually folded down and fit into a small bag she could fit into her backpack, which was another find on another day.

She was on the move, because she had to be. She would come back to this park later on, after she did what she had to do, but she first had something important on her mind.

She packed up her new tent, her new roll of toilet paper and her new half-eaten bag of chips. She saw two men approaching her, and she immediately wanted to run. She had a feeling these men were the rightful owners of the tent and all the items she found, and she didn't want to give these things up.

For the first time in a long time, she kept out of the rain. San Diego didn't typically get a lot of rain, but, for some odd reason, the past few months had been extremely wet. Most of the time, she slept in the rain. She didn't like to go underneath highway overpasses, because these were well-patrolled. She knew lots of people who slept next to her on the sidewalk had tents, but she never spoke to anyone else on the streets, so nobody ever offered to share their shelter with her.

This tent held a ton of possibilities. For one, she could go down to the beach and pitch it, and she could blend in with everyone else, because everybody had some kind of tent or shelter on just about every beach in town. As it was, she knew she stood out like a sore thumb on the beach, because she was always dressed in jeans and a long t-shirt or sweater, and her hair was completely ratty. Everyone else was in shorts and bikinis and swimsuits. Plus, she always got burned when she went to the beach, because she inevitably would fall asleep – the sound of the ocean waves lulled her – and she always woke up as red as a cooked lobster. But, with this tent, she could go down to the beach and hang out and fall asleep all she wanted. She now even had a second sleeping bag to go with her own sleeping bag, and she could roll it up into a pillow.

Just the thought of being able to fall asleep on the beach without waking up with red blisters on her face made her happy, maybe for the first time in a long time. But these men, who were coming up to her, made her afraid she would lose her new booty to them. They probably were the rightful owners of the tent and all the belongings, so she kept on walking, faster and faster. Then she started to run, leaving the trail that led to the parking lot, and running directly up the rocks and grass, desperately climbing and hoping that these men couldn't catch her and take her stuff away.

She made it up the hill and then ran into the women's bathroom. The men were still around. She could hear them outside the bathroom. She was surprised she was able to outrun them, but she knew that the sheer adrenaline coursing through her veins powered her through to run faster than she had ever run before.

"Where did she go?" one of the guys said.

"I don't know, but she took our shit," another one said.

She sat on the cold metal toilet, with her backpack on the soaking-wet cement floor, and held her breath. She could feel hot tears streaming down her face as she realized just how much these meager belongings meant to her. It meant she could maybe hop a bus to Coronado and lay on the beach and hope that maybe, just maybe, she could get a glimpse of her. The golden child who she thought about just about every day of her life. She messed things up with her son. He apparently got too many of her genes and not enough of her ex-husband's. She felt badly for him, knew he couldn't help it. He couldn't control what had happened. He was gone forever, but her daughter wasn't.

Her daughter thought she was dead. She wanted it that way, because, as far as she was concerned, she really was dead. As good as dead. She never wanted her daughter to know the truth about her. She wanted to always be in her daughter's thoughts just as she was before – a beautiful, trim, fit blonde woman who was bubbly, social and fun. She wanted her daughter to think of her as the woman who baked her birthday cakes from scratch, using food dye and small cake pans to make the cake out of layers that went with the colors of the rainbow. One layer was red, the next orange, the next yellow, the one after that green, then blue, then indigo and then violet. Just like a rainbow. Then she decorated it with little roses and tulips she created out of molds. She wanted her daughter to remember her as the woman who would blow bubbles with her on the lawn, flew kites with her on the beach and dressed up with her on Halloween.

She hadn't seen her daughter since the girl was 14 years old. That was the year she broke. A tragedy happened that year, one that her mind simply couldn't fathom or handle. It was still something she couldn't come to grips with, so much so she had repressed it. If she tried to remember what had happened that year, she couldn't. If somebody asked her, she would say she didn't know, and that would be the truth.

She later found out, after her first hospital stay, she was suffering from late-onset schizophrenia. She was 35 years old when she was diagnosed, and before that year, she'd never had any kind of episodes that made her think she was mentally ill. Had never heard voices, never had hallucinations, never even had extended periods of depression. But that year, she had a breakdown that was brought on by a tragedy so horrible that her mind snapped. It was then, after she was in the mental hospital for six months, and her schizophrenia had gone into remission, that she found out that sometimes serious mental illnesses like schizophrenia don't show up until later in life. That was just how it was sometimes, she found out – you go through life without showing any kind of signs of illness, and then, wham! A tragic incident, and the stress from it, brings it on.

Sometimes, when she had periods of lucidity, which was

often the case, she realized her illness was inherited. She remembered that her mother was taken away from her when she was just a small girl, and her father never did tell her where her mother went. But she would remember the police coming to the door and her mother being taken away in handcuffs. She was only 3 when this happened, so she never quite knew why the police were there and why her mother was gone. It was only when she got older, and her father told her that her mother was in a long-term institution after having killed a man because voices in her head told her to, that she understood. Her mother was very sick.

And then she became just as sick. Only she wasn't as lucky as her mother was. She spent six months in the hospital when she had her first breakdown, and then her husband divorced her and cut her off completely. He didn't even leave her on his insurance. He had money, a lot of money, and she should've been entitled to a decent settlement from him, but he was able to afford a high-dollar lawyer, while she had none. He was able to leave her without a penny by showing the judge that all the property the two had owned during their marriage was his separate property. This was true enough, as she came into the marriage without anything at all, but she thought that at least some of their property was considered marital. But her husband cooked the books to make it look like the two had actually lost equity in their home during their marriage and that the investments he brought into the marriage also went down in value. Plus, he had an iron-clad prenup she willingly signed because she loved him when she married him.

So, she got nothing. No property and no kids. She knew that what had happened with her son meant she was a terrible mother, and her mental breakdown also made the judge concerned she couldn't be alone with her daughter.

So, he got full custody of the kids. Which was just as well, because, even after that stay in the hospital, she never got well. She was forced out of the hospital because she couldn't pay anymore, but she certainly couldn't work and care for herself.

She was eligible for disability, but could never get it together to apply.

That was why she considered her mother to be much luckier than her. Her mother, because of what she did in killing that man, whoever that man happened to be, stayed in the hospital and was cared for there. She'd visited her mother and saw she watched television with some of the other patients, she got meds on time, she had a bed to sleep on and was fed breakfast, lunch and dinner. Her mother never had to sleep outside on the sidewalk, she never went hungry, and she even had crafts and hobbies she was into.

The woman thought, after seeing her mother in the hospital, that maybe she, herself, should kill somebody. If she did, then she, too, could live in a mental institution for the rest of her life. She could be taken care of just like her mother was.

But she didn't have it in her to kill somebody. She wished she did.

She didn't have it in her to kill a person.

But her son did.

Chapter Fifteen

AVERY

AFTER CHRISTIAN AGREED to come and work for me on this case, or, rather, I agreed to take him on, things would start rolling. I immediately went to the lessor's office and rented out another space in the suite for him.

My office suite, located on the 25th floor of a high-rise in downtown San Diego, had 15 office spaces. These spaces were all rented out to different attorneys, all of us doing our own thing. I was friends with most of the people around the suite, but I didn't practice with them. We all tried to cover for each other in courts whenever we had a conflict of some sort, and we shot cases to one another for a finder's fee – I would get word of somebody who needed a will, and I would shoot that case over to Don Lombard, who was the estates and trusts attorney, and Don would find out about somebody who needed a criminal attorney, and I would get that case. I might find out about somebody who was injured in an accident, and I would refer the case over to Natasha Watters, the personal injury attorney in our suite, and she might pass along a DUI to me.

And so it went.

There were only two offices available in the suite, so I jumped on one of them for Christian. It was two doors down from my suite, and, like all the offices on my side of the hall, it had a balcony. Just like my suite, his suite featured hardwood floors, 15 foot ceilings, and was about the same size as mine – about 30x30. I told Christian he could decorate it the way he wanted to, and he and I had been in touch for the past few weeks while he was working with his soon-to-be former employer. He had given in his notice when I hired him, and was eager to get away from his old job so he could really dig into the Esme Gutierrez case.

As for the protestors and the threatening emails, things had calmed down. Enough condo dwellers had had it with the protestors, so there was an emergency town-hall meeting to address the situation. It was decided that it was high time that the city repair that particular stretch of boardwalk, so that's what the city did. The city couldn't ask them to leave unless they were disturbing the peace, because they had a First Amendment right to be there. So the city put barriers 100 feet apart on the boardwalk, right in the place where the protestors had stood. That meant that the protestors couldn't stand right beneath my balcony to protest, they had to protest down the walk a little bit. That deterred them, because it defeated the purpose of harassing me.

I was still getting threatening messages, but Christian managed to fix that for me, too. He planted viruses on the servers of every single person who threatened me. That word got around soon enough - if you send me a nasty email, you'll get a virus in return, so, before I knew it, the hateful messages had dwindled to a trickle.

That was how I dealt with the hate mail. For the actual

death threats, I turned those over to the FBI. A few people were arrested, but, mainly, the people sending the death threats managed to cover their tracks. They were generally smart enough to use somebody else's IP address, like the library, taking their laptops up there and sending their messages from that address while using spoofed email addresses. So, it was more complicated trying to track them down, but the FBI was getting to them, one by one, and, one by one, men and women were being brought in for questioning and getting charged with making terroristic threats.

There was only one person who managed to avoid the FBI, though. It was the guy, or woman, who had sent me the email that had chilled me to the bone. The author who had written the message that started out rational, intelligent and almost empathetic, and then ended with the threat I would die if I kept on Esme's case. I didn't know why that person couldn't be tracked down, but Christian told me that this guy was probably a computer genius who was able to cover his tracks better than almost anybody else.

That didn't comfort me. I wasn't too thrilled with having none-too-bright people threatening my life. I really wasn't digging having some kind of evil genius threatening me. I tried not to think about it, because I had to do my job. Esme needed me to keep my cool. But this guy, whoever he was, unnerved me.

I hadn't had a message from him since that first night, but, when I got into the office the morning that Christian was finally going to join me, that changed.

I was monitoring my personal email much better than I was before the threatening messages had started pouring in, so I booted up the computer and logged onto my personal Gmail account.

And I saw it.

The subject line was *Miss me???*

I got into the body of the email and started to read.

Miss Collins,

I believe I corresponded with you earlier. I told you I felt some sympathy for you and your situation. I understand you were in prison, wrongfully convicted, and I can relate to this. I, too, am in prison, and I, too, was wrongfully convicted. So, I get it. You got out of prison and wanted to help as many people like yourself you could.

But Esme Gutierrez is not worthy of your time. She's not innocent. If you free her, you will be freeing a murderer back onto the street. I know you don't want that on your head. Try to look yourself in the mirror after you walk Esme and she goes on to do it again.

I'm sorry, but I must stop you before it's too late. When I wrote you before that if you continue to represent Esme you would die, that wasn't a threat. It was a promise. It's a simple calculation, really — if you get to the court and you get Esme acquitted, then she'll be free to do it again and again. But if you are sacrificed and Esme does not have a high-caliber attorney, then she will be convicted and she'll spend the rest of her life in prison. Where she belongs. So, I must take you out to save society. I'm sorry that it has to be this way. I know you are only doing your job. You seem like a very nice person. But you have to give up this case if you want to live. It's as simple as that.

Do not even try to find out who I am. You will not be able to. Neither will your new associate, Christian. I understand he's a computer genius, but he does not know who he's dealing with. If he did, he would not allow you to go ahead and keep on this case. Trust me on this.

There's the stick, now the carrot.

I have information on who killed your friend, Becky Whitfield. Interested now?

X

I sat there and looked at that email for what seemed like forever. It was as if I thought that it would change somehow or disappear if I just willed it to. I touched the screen of my computer and put my hand to my chest. I felt my heart pounding beneath my fingers, and I massaged the skin on my chest lightly. It was difficult to think about which part of this email terrified me more. Was it the fact he knew that my new associate, Christian, was a computer genius? Was it the fact he even knew I had a new associate? After all, Christian had not yet entered his appearance on this case, so how did this guy even know I had a second-chair? Was it the way he stated as a fact that my client, Esme, was guilty? Was it the casual way he told me he would kill me to save society?

Or was it the fact he stated he had information about who killed Becky?

Did he have this information?

How would I even know? He wouldn't give me information about who he was, and he confidently said that even Christian wouldn't be able to track him down. If this guy was a skilled computer hacker, like Christian, then he could do anything at all to cover his tracks. In fact, he must've been good at covering his tracks, because the FBI had not yet been able to figure out who he was.

I shut my laptop down and went down to see Christian. He was getting settled into his new office, and I noticed that all the women attorneys in the office were spending a great deal of time with him, giving their opinions on his décor and bringing him baked goods and flowers and things like that. I thought that was sweet, but I also knew that these ladies had an ulterior motive for getting to know the newest attorney on the block. Christian was quite easy on the eyes and he had the charm to match.

When I went to talk to him, Alexis O'Neill, an attorney who specialized in medical malpractice, was standing in Christian's doorway, talking to him about something. She saw me and smiled. "Avery, was just chatting with your new associate," she said. Then she turned to Christian. "Well, if you need me, you know where to find me."

"Thanks, Alex," he said, already calling her by her shortened nickname. He was busy unloading legal treatises onto his wooden bookshelf in the corner of the room. "I'll definitely keep that in mind."

I watched Alex walk down the hallway to her own office with suspicion. She was going through a messy divorce, which was being handled by Max, short for Maxine, an attorney in our suite. I heard her crying in Max's office more than a few times, and I knew that her divorce was hard for her, to say the least.

I could be wrong, but I thought I saw her toss her rich brown hair more than once as she talked to Christian, and I saw quite a bit of eye-batting. Why I cared if she was flirting with him, I didn't know, but I only knew that it bothered me.

But not nearly as much as that email bothered me.

"Hey," Christian said, coming over to me with a smile. "What's going on?"

"Well, I thought we could get our schedules lined up on this case. I don't know what you have going on with other cases, so I need to figure things out. I have an interview with Jacob and Colleen tomorrow, the father and the step-mother of the victim. And my investigator, Regina Baldwin, is following up on some leads she got from a friend of hers, Juan Castro. He told her he knew Aria because she was running around with a friend of his named Julian Rodriguez. Regina's going to talk to Julian while I'm going to be talking to Jacob and Colleen. In the meantime, I thought you might start with trying to track down somebody who, sent me an, uh, interesting email."

Christian nodded and took a potted plant that was an apparent gift from one of the other women in the office and put it out on the balcony. He smelled the air with a smile on his face. "You can't imagine how nice it is to work in an office with a balcony. I spent most of my time with my other firm in the library. Lots of windows, but quiet as a tomb. Kinda lonely, really." He walked over to me. "Now tell me about this email."

"Maybe you should come down to my office," I said. "And read it on my laptop. It's gotten me freaked out, if you want to know the absolute truth."

He went down to my office, and I opened up my laptop and logged back on. The email was right there, because I hadn't actually shut down the email, I just shut the laptop when I walked out of the office.

He read the email, his hand on his chin. He narrowed his eyes. "How does he know about me, I wonder?" he said. "That's odd. I haven't even entered my appearance in this case, so how would he even know I'm working with you, let alone I'm a so-called computer genius?"

"I know. That's the weird thing for me, too. I have no idea how this guy seems to know this. And what's up with him using Becky as bait? I mean, what good does it do for him to say he has information about Becky's murder if he doesn't care to reveal his identity?"

He raised an eyebrow. His scent was somewhat distracting me, because he was wearing some kind of subtle woodsy cologne that smelled like it was high-dollar. Everything about this guy was somewhat distracting, but I had to concentrate on the matter at hand, so I tried to ignore my feelings.

"I'm obviously going to have to try to find out where this guy is," he said. "The FBI hasn't been able to find him, though, so it might be hard. He probably is an expert spoofer, which means he can not only spoof his email address but also his IP. But it's not impossible to try to find him. That's actually the least of the issues right here. To me, it's more concerning he knows about me. That would tell me that perhaps he knows somebody who knows you."

I thought about who knew I had hired Christian to work this case. The people at his job were aware of him coming to work for me, because he told them that was where he was going. Esme knew he was coming to work for me. I'd visited her to tell her I would get a second-chair for her trial, and she was quite excited I would have somebody help me. Regina knew about him, too. And my brother knew about Christian. He'd met him when I had Christian over for dinner one night, and the two bros bonded immediately over their shared love for college basketball and Quentin Tarantino movies.

That was it, though. I had no idea how I would work backwards from those people to figure out who this guy was.

"It's creepy that he seems to know about my personal life," I said to Christian. "I mean, if he knows about you, then what else does he know about me?"

"That's what I'm saying," Christian said. "Man, are you sure you don't want to hire a bodyguard?"

"No," I said, shaking my head. "I don't. I got a high-dollar security system that's so sensitive I've set it off more than once, and so has Aidan, and I have a gun and a permit for concealed carry. I think that those steps are as far as I want to take things right now. I don't want some random dude sleeping on my couch, which is what he's going to have to do, because I don't have space for anybody extra in my condo."

"Well, let's try to figure this out," Christian said "Aidan is a law student, in his third year. Didn't you tell me he nailed down a job for when he gets out of school?"

"Yeah," I said. "He's working with a firm that hired him as a summer associate last year. Nixon and Pierce. It's a PI firm, and he's going to be working for them as a new associate in the fall. Assuming he passes the bar."

"And what kind of activities does he do besides go to school and working at Starbucks?" he asked.

"Well, he does some work for the firm that's hired him, Nixon and Pierce. It's low-paid stuff, but it's helping him get acclimated more into the firm. Right now, he's been doing work on involuntary commitments to mental hospitals. I think that's what he's going to be specializing in. He seems to really like the work."

Christian nodded. "So, your brother is representing the people who've been involuntarily committed to mental hospitals?"

"Yeah. The firm takes some of those cases *pro bono*, but they generally try to concentrate on patients who have the money to hire them. They also take cases where people have been confined in mental hospitals because they committed a serious crime. Sometimes these people go into remission from the mental illnesses for a time, and they hire Nixon and Pierce to help them get out. That doesn't usually work out so well, but sometimes it does. Nixon and Pierce represents them in their hearings for release."

"And how involved is he in these proceedings?" Christian asked.

"He does the prep work. Talks to the client, does the legal research, talks to the doctors who are treating the patient. He doesn't represent them in court, of course, because he can't yet. But he does the legwork."

Christian put his hand to his chin and looked at the email. "Let's start there," he said. "Your brother is a friendly guy. He might've made a friend there at the mental institution during one of his visits to the hospital. Maybe somebody who he might chat with about what's going on in his life, and perhaps he casually mentioned that you hired me. It's worth a shot to think about."

"Yeah," I said, feeling apprehensive. I couldn't imagine Aidan chit-chatting about me with a mental patient, but, then again, maybe he would do something like that. "But how would a mental patient have access to a computer to do something like this?"

"I don't know," Christian said. "To my knowledge, people who are involuntarily committed to a hospital don't have access to computers, let alone Wi-Fi. But it's still worth thinking about."

"What about Esme herself?" I asked. "She knows about your working with me for sure. Maybe she inadvertently told somebody about your being my second-chair, and that person is the one who is threatening me."

Christian and I brainstormed ideas until 1 PM, at which time I had to rush to get to court for one of my robbery clients. Chanel McMillan had held up a liquor store because she was desperate to get money to feed her addiction. She'd since gotten clean, but she still had the robbery charge hanging over her head. I took her case because I had a great deal of sympathy for her – I knew women like her in prison, a lot of women like her. Women who were great people who did stupid things while in the throes of an active addiction. This robbery charge was Chanel's first arrest for anything at all, and I was determined to get as light of a sentence as possible for her.

Christian and I had gotten no closer to finding out who the mysterious "X" was, but we had some good ideas on where to start to find this person.

Chapter Sixteen

REGINA

REGINA HAD FINALLY MANAGED to track down the elusive Julian Rodriguez. She'd gone to the address that Juan had given her originally, and found that house was abandoned. From there, it was a matter of talking to Julian's neighbors, until one finally talked to her and told her where Julian had moved to. She went to the address that the neighbor gave her, and he wasn't living there, either.

His social media had gone dark in the past few months. He used to be quite an active poster to Instagram, Facebook and Twitter, but, in the past few months, there had been nothing. No postings at all.

She finally managed to find out that Julian was back in the hospital. He was in a mental health facility in La Mesa. He had apparently had another acute episode with his bipolar disorder, according to a lady she spoke with who was living close to the neighborhood where Julian had moved to.

"He was running naked through the streets, screaming at the top of his lungs," Anna Kent told Regina. Anna was currently a neighbor in his new apartment where he had moved. The apartment complex was in La Mesa, a suburb of San Diego, and was a dark brick building that resembled a motel. The apartments faced a courtyard in the middle, and each apartment was next door to one another in a neat row, ground floor and second floor, with a small sidewalk connecting all the apartments. Julian's apartment was on the second floor, and Anna was right next door.

"Why was he doing that?" Regina asked. "And what was he saying?"

"He apparently went a little bit crazy one night," she said. "I don't know, I know the guy, I don't think he does drugs, but he sure was acting strangely that night. I saw him earlier in the evening, and he talked to me a little bit, but what he was saying was incoherent. I asked him a question, and he responded by telling me about how Vincent van Gogh was persecuted for his beliefs."

"What question did you ask him?" Regina asked. That was weird, to respond to a simple question by talking about van Gogh's persecution. Regina wasn't aware that van Gogh had any controversial beliefs, let alone that he was persecuted for them.

"I literally just made small talk with him," she said. "You know, you see a neighbor, you don't want to be unfriendly to him. And it's not like I can really avoid him if I'm coming out of my apartment to go to my car, and he's going to his place. I had to pass by him on the way to the stairs. I think I just pretty much asked him how he was doing. You know, small talk. What do you think about this weather, do you think it's gonna rain, that kind of thing. It wasn't an important question, but he responded by telling me how similar he was to Vincent van Gogh because he was persecuted for his beliefs, just like van Gogh. I thought that was very odd. To say the very least."

"Have you seen him since? Have you talked to him at all?"

"No. I haven't. I've heard around he might've gone into a behavioral management facility."

"By behavioral management facility, you mean nuthouse, right?"

"Yeah. That's what I mean. Obviously. I don't know which one though. And even if I knew which one, I don't think you'd be able to talk to him. My mother was in one of those facilities, and I know what kind of a strict protocol they keep." She seemed to be mildly offended by Regina's use of the term "nuthouse," as many people were.

Regina silently kicked herself, wishing that her mouth had a bit more filter than it did. But it didn't, and that was just her. Her words flew out of her mouth before she could even engage her brain.

"Thanks for your help. And I'm sorry about using the derogatory term for a mental health facility. Obviously, I didn't know your mother had issues as well."

She shrugged her shoulders. "Oh, I'm not offended. I've heard that from people for most my life. If I got mad every time somebody called a mental health facility a nuthouse, I'd be in a state of perpetual anger. Anyhow, I wish you luck with trying to talk to him. I don't know where he is, and I don't know if you'd be able to talk to him even if you found him."

Well, Regina thought. *This is another dead end.* But maybe she could make the best of it.

Maybe there would be a way to find out where he was, and not only that, go and talk to him.

She was just going to have to think outside the box.

Chapter Seventeen

AVERY

CHRISTIAN and I headed over to the Whitmore mansion the very next day. I had made an appointment with Jacob and Colleen to speak with them about their daughter's death.

At first, neither of the people wanted to talk to me. Which was always the problem with not being able to subpoena people for depositions. Obviously, you don't know a witness will be material unless you speak with them. And, if you can't prove that witness is material, then you can't subpoena the person for trial. A classic Catch-22. Which was why, as I understood it, some states had the option to subpoena people for depositions prior to trial. California was not one of those states, as you had to show the person wouldn't be available for trial for one reason or another in order to subpoena that person for a deposition, and you had to have a court order.

So I was very happy that both Jacob and Colleen were willing to speak with me. I supposed they probably had it in their head that if things fell through with the Esme case, they'd be the prime suspect. Maybe they wanted to get ahead of it.

We went in Christian's car. It was a brand-new Tesla, two-seater, red and sporty. I had to smile. Such a yuppie car, and, I had to admit, Christian was a yuppie kind of guy.

"Nice car," I said. Then I had to rib him just a little bit. "Are you sure you want to come work for me? I mean, I'm not sure if I can keep you in the manner of luxury to which you've been accustomed."

I got in and fastened my seatbelt, and Christian grinned at me. "Don't forget that our arrangement is just my second-chairing this one case for you. Granted, it is a huge case, but I've already got some clients of my own lined up for next week. I'm thinking I'd like to not just focus on criminal defense, but I might also go the personal-injury route. I was talking to Alex, she does a lot of medical malpractice cases, and she told me she can give me some good referrals for other kinds of personal injury cases. Products liability, class actions, train accidents, things like that."

He stretched out a little bit before putting his hand on the leather steering wheel. "I have to tell you, I feel so much freedom doing this job. When I was working at my old job, I really felt like I couldn't breathe. I mean, I couldn't even have a dog at home. Hell, I couldn't even have a cat at home. Or a hamster, parakeet, or anything like that. Maybe some fish – but any other animal, I wouldn't have been able to take care of it. Now, it's just a matter of me coming home at 6 o'clock, and taking care of whatever pet I decide to have. I haven't quite decided that yet, though."

"Let me suggest you look into getting in a boxer dog. I know how much you get along with my pups Harlow and Lola. You're really good with them."

We drove down the highway, heading towards the Coronado Bridge. The Coronado Bridge was what connected the mainland of San Diego to the so-called island of Coronado. It was a so-called island, because it really wasn't. It was more of a peninsula, connected to the mainland of San Diego by a thin strand called the Silver Strand. There was a ferry that ran from Coronado to the Bay every 15 minutes or so, so there were three different ways of getting onto the "island."

The "island" itself was a quaint and upscale little enclave. The main drag was Orange Ave, which was a boulevard lined on both sides with storefronts of every kind. The traffic was horrendous because the streets were so narrow and there were always cars lined up on either side of the boulevard.

At one time, Coronado was mainly a naval base and many of the navy men lived in the houses around the island. In fact, on the beach where everybody hung out, there was a Navy base right next to it. The planes would fly in so low over the heads of the beachgoers you couldn't fly a kite on Coronado Beach. Literally.

What was allowed, at least on part of the beach, were dogs. There was an off-leash dog beach right next to the Coronado Navy base, and I really enjoyed taking Lola and Harlow down there on a regular basis. They would gallop, run and chase each other while making new friends, while I would put my toes in the water, thinking about how nice it was to be able to have the kind of freedom to have my toes in the sand. At one time, I despaired I would never have that kind of freedom again.

On the way to Jacob's home, I thought of Becky and about the mysterious person who'd written me. I wondered if he was just trying to freak me out.

I wasn't alarmed that he knew about Becky. Everybody

knew about her. When I got on the case, there were all kinds of news stories about me, in just about every major publication there was. It was a big deal, I guess, that I was a former prisoner who was now defending people. Ever since I'd gotten out of prison and went to Harvard, there'd been interest in me. There were some offers to make a documentary about my life for Netflix, but I rejected these offers because I had no desire to have my personal life splashed onscreen for everyone to see.

But my involvement in this case made it to where my personal life was splashed for everyone to talk about anyhow. So the fact that my best friend had been murdered, and I was in prison for her murder, was common knowledge amongst the people at large. So the fact that this mysterious X person, whoever he was, knew about Becky's murder, didn't disturb me.

What *did* disturb me, or maybe it intrigued me, was this person's statement he knew who killed her. I was sure it was just him trying to pique my curiosity, trying to torture me, but what if he really did know about it? How would I even find this guy?

And was this guy, whoever he was, somehow tied to the Esme Gutierrez case? Did he maybe have some kind of information about that case as well? Maybe he knew who did it. That was why he was telling me to back off. He wanted Esme to have a court-appointed attorney, so she'd be less likely to win the case. If she got convicted, obviously the cops wouldn't continue to look for the real culprit. That would make sense – maybe this guy was trying to throw me off my game so I lost. At least, I hoped that it was something as simple as that, because if he really was a deranged psycho, I would be in a lot of trouble.

We finally arrived at the Whitmore mansion, which was

actually just one of many homes for the family. At least, that was what I understood. They apparently had houses all over the world, including a penthouse in Manhattan.

This house was one of the few beach houses on Coronado that actually had a bit of land attached to it. Most of the homes in this neighborhood were quite stately, and worth multi-millions of dollars. There were all kinds of different genres of architecture in the neighborhood, from Cape Cods to Colonial to thoroughly modern Frank Lloyd Wright-style , to Spanish style. There was even a house in the Queen Anne style that was called the "Baby Del" that was right down the street from the Hotel Del. The "Baby Del" got its name because it was white with a turret and a red roof, and it resembled a small version of the large and grand hotel.

But one thing I noticed about all these homes was that there was hardly any land for any of them. No real backyard to speak of, and every house was extremely close to one another. It was almost as if one house was built on top of the other. It was somewhat unusual for me to see, because coming from Kansas City, I was used to grand homes having grand lands. Like an acre or more per home. Even the homes in the city always sported a large front yard and backyard. But not Coronado.

The Whitmore mansion was the one exception. It was built on the corner, and the front yard, at least, was enormous. It didn't have much of a backyard to speak of, but there was an attached guesthouse, and I knew that was where Aria was found. The judge had given me permission to inspect the crime scene as well, so Christian and I would head to the guesthouse after we spoke with Jacob and Colleen.

I walked to the gate and up the sidewalk to the enormous wooden door. I knocked on it, and a lady about 25 years old, blonde and blue-eyed, answered it.

"Hello, you must be Avery and Christian," she said. It was then I noticed she was pregnant. She was wearing a loose-fitting frock, but her baby bump was obvious. At least, I thought it was a baby bump. I wouldn't ask her about it, or say "congratulations" or anything like that. It was entirely possible she was simply a little thick in the middle. I'd been embarrassed about making assumptions on more than one occasion, and I wouldn't go there again.

I glanced over at Christian and I knew he was thinking the same thing. I'd told him about what Esme had told me about how Jacob and Colleen needed her as a surrogate, and how she had to sleep with Jacob. I noticed that this maid, or domestic worker, had a thick accent that was much like Esme's. I wondered if she was in the same situation. I wondered if she was being forced to sleep with Jacob and bear his children. Or his child. I wondered if she was being forced to have abortion after abortion, because Jacob was so obsessed with having another male child.

It would make sense, really. I wouldn't imagine that Jacob would be satisfied with having just one child. After all, what would happen if something had happened to that child? Maybe the child got sick with cancer and died, or got run over by a car. What then? Jacob would once again be left without a male heir to run his hotel empire. I imagined he probably would want an insurance baby, and I wondered if this woman was pregnant with that baby.

The woman led us through the enormous house to a small sitting room that was towards the back of the house. It faced a brick patio that led out into an alley. "Wait right here," she said. And then she disappeared.

I whispered to Christian. "So what do you think? Do you think that bun in the oven belongs to Jacob?"

He nodded his head. "If I was a betting man, that's exactly what I would say. But you and I know better than to jump to conclusions. After all, we're lawyers. We need to go on the facts and evidence. But my hunch is that lady is having his insurance baby."

About 10 minutes later, Jacob came into the sitting room. He was a tall, elegant man. He was in his 70s, but he was obviously very fit. His hair was grey, but it was very thick and wavy. His eyes were blue, and his nose was straight and Roman. When he sat down, he had the bearing of a patrician man. His back was very straight in his chair, his legs were crossed, and I could see he was wearing loafers and no socks. He looked like he wanted to be drinking a spot of tea with us, but he didn't. Instead, he brought out some brandy in a crystal decanter, and poured a glass for himself. And then he looked at the two of us.

"Would you like a spot?" he asked us.

I shook my head, because I didn't like to drink on the job. But Christian nudged me, and I thought he was probably trying to tell me I'd be rude if I said no. So I nodded. Then Jacob poured both of us a glass. "Rocks or neat?"

"Rocks, please," I said.

"Neat for me," Christian said.

Jacob nodded his head. He poured the two glasses, and handed them to both of us. "Now, what would you like to ask me?"

"Well, as I was saying on the phone, I'm defending Esme Gutierrez on this case. I wanted to ask you a few questions about what she told me about you and Colleen. I wanted to get your side of the story."

He nodded again. He uncrossed his legs and then re-crossed them on the other side, then sat back in his wing-back chair. "I believe that anything she has told you has probably been a lie. But please, indulge me."

I cleared my throat, suddenly feeling very nervous. The way this guy was just staring at me, his icy blue eyes without any kind of soul or mirth behind them, was setting me on edge. I cleared my throat again. "Sir, why would you say that?"

"Why would I tell you that anything she said to you was probably a lie?" he asked. "The reason why I say that is because almost everything she says *is* a lie. Therefore, the odds are great that anything she told you was also a lie." He continued to stare at me, and I felt a chill go up my spine.

"Okay, I guess that it's your position that Esme lies. And you're entitled to that opinion. Be that as it may, I wanted to speak with you about a few things she said to me. As I said, I want to get your side of the story."

He motioned me with his hand to tell me in a nonverbal way he wanted me to continue.

"First of all, I was curious about one thing. Who is Aria's birth mother?"

"Her mother is Colleen. Any other questions?"

"How old is Colleen?"

He appeared to bristle at that question. "How is that any of your business?"

"I'm simply asking the question. How old is she?"

"She's 35."

I raised an eyebrow, and I looked over at Christian. This guy was certainly defensive. Of course, it was entirely possible he was only being defensive because there was such an age gap between the two of them. News reports had stated he'd just celebrated his 75th birthday. Maybe he was defensive because Colleen was 40 years younger than him.

And she obviously was a gold digger. At least, that was the thought in my head. Because, after all, this guy wasn't exactly a man with a scintillating personality. Granted, he was physically attractive, but I couldn't imagine being in the room with him for two seconds.

In fact, I wanted to leave right at that moment.

"You see, the reason why I ask you that question is because you told me that Colleen is her mother. Now, are you telling me that Colleen gave birth to Aria when Colleen was only 14?" And then I gave him a look like I was trying to tell him *is that what you're saying, are you trying to tell me you impregnated a 14-year-old? Is that the story you're sticking with?*

"Of course not." By the tone of his voice, I could tell he was thoroughly offended I'd even ask that question. "I was simply saying that Colleen is the only mother she knows, the only mother she's ever known. So, for all intents and purposes, Aria's mother is Colleen. Now, what's your next question?"

"Where is her mother? Her actual mother? The woman who gave birth to her?" I asked him.

"That's none of your business. Now, I gave you a courtesy when I agreed to go ahead and sit down for this interview. I'm a very busy man. And, at the moment, it seems you have been wasting my time. Colleen advised me against speaking with you. After all, you are the person who is defending the woman who murdered my daughter. I have an interview with the prosecutor, and there's a reason for me to speak with the prosecutor. The prosecutor is the one who's going to be putting Esme Gutierrez into prison, on death row. Where she belongs. Now, if you'll excuse me, my domestic help will show you out."

"Your domestic help," I said, not making a move to get up. I would put this guy off balance, and see if anything he said gave me something to go on. I doubted he would, but it was worth a shot. "Is she an immigrant? Is she here on protected status? Did she flee a war-torn country?"

"Yes, as a matter of fact, she did. She's here from Syria."

"Oh." So far, I had my suspicions about this other domestic worker. She, like Esme, was a refugee from a war-torn country. She, like Esme, was fair-skinned and blue-eyed. She was also pregnant. "I noticed she's in a family way. What are you going to do when the baby comes? Does your domestic worker, I'm sorry I didn't ask for her name, live here on the grounds with you and Colleen?"

"Calista, her name is Calista. And yes, she does live on the grounds with us. Now, I'm sorry, what was your question?"

"Is the baby going to live with her on the grounds?"

"Again, I fail to see how that is any of your business."

"It's just that when I talked to Esme, she told me you fathered her child. In fact, the way she spoke, it sounded as if the main reason why you wanted her to be here with you and Colleen was so she could have your child. Now, I see you have another domestic servant, who apparently is also a protected refugee from a war-torn country, and she, too, is pregnant. Perhaps you're trying to produce a replacement baby with her? Or an insurance policy, perhaps?"

I looked at him and I thought he might kill me. His blue eyes were no longer cold, but, rather, they were lit from within. Lit with rage, it seemed.

"That girl, I told you she tells lies. Lies are all she's about. I cannot believe you come here into my home and accuse me of something so vile."

I looked over at Christian, who silently nodded. "Sir,

with all due respect, I'd like to meet your son. What's his name again?"

"His name is Jake. Jacob Whitmore II. And you cannot meet him, because he is currently in school."

I leaned back in my chair. I took a sip of the brandy. It was smooth as butter, and its dark richness hit the back of my throat and tickled it just a little bit.

I was getting to this guy. Striking a nerve. And that was my intention, to be honest. I wanted to see if I could rattle him. See what kind of temper he'd have if I said something to him that *really* upset him. And for just one second, the way he looked at me, I thought he had it in his soul to murder somebody in cold blood.

The only thing was, I didn't really understand why he would murder Aria. I didn't quite know how everything was fitting together, but I knew that there was a puzzle here for me to put together.

"Your daughter, did she happen to know the true nature of the paternity of young Jake? Did she know that your domestic worker was the actual birth mother of the child?"

I saw Jacob take a deep breath, and let it out slowly. "I'm going to tell you one more time, and then I'm going to have to ask you to leave. There's no story to tell about the birth of my son. Colleen is his mother. His mother is not Esmeralda. I don't know what you're getting at with these questions. I don't know what you're trying to prove here. Now, as I said, I'm a very busy man. I gave you the courtesy of meeting with you today, and I really didn't have to. In fact, I have meetings all day after I leave you. Calista will show you out."

I stood up. "With all due respect, I also made an appointment with Colleen to speak with her. Is she around?"

"You're going to have to speak with her another time."

"I also have a court order from the judge to inspect the crime scene. Can I do that right now?"

"No, I'm afraid you cannot. Perhaps you can come back tomorrow, or another time. At the moment, I have to leave for work, and nobody will be here for you to be supervised. Please set up another time to come back. I'm not trying to hide anything, it's just I'm a very busy man."

"So you said."

At that, Christian and I stood up. Calista came to the door, smiled at us, and showed us out.

"I'm very sorry, I know you wanted to speak with Mrs. Whitmore," Calista said. "I'm afraid she's taken ill. She gets migraine headaches sometimes, and she's now in her bedroom with the shades drawn, the lights out, with a cool pack on her forehead. Perhaps she can speak with you on another day."

"Maybe. But maybe you'd like to talk to me."

"What would I say to you? What kind of information could I possibly give you?"

"You could give me a lot of information. For one thing, you could tell me what kind of environment you're working in. And I really hate to be nosy, but I'd really like to know who the father is of your baby."

She's looked down at the floor, and then looked around as if she was afraid. I knew why she was scared. If Jacob had seen her still talking to us, by the front door, he probably would've fired her, or worse. I wondered if she was in a tenuous situation, much like Esme. I wondered if the Whitmores constantly threatened her refugee status, constantly threatened her with going to ICE and turning her in for some imagined violation. I wondered if the Whitmores had threatened to plant drugs on her and call the police. I wondered if she was being treated as poorly as Esme was.

"I don't know why you ask me that question."

I looked over her shoulder, to make sure Jacob wasn't coming out to see me talking to her.

"What is your legal status in this country?" I asked her.

She bit her lower lip. "I came here from Syria, just two months ago. I was very lucky I was able to make it this far. I know that in this country that refugees aren't being welcomed as much as they used to be in the past. I understand what kind of place this country is. It's a much better country than the one I came from, but I'm not so welcomed here. I've applied for protected status, but I don't know if it's going to happen. I do know that Mr. Whitmore has ways, or so he says, of making sure I can stay in this country. But that is all I can really tell you."

I nodded, knowing what this woman was going through, which was something similar to Esme. Always afraid she would be sent back to her country to be murdered. I knew she probably had seen the same kind of atrocities and horrors as Esme did on her journey over to this country. I knew she probably had been sexually assaulted, beaten, tortured. I could see the fear in her eyes. It was palpable. It was almost as if the fear in her body was an independent thing. Like I could touch it. That was how strong of a vibe I got off this woman.

"Just be careful," I told the frightened woman. "Please. Esme was in the same situation as you. Now she's in jail, awaiting trial. It's possible she might end up on death row. Now I don't know exactly what happened, but I do have my suspicions about what's going on here behind closed doors. And I just want you to be careful. These people, these Whitmores, they don't have your best interest at heart. They might have their own agenda."

She nodded her head. "I know. I know they have their own reasons for doing what they do. And I know I'm trapped in my situation. But you have to believe me, anything is better than going back to my country. Have you seen what happens to people when they inhale chemical poisoning? Have you seen the burns on the skin? Their eyes water, they choke, their lungs are burning, they can't breathe. Do you know what it's like to see your own child die from a chemical attack?" She hung her head, and tears came to her eyes. "You can't know. You can't understand what it is I've gone through. And I will never, ever, go back to that. So I do what I can to stay in this country."

I knew I had to speak with her a bit more, but then, at that moment, Jacob was coming down the hall. I was afraid he would say something to Calista, maybe tell her she needed to make sure we left. I was afraid he would maybe fire her, because she was obviously speaking with us for too long.

"Thank you very much," I said to her. I figured that was an innocuous enough thing to say to her, so that Jacob didn't necessarily know what we were talking about.

She nodded, and shut the door behind us.

Christian and I walked to his car, and I got in after he pushed the button to unlock the door. "So, what do you think about all that?"

"I don't know. He certainly was stonewalling, but I don't understand why he agreed to talk in the first place. You know he didn't have to."

"That's true, and I was kind of wondering the same thing. What did he think he would gain by talking with me?

All I know is he's hiding something. I don't really know quite what."

I didn't know what he was hiding, but I was certainly going to find out.

Chapter Eighteen

REGINA

REGINA WAS BEING STYMIED in trying to find this Julian person. Anna was certainly helpful in that she told Regina where Julian probably was. However, as Anna said, it would be very difficult to find out exactly in which hospital he was being held.

That was a frustrating thing, to say the very least. Regina had a feeling this guy had the keys to this entire case. Not that she thought that when she saw him, everything would become clear. But she certainly thought that since he was friends with Aria, maybe he'd have some kind of a clue as to exactly what happened to her.

So she decided to call her boss, Avery, and meet with her. She remembered that Avery had told her that Christian was apparently a computer genius and a hacker. She also remembered that apparently Aidan was working for a law firm that defended people involuntarily committed to a mental hospital.

She called Avery from her car. "Hey," she said when

Avery picked up. "I got a hot lead here, Julian Rodriguez. You remember me telling you about him?"

"Of course, how could I forget about that? He was a guy who lived in the barrio, and apparently had some mental issues, but he knew Aria. How are you coming along with trying to find him?"

"I'm not. Nah, scratch that. I'm trying to find the guy, but he seems to be in some kind of a nut house. I don't know where. That's all his old neighbor, Anna, seemed to say to me. He apparently ran naked through the streets, screaming at the top of his lungs. The next thing she knows, he's being taken away in a police car. She assumes he was put into a mental institution of some sort, but she doesn't really know. I need to track this dude down. I think this dude has some information that'll break this case wide open. I need to find him but I don't know where to begin."

"We can start with all the mental institutions in the La Mesa area, because didn't you tell me he'd moved to La Mesa? He would've gone to Alvarado Hospital or maybe Sharp over on Grossmont, and then was transferred to more of a long-term care facility if he needed it. I know there's a few of them in that area. Maybe we can start with ones around his old apartment."

"That's a good idea, but you know those places are tighter than a rich bastard's wallet. They ain't gonna tell us crap. I mean, we can't just be calling them and being all, 'hey, do you have a dude named Julian Rodriguez squatting in one of your rooms?' They'll be like 'bitch, don't be bothering me with this crap.'"

"That's true enough. So, anyhow, here's what we do. Meet me in my office in a half-hour. Christian and I will be there to meet you. We're going to have to do something a little bit extralegal. Christian can get access to the databases of the hospitals around town. He can also get access to medical records. Of course, both of us would be disbarred if anybody found out about what we were doing, but sometimes it's important. Because you're right, I think it's odd that Aria was friends with somebody who came from a much different world from her. I just wonder why. What brought them together?"

"That's good," Regina said. "But listen, I think you also need to talk to your brother and ask him to get in on this. Because even if we figure out where he is, that doesn't mean we're going to be able to just go on in there and be all like 'yo bitch, I want to see Julian Rodriguez right now.' They'll slam the door in our face. They'll laugh us out of the place. But your brother, he probably has some kind of pass. Something that allows him to get in behind those doors. Maybe he knows people?"

"Good thinking. You're right. We probably need Aidan to be a part of this whole situation. I'll give him a call and maybe we can all meet up at my condo. He won't necessarily want to come to my office because you know he's always busy. But hopefully he'll be around this evening. Maybe we'll order out, you can come on over, and we'll all brainstorm exactly how we can talk to this Julian Rodriguez person."

"I'll see you then."

Chapter Nineteen

AVERY

I MET Regina over at my condo that evening. She came over with a bottle of wine. Christian was also over at my condo and my brother was expected at any moment.

My brother was very important to this entire operation, because, as Regina said, even if we managed to track down Julian Rodriguez, it didn't mean that we'd be able to see him. Mental institutions were very tight with who was allowed to see their patients. To see a patient, you had to be on a list, or be given a patient code, before you could even get in the door. As an attorney, I could possibly get a court order to see Julian, but I didn't know if I could show the judge he was a material witness. All we knew at that moment was that he knew Aria.

Regina and I sat down at the table, while Christian was in the kitchen getting plates for us. We'd ordered out through Uber eats and were soon going to be sitting down to some Thai food. Regina was busy going over with me what she'd found out in her preliminary investigation. She'd not only spoke with some people in the barrio, but she also did extensive background research on Aria herself. She went through her school records and every other kind of record available.

"Well, there's one thing odd about this chick," Regina was saying.

"What was that?"

She shrugged. "It didn't seem she was all that interested in the piano until she was about 14." She nodded. " I couldn't see any musical lessons she'd been given or received when she was younger. Which might mean nothing, because from what the story is about her, she was some kind of a genius. She started playing at the age of three or some shit, hell, maybe she was playing when she was a newborn. The story is she was a regular Mozart. You know in that movie, *Amadeus*, where Mozart's a little kid and he's playing the piano with a blindfold over his eyes? That's Aria, if you want to believe the stories. But I ain't buying it."

"You're not buying it? And why is that?" I asked her.

"Because I told you I saw nothing in her background that told me she was even playing the piano until she was 14 years old. And then she turns 14, and all of a sudden, wham! Chick's playing Carnegie Hall."

"Are you being sarcastic? Or was she really playing Carnegie Hall at the age of 14?"

"Not really. I mean she really was playing Carnegie Hall, but when she turned 16. I found a YouTube video of her and she was goddamn good and I don't know a thing about piano music. So why was there no evidence of her playing the piano before she turned age 14 if she was that damn good? And the weird thing is that when she was 14, she started posting videos of herself on YouTube playing the piano. She had her own goddamn YouTube channel at the age of 14. She had 10 million subscribers at one time.

She was making money hand over fist from that thing, which I guess is a good thing, because apparently her own dad refused to pay for her schooling at Juilliard. I know she got scholarships and all, but it's damned expensive to live in New York City. Anyhow, before the age of 14, she didn't even put up a single video of her playing the piano."

I tapped my fingers on the table, trying to figure out what was going on. "Okay, so you're saying that before the age of 14, there was no evidence she was even interested in the piano. And that at the age of 15, she suddenly started posting videos of herself. That isn't necessarily evidence she didn't start playing the piano before the age of 14. Maybe she was just shy and didn't want to post videos of herself playing piano, and then she suddenly decided she wanted to. She got a little attention for it and she just kept going. Just because she didn't have a YouTube video posted before age 14 doesn't necessarily mean she wasn't playing piano before that."

"Yeah, but I couldn't find any evidence she had any kind of recitals before the age of 14. That's what's so weird. You know how it is, you're playing the piano, you're good at that, you're gonna have recitals in front of people. Even crappy piano players have recitals. She's some kind of a genius, some kind of a lady Mozart, the next coming of Beethoven, and she's not having recitals when she's young? Not even one?"

"Maybe she was a late bloomer," I said. "Maybe she didn't even know she could play the piano until she sat down and started playing one day and realized she was a natural. I know the story was she started playing at the age of five, but maybe that's just the story."

Regina shook her head. "I'm not buying it. Somebody who's good enough to be playing Carnegie Hall at age 16 doesn't just sit down at age of 14 and suddenly discover they can play. You gotta be practicing for years before you're good enough to play at Carnegie Hall, and somebody who has that kind of a talent will know about it before she's 14. There's something really off about this entire situation and I don't quite know what it is."

Christian came out with some plates, and I got up and got my martini shaker out. I would make everybody a dirty martini. I knew that would not necessarily go with Thai food, but I was really craving the taste of olive juice.

"Tell Christian what you told me. Maybe he has an idea about what's going on."

I saw the two of them in there talking. I thought about what Regina was saying to me, and I knew there were all kinds of logical explanations for it. Regina was a very intuitive person, and if she thought there was something amiss, there probably was. There *was* something about the fact that Aria wasn't quite the piano prodigy everybody said.

I got out my metal martini shaker and poured some Grey Goose vodka into it. Then I poured some vermouth and a whole lot of olive juice. I shook everything up and put some green olives on some toothpicks over the top of each glass. Then I went into the dining room and put the martini glasses in front of both Regina and Christian.

"So, Christian, what do you think about what Regina was saying? Can you think of any reason why there's no evidence of her playing piano before age 14?"

Christian shook his head. "I don't know. That's the strangest thing. But I'm with you – maybe she was playing before the age of 14, but was just shy about it. Or maybe she got hit on the head. You know, I've heard about things like that happening – people get hit on the head and suddenly wake up and have abilities they never had before. You ever hear about people who come out of a coma and are suddenly able to speak French or Mandarin Chinese? I listened to a podcast one day that was talking about that. They were talking about people who come out of a coma and are suddenly fluent in a certain language. Maybe she had an accident at the age of 14, went into a coma and came out of the coma playing the piano like Liberace."

Regina took a sip of her martini and nodded in approval. "Now that you mention it, that's another thing I found out when I did my investigation on Aria's background," she said. "She *was* in a car accident at the age of 14. Down in Mexico. I couldn't find out much about it, except they had a report of an accident involving her and she went to the hospital down there. In fact, I went down to TJ, which is where the accident happened, and I went to the hospital to find out how long she'd been there. I couldn't find out much because of confidentiality laws, but I found out she was in this hospital for six months."

I nodded. "There you go. She got into an accident at the same time she suddenly started having piano abilities. Christian is right. I've heard of patients coming out of a coma being able to speak a language they never knew before. If that's the case, certainly somebody can come out of a coma and have an ability such as playing the piano. I'm sure that's probably all it was."

"Maybe." Regina looked unconvinced. "That makes sense. I mean, I know it's not a coincidence she got into a car accident in the same year she started playing piano, but I wonder if there's something more. That's all. I don't quite know what, but there's something more to the story."

"Maybe there is," I said. "But I think that sounds pretty good to me. She got into an accident and started playing the piano. That's kind of logical. It wasn't just a coincidence, was it?"

Regina bit her lower lip. "I don't know. My spidey sense is telling me there's something else we're not seeing. I'm an investigator and I go with my gut a lot of times. You're an attorney. You look at facts and evidence and you take those facts and evidence to put together a working theory. That's what you do. That's how you win cases. I don't know if your intuition is the same as mine. It's probably not. You know, with all those years I spent on the streets, I've had to develop my sixth sense."

I took a sip of my martini. "Is there too much olive juice in these martinis?"

Both Christian and Regina shook their heads. "It's good," Christian said. "I like a lot of brine."

"I agree," Regina said. "I like a lot of olive juice as well. But, we need to talk about this. I'm not convinced that accident had anything to do with her being able to play the piano."

I opened my mouth to say something, then turned around and saw Aidan was coming through the front door.

"Hey, everybody," he said. "Man, I'm beat. I just want to take a hot shower and get in my bed. I don't think I've ever been so tired."

"Why're you so tired?" I asked him.

"I think I've just been doing too much. Too much work, too much partying, too much school. Just too much. I gotta cut down on one of those things, and I can't cut down on work or school. So looks like I'm going to have to cut down on the partying. But I see you guys are drinking dirty martinis, and I could be persuaded to have one of those."

"I got one with your name on it," I said as I got up and made Aidan his own dirty martini. I brought it into him and he sat down at the table with us. "Listen, I know you said you just wanted to go to bed and you're really tired. But it's early on a Friday night. Something tells me you going to bed early won't happen. Even though I know you have to be at your job at Starbucks tomorrow morning at 6 AM, I know you're going to be burning the midnight oil like you always do. And you need to be here at the table to talk to us. We need to find somebody and we need your help."

"Who you trying to find?" Aidan asked us.

"A guy by the name of Julian Rodriguez." I then told Aidan all I knew about Julian, about how he was in a mental institution and about how we probably would be unsuccessful in tracking him down because of HIPAA laws.

"So you need me to go on in there and try to find him for you guys? Just because I'm working on involuntary commitment cases doesn't necessarily mean I'm gonna be able to get in there either. Unless you're gonna tell me something I'm not seeing, I don't see how I can possibly help."

"Aidan, how do you get those cases?" I asked him. "How do you get the involuntary commitment cases referred to you?"

"They're usually referred to us by a caseworker. A patient is held for 72 hours if he or she is showing acute psychiatric symptoms. If the patient needs to be held longer, they have a hearing. That's where we come in. We represent them in the hearings. Sometimes the person is a danger to himself or others, and then he can be held an additional 14 to 30 days without a hearing. But they eventually have a hearing and that's where we step in. We represent them in court."

"Listen," I said to Aiden. "Here's the thing. You're known at just about every mental health facility around town, aren't you? Aren't you pretty much on a first-name basis with people who staff these hospitals? Do you know the people who run the mental health wings of the hospitals around town? If we can figure out where he is, you can sweet-talk your way into seeing him, can't you?"

Aidan sighed. "Are you really going do this to me, sis? Are you really going to ask me to do something like this for you?"

"Damn right. What am I really asking you to do except to talk to this guy and find out how he knows our victim? I've never been inside one of those institutions and I don't think Regina has either. Neither has Christian. None of the staffs in these institutions know any of us from Adam. But they know you. So yes, I want you to go in there and talk to him. That's all." I raised my eyebrow. I knew he knew what I was thinking – he was staying here on my dime. I wasn't charging him anything to live in this beautiful beach condo. He owed me. This was the least he could do.

"Okay," he said. "If it that's important to you, I'll do it."

"Good," I said. "Now, I'm going to put Christian to work in hacking into the databases for all the mental health facilities around town. I'm going to have him start with the ones in La Mesa, because that was the last place Julian lived. After that, he's going to be looking at the mental hospitals around the San Diego area. When he finds him, I want you to go down there and see him. I don't think Christian's going to be able to get the codes for the patients. I don't know if these codes are in the database, so you will have to go down there and ask for him by name. They'll let you see him just because they know this is the kind of work you do."

Aidan rolled his eyes and then flopped on the couch. He picked up a football laying next to the couch and tossed it up in the air, again and again. It was a sure sign he was annoyed, because he always tossed around that damned football when he was pissed.

"Sure thing, sis. I'll do what you want me to do, but just because I don't want to become homeless."

"I'm quite sure you wouldn't be homeless," I said, "even if I kicked you out. Not the way you look. Some woman would take you in for sure."

Aidan gave me a look that said *are you really going there?* Then he shook his head and threw the football up in the air again. "Whatever."

At that, I sent Christian into the bedroom to get on my computer.

An hour later, Christian came out to see us. "Found him. He's at the Alvarado Behavioral Health System in La Mesa, over on Parkway."

The doorbell rang and I went to get it. It was the Uber driver with our Thai food. I took the food from him and gave him a five dollar tip. "Good. We know where he is. Now, Aidan, you just need to see him."

"Yeah. I guess I'm gonna have to. When do you want me to do it?"

"As soon as possible. We need to figure out what this guy knows. From there, I'll be able to do the rest of my investigation."

All of us ate our Thai food as we brainstormed some more about the case. We were getting closer to getting a missing puzzle piece and I was feeling better about the case by the second.

Chapter Twenty

AIDAN

AIDAN WENT DOWN to the Behavioral Health Institute the very next day. It was a nondescript one-level building in a residential neighborhood, with a pot shop called Well-greens right next to it and a church right behind it. Just like his big sister said, he was a well-known person in this particular place. He had had quite a few patients who he'd represented that were housed in this facility because it was a long-term care facility, so he had no doubt he could see this Julian Rodriguez person.

He brought a list of questions to ask him but preferred to freewheel it, especially when he was dealing with somebody who was perhaps in the middle of an acute mental breakdown of some sort.

He went into the place and saw Sally at the front desk. "Hey," she said to him. He was happy that it was her at the front desk, because she was perhaps the friendliest with him. "Aidan. Long time no see, huh?"

"Too long," he said to her. "Way too long. Anyhow, I'm here to see a client of ours. His name is Julian Rodriguez."

She nodded and got on the computer. "He's in the east wing. I'll buzz you back there." Then she wrote down the number of his room on a piece of paper and hit the buzzer. "Don't be a stranger for so long next time, okay?"

Aidan smiled and nodded. "I won't. At least I'll try not to. Hey, Sally, it's good seeing you."

"You too."

Aidan went down the hall to the room, which was 135. On the way there, he said hello to some of the doctors and nurses who were on the floor, all of whom knew him well. After all, he he'd been working for this law firm, off and on, for the past three years. And the entire time he was working for them, he was working on involuntary commitment proceedings. He was a well-known person to every psych hospital and wing around town.

He knocked on the door to the room, which was open. Julian had a typical hospital room. He had a roommate, who wasn't there at that moment, and he was sitting in a chair and watching television. His hands were clasped in front of him and he was staring at the TV intently. In fact, he didn't even notice when Aidan came in.

Aidan went over to the bed and sat next to him. Julian finally noticed him, looking right at him. "Who are you?" he asked Aidan.

"My name is Aidan Collins," he said to the man. "I'm assuming you're Julian Rodriguez?"

Julian nodded. "Why are you here?"

Aidan knew what he was supposed to say. He was scared to death this guy would complain and word of this unauthorized visit would get back to his firm, which would inevitably lead to his firing. It would also draw an ethics violation against him. All because his sister wanted him to do something a little bit shady. Not that doing shady things was necessarily out of his repertoire. It was just that he was sitting for the bar in just a matter of months and didn't need any kind of a report on his record. So he had to finesse this delicately.

"I needed to talk to you about a few things. I understand you might be in here involuntarily. And my firm sent me down here to speak with you to see if there's anything you need."

He shook his head and then started watching television again. "No, amigo. I mean, I was put in here against my will. But I kinda like it in here. I don't really want to leave. So I guess you're kind of barking up the wrong tree, aren't you?"

Aidan took a deep breath. "I was also going to ask you about a girl you knew. Her name was Aria Whitmore. Do you know anything about her?"

He looked at Aidan and then turned his attention to the TV again. "I don't know nobody named Aria Whitmore. I know somebody who said she was Aria Whitmore but really wasn't. I could never forgive her for doing what she did, but I could kind of understand it."

"What do you mean? What do you mean when you say you knew somebody who said she was Aria but really wasn't?"

"I had an amiga, her name was Sophia Delgado. She came up with me out of Nicaragua. I got to come over here legally. I was a winner of a lottery visa and I brought her with me. She wasn't legal. She had no papers. But she had to get out of Nicaragua because there were some gang members who were trying to kill her. She was a prostitute but she got in with the wrong crowd. The very wrong crowd. The worst kind."

Aidan was confused as to why this guy was talking about

this Sophia Delgado. "Okay. So you knew somebody by the name of Sophia Delgado. She was in this country illegally and she came over with you. And you are here legally. Is that what you're saying to me, dude?"

"Yeah, that's what I'm saying. So she goes and she's with this rich couple. A couple of rich weirdos over on Coronado. Sophia. She goes over there, pretending to be their daughter. All of a sudden, she's going by a different name. Calling herself Aria or some shit. I told her she shouldn't be doing it but she told me she had no choice. She told me there ain't no way she's going back to Nicaragua. She goes back to Nicaragua, she's a dead woman. She stole money from some gang members down there. You don't do that unless you want to get burned alive. She told me this family said she could live with them and call herself Aria, and they wouldn't turn her into the authorities."

Aidan was extremely confused as to what this guy was saying. "Wait, so you're saying she lived with this couple and she said her name was Aria?"

"That's what I'm saying, amigo. I'm saying she went to live with this couple and started calling herself Aria. I didn't agree with what she was doing. I thought it was weird. I mean, they had some dead girl by the name of Aria, or something like that, I don't really know, all I know is that's what happened to her. That was okay. I was happy I could still hang out with her. We were just friends, nothing more than that. And she came around with me a lot when she could sneak out of that house. That dungeon she was living in. I just don't know how anybody could live like that. Those were two strange people, those Whitmores."

Aidan had no idea exactly what was going on here. He didn't even know if he could believe this guy. After all, he was apparently mentally imbalanced in some way. Aidan obviously wasn't privy to his chart. He could've asked for it if he wanted to. They would've given it to him, but he didn't want to go that far. He knew he was in danger of getting into hot water as it was, just by being there.

"Can I ask a question?" Aidan probed.

"Sure, ask away."

"Your friend, Sophia, did she happen to be a genius on the piano?"

"Yeah. I mean, she never really was able to play an instrument when she was living in Nicaragua. Too poor. But she was always writing music, always, and I've known her since the age of five. She wasn't able to even afford to buy those sheets where you can put the notes on, so she made her own. I don't know, she was doing that before she could write her name. But yeah, she came up here, saw the piano and started playing it like she'd been playing it her entire life. She had it in her. Why do you ask that question?"

"I was just wondering." Aidan was starting to get the picture, but it was still just a little bit hazy. His sister had told him there was an issue with Aria and she'd been in a car accident at the age of 14. But how this Sophia Delgado person fit into all of it, he didn't know.

"And where is Sophia Delgado now?" Aidan asked him.

"Dead, man. Got strangled in the guesthouse of the home she lived at." Then he started to speak in Spanish. "When I found out she'd been strangled, that was when I went crazy. I started having delusions, started hearing voices talk to me. That's how I ended up here, because the voice told me to take off all my clothes and run naked through the streets. Then I started screaming as I was running, because I felt somebody chasing after me."

"What did Sophia look like?" Aidan asked.

"She was a Guero," he said. "Do you know what that is?"

"That means she was fair, is that right?" Aidan asked.

"Yeah. White. Blue eyes, blonde hair. Looked like a Barbie doll."

"You don't happen to have a picture of her, do you?"

"Yeah. I do. I got my phone here. They let me have phone privileges here because I haven't been acting up or nothing. Let me get it."

He went over to his drawer and got the phone out of it. Then he went to look at it, scrolling through the pictures, smiling as he went.

"Here it is, a picture of me and her."

Aidan looked at the picture. It was Aria. He'd seen her picture in the papers, in magazines, online, everywhere.

"This is the woman who's known as Aria," Aiden said kind of dumbly.

"No shit, amigo. That's what I was trying to tell you. I told you she came to this country and then became somebody else."

"So, when she became this other person, did you say anything to anybody about it?"

"No, man. She told me not to say a word. She told me she had to do it, because the people she was staying with, they would do something that would get her deported. She was afraid of those people. She said that if she didn't play their game, they'd have her deported. So she told me I can't say a word about who she really was. And I wasn't gonna say nothing. Why would I say anything to anybody? Why do I really care? I mean, I didn't like that she was walking away from who she was, I thought who she was was great, but, at the same time, I knew she had her reasons for doing what she did. And that's all I knew."

"Who else knew this person going by the name of Aria was actually this Sophia person?"

"Nobody knew. Just me. The only reason why I knew was because she came up here with me. It was just the two of us. So nobody knew."

Aidan didn't know what else to ask this guy. He was anxious to see his sister and tell her what he found out. And then maybe Regina could get to the bottom of exactly what had happened.

This entire scenario somehow fit in with everything else he had learned about Aria from his sister and from Regina. Namely, that Aria was in an accident at the age of 14 and didn't play the piano when she was younger. It all fit in. Perhaps the real Aria died in the car accident and this Sophia person took her place? But that didn't make much sense to him. Why would a family do something like that? It wasn't like the family was desperate to have another daughter, because, after all, apparently this Jacob guy only wanted sons. And he ignored her anyway.

So if she died, she died. If the real Aria died, why would they would just replace her with an imposter? And how would that even work? You can't just substitute one person for another. Everybody would be suspicious about that. The teachers, her friends, everybody.

There was something else he wasn't seeing. And, of course, there was always a possibility that this Julian guy was mistaken about this entire thing. After all, he was in the mental institution because he'd been having delusions. Perhaps he was delusional about Aria being somebody else. The whole thing could just be fabricated in his head.

But, at the same time, it all made a kind of sense. Because he couldn't figure out why a rich girl like Aria would've been hanging around with this Julian person to begin with. How would she have even known him? It was entirely possible that perhaps, like Regina had said, she was doing drugs and palling around with people in that area. But, at the same time, Julian was not known to be a drug dealer. So that wouldn't explain why she would've been palling around with him.

Aidan stood up and held out his hand. "Listen, I'm really glad you were able to meet with me. You've been a big help. More than you know."

"My pleasure, amigo. De nada."

Aidan left and immediately planned to call his sister. He was anxious to tell her what found out from this guy.

But as he was walking out of the building, a van pulled up. Before he knew what was happening, two guys with masks forced him into the back. Before he had time to react, somebody had put something over his mouth.

And that was the last thing he could remember.

Chapter Twenty-One

THE HOMELESS WOMAN

THE WOMAN gingerly got out of her tent. She'd pitched a tent on the beach, and, for the past two nights, she'd been lucky enough to stay there. Usually nobody could stay on the public beaches overnight. The beach cops would come along and make sure everybody was gone by a certain time, usually around 3 AM. But she was lucky enough that nobody had chased her off just yet. And, in her sleeping bag, inside the tent, listening to the ocean waves at night, she was able to actually sleep through the night for the first time in she couldn't remember how long.

Because she was getting more sleep, her mind was clearing up.

She would have to see Avery Collins. She'd finally read in the paper that her daughter, Aria, was murdered. At first, she was devastated.

But then she realized she had really no reason to be devastated. Because Aria *had* died, but she'd died years before. Somehow, her brain hadn't let her imagine that to be true. Somehow, she'd always thought that her daughter, the young girl she dearly loved, was still alive. She thought she could see her again.

She was lucid these days. She was living in reality and the reality was that her daughter was dead, her son was in and out of mental institutions, and her husband hadn't spoken with her in years.

Not that she really cared that Jacob hadn't spoken with her in years. He was the cause of most of her problems. After all, he was aware that her mother had an issue with schizophrenia. He knew there was a good chance she, too, would also be schizophrenic, because schizophrenia was inherited.

Yet what he did to her after her daughter had died, and she was on the edge, pushed her further over the edge. She was showing signs after her daughter had died that she was ready to go off the deep end. She was hearing voices, she was imagining her daughter was still there and she was also imagining her mother was there. She was talking to people who weren't there. Her husband had seen that. And when he did, he pushed her even further over the edge.

It took her a long time to realize that what had happened was that her son apparently had killed her daughter, and after that, he was put into an institution. He was never tried for her murder though. Why was that? That was still a black hole in her brain. She didn't know exactly what happened after she went into the institution. All she knew was that, according to the entire world, Aria had never died in the first place.

But sometimes when she was lucid, she understood exactly what happened. This was one of those times. This was one of those rare times when she understood exactly what the reality was. And she understood that her daughter really had died all those years ago. And somehow, someway, somebody else had taken her place. Someone she didn't know.

And that new person was now dead.

She had to see the attorney for Esmeralda Gutierrez. She had to see her and tell her the truth.

It was very important because she knew her husband was a murderer.

Chapter Twenty-Two

AVERY

I WAS IN MY CONDO, pacing the floor. The dogs were on edge along with me. Something was wrong. Very wrong. Yesterday, I'd sent my brother over to talk to that Julian Rodriguez. Aidan hadn't come home since. Not only that, he wasn't answering his phone. I had no idea what had happened to him. I only knew it wasn't like him just to do this.

Aidan was sometimes a bit of a flake. He had the surfer mentality, where, on his days off, he loved to ride the waves. He was very good at it. And, like a lot of the surfers around, he did indulge in his share of cannabis. It was legal, so why not? It wasn't like he could possibly lose his job, or not be able to sit for the bar, because he might get busted for having marijuana. That wasn't how it was in this state. So he indulged in the pot, sometimes a little bit too much for my taste, but I didn't say anything.

I thought at first that maybe he decided to see his buddies and toke up with them. I was annoyed all yesterday because I couldn't get in touch with him. I imagined him sitting around with a group of guys, passing around a bong, getting wasted, and not answering his phone.

I was boiling by the end of the night.

When I woke up this morning, and saw he still had not come back, I thought something had gone wrong. I needed to get information from him about that Julian Rodriguez and he'd stood me up. But what if something worse had happened to him? What if somebody really didn't want him to talk to Julian? Would I be in danger as well? Would Regina? After all, Regina found the name of Julian Rodriguez in the first place.

I knew what I would have to do. I would have to call Regina and Christian to come over and the three of us would have to figure out how to find my brother. I couldn't just sit there, pacing and fretting. I had to have a plan.

Christian and Regina showed up an hour later. "Dude," Regina said to me. "You still haven't heard from your brother yet? What the hell happened to him? He goes over to the funny farm yesterday, talked to that guy, I guess, who knows if he talked to him. And then what, he just never shows back up here? What the hell?"

I looked over at Christian. My hands were shaking and he walked over to me and put his hands on top of mine.

"What did I do?" I asked him. "I sent him over to talk to that Julian Rodriguez and now something happened to him. If something really did happen to him, how can I ever forgive myself? I'm the reason he was over there in the first place. He didn't want to go over there and I forced him to. I told him, point-blank, if he didn't do this for me I would kick him out of the house. What kind of sister am I?"

"Relax," Christian said, looking me in the eye. "We're going to figure out what happened to him. More importantly, we're going to find him. With my computer hacking skills and Regina's investigative skills, we'll figure it out. Just relax. You're in good hands."

I clasped my hands in front of me and looked down at the hardwood floor. My brother was really the only thing that had grounded me all these years. He was the only thing that had been a constant in my life ever since I got out of prison. He was the one person who'd known me the best. Regina had been a good friend over the years. I just met Christian, but he seemed to be a pretty solid guy. But nobody had grounded me the way Aidan had.

If something had happened to him, especially if it was my fault, I didn't know if I could ever recover.

"Okay, then, where do we begin?" I asked.

"The first thing we need to do is figure out if there's any way we can possibly track his cell phone," Christian said. "Did he install some kind of Find My Phone type app? Anything like that?"

I shook my head. "I don't know, but I don't think so. There must be some other way you can figure out where his phone is."

"I'm going to start with that," Christian said. "I want to try to locate his phone. Even if its GPS is turned off, I can still locate it. It'll be a lot tougher to do, but I can do it. But if his phone is turned off, all bets are off. I can find where he was when the phone was turned off, but if somebody abducted him, I don't think they're going to let him have a live phone. That would just defeat the purpose of doing what they're doing."

"Okay, Christian, so you're going to try to locate Aidan through his phone. And what are you going to do, Regina?" I asked her.

"Obviously, I'm going down to that Behavioral Health Institute place and talk to people who know him down there. Maybe somebody saw him being abducted, if that's what happened to him. Maybe somebody saw something. I mean, maybe —"

It was then that I heard the door rattle.

I screamed as I saw who it was.

It was Aidan.

Chapter Twenty-Three

"AIDAN!" I screamed as I ran over to him and threw my arms around him. "Where have you been?"

"Nowhere. Listen, sis, I'm sorry, but I wasn't able to see that dude. I thought my usual charm would carry me through and I saw everybody I knew down there, but they still wanted to have a patient code for him. They usually trust me but not this time."

My heart fell. "That's too bad, but I guess he was a patient there? Did you at least find that out?"

He shook his head. "I couldn't even find that much out. Sorry sis."

"So where have you been?" I demanded, suddenly feeling enraged. "You went over there yesterday afternoon and you haven't been back since. I thought something had happened to you."

"Sorry, man. What can I say, I got distracted. I was so disappointed about not being able to see that dude that I went over to Tommy's house and we smoked a bowl. Next thing I know, I'm waking up on his porch and I don't really remember what happened yesterday."

I wanted to kill him. Strangle him with my bare hands.

"And your phone? I've been calling you since yesterday. Aidan, I don't think I need to put up with this crap from you anymore. I ask you to do one thing, one goddamned thing, and you can't get it done. I understand you can't get it done. If they're not going to let you see him, then they're not going to let you see him. There's not much you can really do. But to disappear like that, and not even call me, that's just...." I shook my head and started pacing the floor. "I thought you were dead. Dammit, I thought you were dead and it was my fault. And now here you are, telling me you're not dead but just stoned. At this point, I wish you were dead."

Unfortunately, Regina was witnessing this entire melt-down I was having at my brother's expense. Christian, thankfully, was in the other room. He was working on my computer, trying to find my brother.

She came over to me and looked me in the eye. And then she looked right at Aidan. "Aidan, why don't you tell her what you really were doing yesterday? And tell me, while you're at it. I don't believe the story you're telling us, not at all. I think you saw that guy and for some odd reason you're now telling us you didn't. You better come clean. This is important. We need to talk to this guy and find out what he knows. I can tell just by looking in your eyes that you're a lying son of a bitch."

"I'm not lying. I'm telling the truth," Aidan protested. However, when he said that, he looked at the floor. Before, when he was talking to me, he was looking me right in the eye. But after Regina had called him out on his lying, he decided to not look either of us in the eye.

"Listen dude," Regina said. "You can try to play your shady games with your own sister all you want. You might be able to bullshit her, but you can't bullshit me. I'll call you on it every damn time. Now you're obviously not telling either one of us the truth and I don't really know what the truth is. But I at least know with reasonable certainty that Julian Rodriguez really was at that nuthouse you went to yesterday. Because if you really were unable to see him, you wouldn't come here and lie to both of our faces. I think you saw him and I think someone got to you. How close am I?"

It was then that I saw Aidan's face flush. "I don't have to put up with this crap." And then he went into his room and shut the door. Ten minutes later, he came out in a wetsuit.

And then he went out onto the balcony and got his surfboard.

"Aidan, what do you think you're doing?" I asked him.

"What does it look like? Let's see, I'm in my wetsuit, I've got my surfboard, I'm going out the front door. I can see the waves are pretty tasty today. Lots of my friends are out there already. It's a Sunday. I'm not working. I don't have school. I think that even a woman like you, who doesn't exactly have the skills of Sherlock, can figure out exactly where I'm going. Later."

"Aidan, you go out that front door, I swear to God, I'm going to change the locks," I said. "You're not going to be able to come back in here."

He raised an eyebrow, opened the door, and stood in the doorway. He hesitated before he left.

"You're going to change the locks?" He shook his head and grinned. "Don't threaten me with a good time."

At that, he slammed the door.

I was back to feeling enraged. How could he do this to me? After all I'd done for him? I was letting him stay with me, not charging him a dime, and this was how he treated me?

"Dude, you can't be mad at him," Regina said. "Your brother knows something and he can't say a word to you about it. I don't really know why exactly he can't tell you, but I can almost guarantee you that he knows a lot more than what he's supposed to know. I think that somebody's gotten to him and they made a threat to him that has got him running scared."

"And why do you think that? Why are you so sure he's hiding something and he's not just a lazy slacker who blew off the assignment I gave him?"

"You're too close to this. He's your brother. He's done crap to you in the past that pissed you off. You're automatically gonna think the worst about whatever he does. I'm just a neutral observer. And, you forget, I'm an investigator. I've shaken people down on more than one occasion. I know when someone's lying and that dude was definitely lying. I'll shake him down later and come up with the truth. But maybe I shouldn't come up with that truth. Because maybe if I did, all of us will be dead people. I think we've touched a nerve. Somebody is pretty desperate to keep whatever Julian Rodriguez knows away from us. That's all I know."

I thought about what Regina was saying and I realized she probably was very right. She was an investigator. She dealt with nonverbal cues like nobody I'd ever known. I was an attorney. I dealt with facts, logic and evidence. And the facts, logic, and evidence all pointed to my brother being a flake who blew off the one thing I asked him to do, didn't bother to tell me about it and went and got high with his friends. But Regina was seeing something else I wasn't seeing, so perhaps I needed to give him the benefit of the doubt.

Christian came out of the bedroom. "I'm guessing your brother's phone isn't turned on because I can't seem to track it down. Sorry about that."

When he said that, for some reason, I grinned. And then I started laughing hysterically.

"I have to say, I wasn't expecting that kind of reaction from you," he said. "I tell you I can't find your brother, he's still missing, and you're laughing?"

My brother's phone was on the table. And, just like Christian had said, it was turned off. By now, I was laughing so hard that tears were running down my face. I could do nothing but point at the phone on the table, and I collapsed on the sofa, still laughing my ass off.

Christian looked over at Regina, who just shrugged. "Aidan came home. He's out surfing right now. I think the reason why she's laughing is because the reason why you couldn't get in touch with his phone is because it's here. Turned off."

"I guess I don't understand. What do you mean, Aidan came home? Why didn't anybody come in and tell me about it?" Christian asked.

"We would've, but homegirl over there was pretty much spending the whole time he was here reaming him a new one. I was just trying to referee between the two of them, so none of us thought about calling you in. Sorry about that."

I finally stopped laughing. And then I looked Christian in the eye. "I'm sorry. You're probably thinking I'm insane. I think I just needed a pressure release valve and sometimes I laugh when I should be crying. Aidan came home and told me he not only didn't talk to the person he was supposed to be talking to, but after he left the Behavioral Health Institute place, he went over to his friend's house, got stoned and didn't bother to call me. However, Regina thinks he's lying about all that and she doesn't quite know what the real story is. I don't really know what the real story is either. All I know is that we're no closer to figuring out what this Julian Rodriguez knows than we were yesterday."

It was then that the doorbell rang again.

"It must be Aidan. He probably forgot his keys."

I opened the door and it wasn't Aidan.

It was some woman I'd never seen before. She was probably about 90 pounds. Her hair was extremely ratty, what was left of it. She had bald spots all over her head. She was dressed in a heavy coat, even though it was probably 80° outside. She had a backpack. She had shoes on with holes in the toes. She smelled like somebody who had urinated in her pants over and over again. It was the same smell I would smell when homeless men used to get on the trolley. Her blue eyes were bloodshot, her lips were cracked.

Yet, I could see where at one time, maybe before she became homeless, which she obviously was, she must've been an attractive woman. Under all the cracked, leathered skin, I could see elegant bone structure in her face.

"Avery Collins?" she asked.

I was apprehensive. To say the very least. I didn't know if this was another of my stalkers. So far, the only stalker who'd been bold enough to come into my house was the one who'd threatened me with a knife. I never did find out who that was.

I cleared my throat. "Yes?"

She extended a weathered and shaking hand. "My name is Lauren Whitmore. I'm Aria's mother."

Chapter Twenty-Four

"ARIA'S MOTHER," I repeated dumbly. "Come in. Come in."

She stood in the doorway, looking unsure of herself. She peeked around my shoulder, as if she was looking to see who was in the room with me. I saw her hand going up and down on the strap of her backpack as she stood there, looking like she didn't quite know what to do.

"I don't mean to intrude, I mean, I see you have people here. I'm sorry, I don't really know why I'm here." Then she shook her head. "No, I do know why I'm here. I have really bad days. Most days are bad days. But today's been a good day. I've slept, more than I've slept in a long time. I've been sleeping on the beach. They haven't chased me off yet. And, it's just been a good day. I finally know what has happened in my life. I remember everything. For the first time in a long time, I remember everything. And I need to tell you what I know. I need to tell you."

She was still standing in the doorway and I was anxious for her to come in.

"Come in, please," I said. I beckoned her into the living room. "If you'd like to, you can use my shower. I even have some clean clothes you can change into. Would you like that?" I asked her. I hoped I didn't sound like I was being condescending, rude or presumptuous. But I had a feeling that was exactly what she needed.

She swallowed as she took one tentative step into the living room. "Do you happen to have a Jacuzzi tub?" she asked. Then she closed her eyes while her hand started stroking the strap of her backpack on her shoulder again. She shook her head and mumbled something.

"I'm so sorry," she finally said. "I shouldn't have asked that question."

"No, no. Of course I have a Jacuzzi tub. I have one in both the bathroom in the master bedroom and the bathroom in the hall. The one in the hall is a nicer bathroom, so maybe you might go in there."

She took another step into the living room and then looked over at Christian and Regina with wary eyes.

"I'm so sorry. I don't mean to be bothering you guys. I need to talk to Avery and I think I really need to wash up. I'll admit it, I haven't had a decent shower in so long I don't remember the last time I've had one. Sometimes I'm able to go to a shelter, but it's almost impossible to get into their showers because there are so many people lined up for them. I honestly can't remember the last time I've even seen a bathtub. I think that if I could take a long bath in a Jacuzzi tub, I'll feel like I've died and gone to heaven."

Regina came over to her and gave her a spontaneous hug. "I'm glad to meet you," she said to Lauren. "And don't feel like you're bothering us. We're really happy to see you."

At that, Lauren took a few more steps into the living room. She looked over at the bathroom with longing eyes.

I put my hand on her back and guided her over to the bathroom.

"There's towels in there, stacked up on some shelves I've had built into the wall. And I also have a cabinet with all kinds of bath salts, bath bombs, bubble bath liquid and all kinds of stuff. Feel free to just go through and use whatever you like in there," I said. "I even have some candles on the side of the tub. Feel free to light them."

She looked over at me, tears in her eyes. "Thank you. I'm a stranger. You don't know me. You don't have to do this for me. But this is probably the most kindness I've experienced from anybody for as long as I can remember."

Then she shut the door to the bathroom and I could hear the faucet running in the bathtub.

I went over to Regina. "What the hell? Did that just happen? Did we just meet Aria's mother and she's now in my bathtub? Did I just imagine that?"

Regina grinned. "No, dude. That totally just happened. Now if she really is who she says she is, we're in business. Who needs Julian Rodriguez when we have Lauren Whitmore?"

I went over to Christian, who was sitting at the dining room table, still looking at my computer.

"I'm looking at some of the pictures online of Aria," he said, "trying to see if I can find a picture of her with her mother. So far, though, all I've seen have been pictures of her with Colleen, her stepmother. I'm trying to see if I can find a picture we can possibly compare to this woman who just came in the door. Because, for all we know, she could just be some random homeless woman who's taking all of us for a ride."

Regina and I sat down with him, and the three of us went through the pictures online.

I finally saw exactly what we were looking for. It was a picture of Aria when she was about 10 years old. She was standing between a man who was clearly Jacob, and a woman. I looked closely at that woman.

It was hard to reconcile the homeless woman who had appeared at my doorstep with this woman, but I could clearly see the woman who was currently in my bathtub was most likely the same woman who was in this picture. The eyes were the same shape – the woman in my bathtub, and the woman in the picture, both had eyes that were round but slanted down just a tiny bit. The lips were the same – both the woman who was at my door and the woman in this picture had full lips. Granted, the woman who called herself Lauren had cracked lips, but they were the same shape as the woman in the picture. The nose was exactly the same, the cheekbones were the same.

No doubt about it. The woman who called herself Lauren was weathered, beaten down by life. She was quite a bit skinnier than the woman in this picture. But you could always tell a person by their eyes. Those were usually unique. And the woman in this picture and Lauren had the same eyes.

"That's her," I said as I felt myself tearing up. What had happened to her? Her her ex-husband was a billionaire, for the love of God. What happened to her that she'd become homeless? She probably had some kind of mental illness, but why would her husband just let her be homeless? What kind of person was he?

I had a feeling that when she came out, I would find out exactly what kind of person he was.

———

SHE FINALLY CAME out of the bathtub about two hours later. "I'm so sorry, I almost fell asleep in there. I felt human for the first time in years sitting in that bathtub." She was dressed in a pair of jeans and a sweatshirt I'd laid out for her. I'd also given her a pair of my socks and a pair of my shoes. My jeans and my sweatshirt hung on her tiny frame. I was not a heavy woman by any stretch of imagination - I was about 5'6" and 115 pounds. But this woman was my height and probably a good 30 pounds lighter. She was literally skin and bones.

She shyly came over to where we were sitting. I stood up and took her hands.

"Sit down," I said. "Regina is in the kitchen, making dinner for us. She makes a mean roasted chicken with all the fixings. Mashed potatoes, gravy, cornbread, salad, asparagus. I hope you're hungry."

Lauren smiled. "Of course I'm hungry. I haven't eaten in several days. Sometimes I'm able to get over to the food pantry and sometimes I can get into the shelter and eat. And sometimes the dumpster diving is pretty good. You can find some pretty good things in a dumpster. You'd be surprised. But I haven't had much luck the past few days. So, yes, I'm starving."

I nodded. "Good. This is Christian. I don't think I've formally introduced the two of you. He's going to be working with me on the Esmeralda Gutierrez case."

She looked over at Christian and nodded shyly. "Pleased to meet you," she said.

"Pleasure's all mine," Christian said.

Christian went in to help Regina get some food on the table, and then the two of them set the table and brought out all the food.

"Looks like it's ready to go," I said to Lauren. "So let's eat."

The four of us chowed down and it was clear that Lauren really hadn't eaten in quite a while. She savagely tore into a couple of chicken thighs, a chicken leg and a breast. She ate second helpings of mashed potatoes and several pieces of cornbread. She occasionally glanced up from her plate and smiled sheepishly, as if she was trying to tell us she was not really a savage - she was just starving.

After dinner, we all went out onto my balcony. There was a table and chairs out there, and it was a nice evening. I could hear the waves coming in, which never failed to calm me. I could tell the sound of the waves was very calming for Lauren as well. I wanted her to be as comfortable as possible because I needed to get some information from her. Plus, I really felt for her.

"Okay, Lauren. Tell us what you know."

She nodded. "That's why I'm here."

Chapter Twenty-Five

"WHERE DO I BEGIN?" she asked. "Aria was a beautiful child. And we had a beautiful life. I mean, we had problems, just like everybody else. Who doesn't have problems? But, you know, everything was pretty good. I met Jacob when I was only 19. We had our daughter Aria and then our son, Brad."

"Your son? Aria had a brother?" I asked. This was something new.

She nodded. "He had problems throughout most of his life. In and out of mental institutions. He's a brilliant man. Or at least he was a brilliant boy. His IQ is just off the charts. But he lives in his own world even now. I visit him from time to time. He lived in a group home but doesn't anymore. He was really interested in computers. Very very interested in that. He was very good at that. But, as I said, he had a lot of problems."

When she said the words he was good at computers, it triggered something in me. I instantly started wondering if maybe he was the one who had been sending threatening messages. That would make sense. After all, I was defending the woman accused of murdering his sister. That would give him a reason to threaten me.

"So you say he lives in a group home?" I asked her.

"He used to, but not anymore. He doesn't work much. He collects social security. He can barely make ends meet, but he's really brilliant. Especially on the computer. He can do things on the computer that experts can't even do."

For some odd reason, as this woman was speaking, chills were running up and down my spine. I thought about the guy, or woman, who had stalked me, coming to my house with a knife. I wondered if he was the kind of person who would do that.

"Does he know about me?" I asked her.

"You mean, does he know you're defending Esmeralda Gutierrez?" she asked.

"Yes. Does he know that?"

"Yes. He definitely knows that. I talked to him about it. We've talked about this case. He's not very easy to talk to, not all the time. He does have some areas of his life where he knows what's real and what's not. In other areas, he doesn't have that same line. I'm the same way. Or, rather, with me, I have periods when I know what's real and other periods when I don't. It kind of goes like that with both of us. But yes, when he and I have both been thinking rationally, and living in the real world, we talked about this case."

"And you tell me he's a computer genius? Is there any way he would've known that Christian would be second-chairing Esme's case before Christian had even put a notice in with the court that he was on this case?"

"I'm not sure."

My heart started to race. This woman was giving me

more answers than I ever thought possible. All of a sudden, I had a feeling about who was sending me those threatening messages and who had broken into my home.

"Is he dangerous?" I asked her.

She shook her head. "I thought he was at one time. I thought he killed my daughter. I thought that until just a few days ago. That is, when I wasn't thinking my daughter was still alive. I would go to the beach and still see her. I've had very confused thoughts. But, like I said, I'm more lucid today than I've been in a long time. And I have to tell you everything before things go back to the way they were before. I don't know how long I have before I go back into my shadow self. So I have to tell you that I don't think my son is dangerous."

She took a deep breath.

"I don't think he is," she said. "But I think my ex-husband Jacob is."

Chapter Twenty-Six

"WHAT DO YOU MEAN, your ex-husband is dangerous?" I asked her.

"I just believe he is. You see, my daughter Aria was murdered. Years ago, she was murdered. Beaten to death." She hung her head and then wiped away some tears. "Her father never wanted her. Never liked her. He only wanted boys. So he really doted on Brad and didn't even know Aria was alive. She was very shy, quiet. Didn't have any friends. I felt sorry for her. I wanted her to make some close friends but she never did. She was always trying to get her father's love. She had my love but she desperately wanted her father's love. And he would never give it."

I felt like I was holding my breath as I waited for her to go on.

"When Aria was only 14, something happened. Jacob told me it was Brad who did it and I believed him because Brad had always had so many problems. But I didn't believe it at the same time. I mean, Brad had his issues with delusions, voices, things like that. Hallucinations where he thought people were talking to him in his bedroom when they really weren't. But he was harmless, I thought. My husband, Jacob, convinced me otherwise. Aria was in her bedroom and she had been smacked over the head with a rock. She had this rock she got from this geological field trip she went to. It was this beautiful rock, had little crystals in it. Very shiny when held up to the light, would sparkle like diamonds. She was laying on the floor when I went up there and the rock was right next to her. Jacob came running up the stairs and immediately started screaming at Brad about what he did. He was screaming at him about how could he do this to his sister. Brad was only 12 and had been in and out of institutions for most of his life. He just happened to be home that weekend."

"So wait," I said to her. "Are you positive Jacob killed her? And not your son Brad?"

"I think so. Like I said, he never cared for her in the first place. He never wanted her around. And there's also one thing kind of peculiar that I think might've been related to the reason why he would've killed my daughter. I was helping her do a genetic test. She was doing it for school. You know, she went to a private school, where the kids in her class can afford things like genetic tests they do online. You know when you swab your cheek and send it in. And then you get this report telling you about all kinds of stuff, like if you tolerate caffeine, if you like cilantro, what kind of genetic diseases you might be prone to. That sort of thing. But it also tells you a lot about who your relatives are."

I knew what she was talking about. Everybody knew what she was talking about. Those genetic tests were ubiquitous anymore. Everybody was doing them. But, this was seven years ago that Aria was doing them. They weren't as common back then, as they are now, but I knew they were still around.

"So I helped her do this DNA test," Lauren said, her blue eyes wet with tears. "I told Jacob what she was doing and he went absolutely crazy. I mean, he's always had a hair-trigger temper, but I'd never seen him the way he was when I told him about that genetic test. He was screaming at me about how could I let her do that? Was I trying to ruin him? I had no idea what he was talking about. I thought it was a fun thing. You know, a lark. Everybody wants to know where they came from. Everybody wants to know their unique characteristics. And it was a school project."

As she spoke, my mind was turning over. There was something about that DNA test that really freaked out Jacob. That was for sure. I had to wonder what it was. I had to wonder what he was trying to hide.

I wrote down on a piece of paper that I wanted to talk to Christian after Lauren left and see if he could hack into the database and find out the results of that DNA test. I had a feeling that doing that would illuminate a lot.

"Did you ever find out exactly what it was that made them freak out about her doing that Ancestry.com test?"

She shook her head and then dabbed her eyes. "No. All I know is that when I told him she'd sent in her DNA to be examined, he completely melted down. I don't even know if she got the results of the test. It takes about six weeks to get the results. She was dead before those results came in. By that time, I was out of the house, so I wasn't able to get the mail to see if I could find out what the results were. But there was obviously something in there that really upset him. I still think that whatever it was in those test results were what made him kill her. I think that now."

"But he accused your son of killing her, right? Your son who was only 12 years old at the time?"

She nodded her head. "Right. He accused him and because Brad was having problems anyway, I believed him. Brad was very impressionable anyway and was having delusions, in and out of the hospital, so it was very easy to convince Brad that he killed his own sister. I remember him crying hysterically, apologizing over and over. My husband was beating him. He kept slapping him on the face and shaking him. He boxed his ears and even punched him a few times. The whole time, my son was just crying. All he wanted from his father was his love and approval. Just like every 12-year-old boy. So it was devastating to him to be accused of killing his sister and to believe that's what happened. And I believed it, too, for the longest time, because I've had a hard time with trying to stay in reality. I've never really understood in my life what's been real and what's not real. So I just assumed Brad killed her."

"You remember what happened that night? The night you found your daughter dead in her room?"

She shook her head. "No. When I saw her, I lost all sense of reality. I never quite accepted she was dead. For the next few weeks, I just saw her coming to me in the backyard. It was weird. There was a part of me that knew she was dead, but there was a part of me that was still seeing her talking to me. I didn't really know what happened to her. I couldn't remember what happened to her. And then my husband started giving me LSD. He knew I was having problems with having visions of my daughter, and seeing my mother, and talking with both of them. I kind of knew they weren't real, but I kind of thought they were real at the same time. My husband told me that if I started taking LSD that it would cure my mental problems. He gave me an article he had cut out of a magazine. I think it was *Time*, or *Newsweek*, something like that. This magazine said that people were being treated with LSD for their mental problems. I didn't really read the article itself. I just read the headlines. I believed my husband. I believed everything he told me. If he told me the sky was green, I was gonna believe it."

While she was talking about the LSD thing, I saw Regina on my computer. Her head popped up. "When she was talking about the LSD thing, it sounded familiar to me. And she's right. LSD is being used to treat some kinds of mental problems. But it's used in microdoses. That means very small doses. Let me guess, Lauren, your husband gave you a shit load more than a microdose. How close am I?"

Lauren smiled wryly. "Pretty close. He gave me a lot more than what he was supposed to. And he dosed me all the time. I started hallucinating more than ever. At some point, I lost complete touch with reality. Full-blown psychosis. I went into an entire alternate reality where none of it had ever happened. My daughter was alive and she was with me all the time. I was told that later on, I tried to kill myself. I started hearing voices and the voices were not of my daughter, but of somebody else. I don't really know who. And I heard the voice tell me to kill myself. So I tried to. I slashed my wrists and the next thing I know, I'm in the mental hospital. The whole time I was in a mental hospital, I really was not living in this world. I didn't have any periods of lucidity like I have right now. It was six months of just living in a world where my daughter was next to me the entire time. And the whole time, I was hearing the voice. I was hearing the voice that not only was telling me to hurt myself, but it was also telling me things about myself. Like, the voice would tell me I was supposed to warn the president that aliens would be attacking the United States. And I guess that, according to my chart, which I was able to read before I got out of the hospital - I was lucid at that point - I ran around the hospital screaming that I needed to get out of there because I needed to go to Washington to talk to the president. I needed to save the world."

"What happened when you got out of the hospital after six months?" I asked her.

"Well, as I said, I was fairly lucid at that time. I was lucid enough that I could read my chart and understand what had happened. So I got on a bus. I went to my house. That's when I saw her. She was Aria, but, at the same time she wasn't. She looked like her. But she really didn't. Then I saw a neighbor, and she told me that Aria had been in the hospital in Mexico and had plastic surgery. That was why she looked different. And that's when I started to lose my grip on reality again, because I again remembered that Aria had been killed. I was very confused. Then my husband told me I had to leave because he had a restraining order against me. I couldn't be around the house. I couldn't be around the kids.

So, I left. I was so broken, so beaten down. I just didn't have the will to fight. I just got back on that bus and left. I didn't have a place to go, so I lived on the streets. I've lived on the streets ever since. And, as I said, I've had good days and bad days. This has been a good day. A very good day. But I know it won't last. I know that at any moment, I'll just cave into what I call my shadow self. It's that part of me that takes over and my reality will be fragmented. At best. That's why I'm here talking to you now. I have to tell you my story, before I lose touch with what my story is."

I felt for her. I knew what she was going through. She was feeling isolated, like nobody was there for her. Nobody had her back. She'd lived in a world that was of her own making, and not always a good one. I'd lived in a prison. I'd wished that when I was in the prison I could somehow go to another world.

"Would you be willing to testify in court?" I asked her. "Or would that be too much for you?"

She shrugged. "As I said, I have good days and bad days. Mainly bad days. Or, at the very least, not good days. I don't usually have a day where I'm this aware of my reality. So I can't guarantee I will be in any kind of shape to testify in court. But, if I'm feeling good, like I am today, then I certainly will testify."

I had to game out exactly what she was saying to me and exactly how it was all going to fit. I suddenly realized that if what she was telling me was true, I not only had a new direction to go in this case, but I would have a difficult time trying to prove it to a court of law. I would have a hard time trying to even show exactly why this woman would be a necessary witness. I was just going to have to put together a theory of what had happened, but I had no idea if I could prove it.

But there was one thing I knew I had to do.

I would have to ask for a new autopsy. In the previous autopsy, there was no need to identify the body. That meant that there were no dental impressions that were compared to previous dental records. That also meant the fingerprints weren't processed. I was definitely going to have to go to court and show exactly why I would need those things to be done.

I only hoped it wasn't too late.

Chapter Twenty-Seven

AFTER LAUREN GAVE me the information she gave me, I knew I just couldn't turn her back out onto the streets. She told me, the next day after she talked to me, she was not quite living in reality. I let her stay another night, giving her my bed to sleep in and I slept on the couch. I knew she probably hadn't had a warm bed to sleep in for quite a while. Then, when she woke up, she was afraid, because she didn't know where she was.

I arranged for her to go to a much nicer place than she was used to. I found a place called Bridges to Recovery up in the Pacific Palisades in the Los Angeles area. I found it online and it looked like the perfect place for her. It was a luxury mental institution where she could hopefully try to really recover. The place featured acupuncture, massage, yoga, meditation and personal training, in addition to the usual services a mental institution might provide - psychiatry, psychotherapy, medication management. And it was all administered in a beautiful Los Angeles neighborhood in a luxury home.

The whole thing would be costing me $50,000 a month. I wouldn't be able to foot the bill for too long, maybe for six months, but I hoped I could at least get her on the road to recovery. What she gave me was invaluable information, so the least I could do was make sure she was well taken care of.

After she left, I got to work. I went into the office and met with Christian there. "Okay, the first thing we're going to have to do is –"

He smiled. "I know, we're going to have to make a motion to the court to have the autopsy reopened. We're going to have to ask for dental records and fingerprints. But there are some major issues with that. The first issue is that you have to understand one thing. This imposter, this person who took the place of Aria, she took her place when she was 14 years old. Probably the dental records will match the body, because we're probably going to get the dental records of the imposter. We can't very well ask for the dental records for when Aria was a child, because those dental records aren't going to match the ones on the body, nor should they. The prosecutor will make a good case that the reason why they don't match is because they're too old. They were taken when she was a child. I mean, I understand you're probably going to ask for the dental records, and I would too. But just be prepared that the prosecutor's going to shoot that down."

"I understand. And the fingerprints –"

"They probably won't be dispositive, either. You have to understand that after the imposter was autopsied, her body was released. Presumably, Jacob and Colleen had her buried in a funeral, but she might've been cremated. We don't know that. If she was buried, we're going to have to have her exhumed, and we'll be lucky if we can get good finger-prints from her."

I sighed. "So, are you telling me we might not be able to prove the woman who was murdered wasn't Aria?"

"That's what I'm saying. We might have to prove it the old-fashioned way. We might or might not be able to get Lauren to testify for us. But even if she does, the prosecutors will be able to shoot her story full of holes. She even admitted to us that she wasn't quite clear on whether or not her daughter died. The prosecutors will be able to show she just imagined that and was having issues with her brain at that time. I'm sorry. I know I'm discouraging you in this. I don't mean to be. But I just want you to be realistic. We might not be able to prove there was an imposter who was killed in Aria's place."

I stood up and went to my sliding glass window. I went out on the balcony and breathed in the fresh air. In the distance, I could see a Carnival cruise ship. I thought about the people on the cruise, how relaxed they were. I took on a cruise myself one time. It was seven days filled with food, alcohol, Vegas-style shows, casino gambling, piano bars, wave pools, live bands, the works. I'd never been so happy and relaxed in my entire life. Sometimes, when I would get really stressed out, it helped me to just concentrate on those boat and think about my state of mind when I was on my own cruise ship, and just go to my happy place.

Christian was absolutely correct. There was a good chance that we could never prove it wasn't Aria killed in that guesthouse, but, rather, an imposter.

And he was also correct that since the body had been released to Jacob and Colleen Whitmore after the autopsy had been performed, chances were excellent that they couldn't get a legible fingerprint. Chances were that the imposter was cremated. I would have to try, however. That was the only thing I could really do.

"Okay. So let's just say for the sake of argument that we were able prove Aria was replaced with an imposter,"I said. "Then what's a theory of the case as to who killed the imposter? After all, we aren't going to trial on the death of Aria all those years ago. We'll be going to trial on the death of the imposter. Who killed her and why?"

"The father," Christian said. "Obviously. Think about it – this new person, this imposter, had information that could ruin him. Namely that she was not Aria Whitmore. That would be easy enough for her to prove, wouldn't it? All she would have to do is go to the authorities and give them her fingerprint and she could prove she wasn't Aria. Jacob had to live with that knowledge all these years - this new woman could ruin him at any time. Maybe something happened. Maybe there was some kind of a close call where she was arrested. Or something of the sort. Or maybe she almost got arrested. You have to understand that if the imposter ever got arrested, the jig would be up. They would take her fingerprints and run them in the database and find out her fingerprints did not match those of Aria's when she was born. The whole house of cards could've come down at any moment. Jacob had to live with that. Until he didn't."

I thought about what he was saying and I realized he was absolutely right about that. The key to this case was obviously proving that Aria was not Aria at all. At least, that would be a springboard. That still didn't tell us exactly why he would've gotten rid of the imposter, but it certainly would be a start.

"Okay, so the first thing we're obviously going to do is make a motion to the court to have the autopsy reopened. In the meantime, maybe you can think about trying to hack into the Ancestry.com database. Obviously there was something in those test results that freaked him out thoroughly and I wonder what it was. It was enough for him to have killed her. So it had to have been something very serious."

"Good thinking."

So, that afternoon, the first thing I did was work on that motion to have the autopsy reopened and for the DNA and dental records to be compared to those of Aria.

I wrote the motion, filed it online, and straightened up my desk. It was a mess, as usual. I tended to be the kind of person who would have an extremely sloppy workspace, and then, one day, all at once, I wouldn't be able to stand the sight of it. So then I would spend several hours filing and straightening everything. I would put every pen, pencil and paper clip in their proper place. I would take all the files laying around my office and on top of my desk and file them away in an enormous filing cabinet I had in an alcove in my office. Then it would start again, as the desk would get messy again, and I would do the same thing. Rinse and repeat. I wished I was the kind of person who could just take five minutes a day to make sure things were straight, but I just wasn't. That wasn't how I was wired. So be it.

15 minutes later, Christian came into my office. His eyes were wide. His hands were shaking. In his left hand was a sheet of paper. I could see he had test results in his hand.

I got excited, knowing that Christian probably now knew exactly the reason why Jacob would've killed Aria.

"I got Aria's test results, for the Ancestry.com she did," Christian said. "And you're not gonna believe what I found."

I held out my hand and he gave me the paper he had.

I read it, and I knew exactly why he was so shocked.

"Oh my God," I said. "That explains a lot."

Chapter Twenty-Eight

I WAS in court the very next day. Time was of the essence, because with every day that passed by, I knew that evidence would be more difficult to get, especially fingerprints. Because of this, the judge called an emergency hearing for us.

I went up the steps to the San Diego Superior Court, which was a newish building in the downtown area. The lobby of the building had an almost open air feeling to it. The ceilings were extremely high and there was plenty of light that streamed in from the floor to ceiling windows. My heels clicked along the terrazzo floor and I showed my identification to the guard, who nodded as I walked on through. I was wearing a navy suit, with a red top, and heels that matched my top. My dark hair was in a loose bun and I felt ready to go to war.

The prosecutor, Brent Atwood, had already called me about my motion. He thought I was crazy. Brent was a gangly redheaded guy, pale and freckled, which was a very bad combination to have in sunny Southern California. I imagined he probably didn't go to the beach very often, because if he did, he would end up red as a cooked lobster. When I sent him a PDF version of my motion, he called me right away.

"Avery, what the hell do you think you're doing? You want to disturb a body? You know that body had already been released to the parents and they said their goodbyes. They had a funeral. She's in the ground. Hell, she might've been cremated, I don't know. The autopsy was done. And now you're going to try to have the autopsy results reopened? I'm sorry, but I think you're crazy. I don't think Judge Warner will indulge your little fantasies. I think you've been watching too many *Criminal Minds* episodes or something."

I tried to ignore the inherent sexism in his comment. I didn't think he would've called a man crazy for wanting to have the autopsy reopened. He had to have known there was no way I would go to such a drastic step unless I really thought there was good cause for doing it.

"Listen, all I know is that I have cause to believe that the girl who was killed in that home was not Aria Whitmore. And that's all I can tell you."

"Okay. I'll see you in court tomorrow then. But don't be surprised if you're laughed out of court."

I sighed as I realized he was probably correct. The judge might be inclined to call a full hearing, which would mean I would have to put Lauren on the stand. After all, she was the one who told me the story about Aria and the imposter.

But, at the moment, she was in the rehab facility in the Pacific Palisades. I had called about her, giving her patient number to the person who answered the phone, and that person told me she was resting comfortably but could not come to the phone because, presumably, she was not well. I knew that, when she left my house, she was relapsing.

Without her, I really didn't have anything. I didn't have any reason to have the autopsy reopened.

I called Aidan. I had hoped that maybe, if he knew something, he'd tell me.

"Yeah, sis, what's up?" he asked me.

"You at home?" I asked him.

"Yeah. I am. Why? Why are you calling?"

"I wanted to talk to you about the other day when you blew off what I asked you to do and then came home and acted like such an ass. I have a hearing tomorrow on whether or not the autopsy for Aria Whitmore should be reopened. Do you have any information for me that would help me out in this regard?"

Then he told me something I wasn't expecting to hear. "Find out for yourself. Julian Rodriguez has been released from the hospital. I have his address. He lives in La Mesa, in a trailer park over off of Lake Murray Boulevard. I ain't getting involved with it anymore. I don't need this. I'm sitting for the bar and I need to keep my job. So I'm washing my hands of this whole situation. But you can talk to him."

I felt excited. "How did you find out he was released from the hospital?" I asked him.

"I called the behavioral health center and asked them. They know me and told me he'd been released. Dude gave me his address when I went to see him." When he said that, he kinda gasped, like he told me something he probably shouldn't have. "I mean, crap, I might as well just come clean. I saw Julian. I'm quite sure you're not surprised when I tell you that. But I did see him. Nice dude."

I drove my fingers on my wooden desk, closed my eyes, and counted to 10. "Aidan, why did you lie to me?"

"Man, you would ask me that. Suffice to say I was kind of freaked out by something that happened to me in the parking lot of that place. A couple of dudes jumped me, forced me into the van, and then literally took me to a warehouse in Lakeside. They didn't hurt me, but they scared the living shit out of me. They told me I needed to back the hell off, and if I didn't, bad shit would happen to me. They told me they knew what I did, going in there and seeing a patient who wasn't related to my law firm. They would tell my firm what I did and then they would go to the bar and say I behaved in an unethical manner. They told me to back the hell off, so I backed the hell off. I was afraid you would make me go down there again and talk to him, and I wasn't gonna do it. So, that's why I lied to you."

"How long were you there in that warehouse?"

"An entire day. They took me there, dumped me off and locked the damn door. I was in there, in the dark, freaking my shit for a whole day. I slept on the concrete floor. Then they came back the next day and that's when they came in and threatened me."

"Oh my God," I said. "I'm so sorry that happened to you." I put my hand to my mouth and put my head on my desk. "I'm so sorry."

"No biggie. I just don't want to be involved anymore."

"I don't blame you," I said.

"Good, because my ass is in the fire on this one. No thanks to you. I'm not saying a damn word. I'm on notice. I gotta keep my nose clean. Otherwise, I'm gonna end up working at Starbucks for the rest of my damn life. If you ever want me to be a paying renter of your gorgeous condo, you're gonna just let this one die. But you can go and see him. Or, better yet, have Regina go and see him. She can shake him down. That chick can shake anybody down."

"I'll have her do that or I will. I have an emergency hearing tomorrow and I need for Julian to meet me at the courthouse. If the judge wants evidence on why I want that body exhumed, I need somebody to tell the story on what they know. Lauren, Aria's mother, is out of the question. She's at a rehab facility. She's not lucid anymore. But if Julian can back up the story, then I need him to tell it. Otherwise, I don't think I'm going to get what I want, which is a reopening of the autopsy results."

"Nobody's stopping you from going to see that dude. Listen, I gotta go. I got to meet up with my study group. Got a mock trial next week. Later."

After I hung up the phone with Aidan, I tried to get in touch with Regina, because I needed her to see Julian right away. Unfortunately, she, like Aidan, was busy.

"I'm down in TJ," she said, referring to Tijuana. "I can try to see that dude later on if you want. Like this evening, but I'm going to be down here for the rest of the day."

I put my head on my desk, wondering what the hell had compelled me to try for an emergency hearing before I could get any witnesses lined up for it.

No, I knew why. The reason was simple. I had to get a hearing as soon as possible, because if I didn't, there would be less of a chance of us getting a good fingerprint.

I checked my watch and went out to see Sarah. Sarah was not only our receptionist, but she also was kind of an assistant to all of us. Whenever any of us needed some kind of help such as scheduling clients or telling clients they needed to be rescheduled, or something like that, she was our girl. I wanted my own assistant, of course, but it was difficult to have one in the situation I was in. I only had my one office and Christian's office down the hall. There really wasn't a place to put an assistant.

"Hold my calls, please. Also, I have a client scheduled in an hour. Could you please call this person and reschedule him for tomorrow?" I had a guy coming in by the name of Bill Nadler. He was supposed to meet with me about a DUI case he had. He would have to wait until tomorrow. It was important I went down and saw Julian right that second.

Chapter Twenty-Nine

I GOT to the mobile home complex that allegedly was the new home of this Julian Rodriguez person. Julian's unit was a typical trailer. It was a single wide, not a double wide, small and white with a bay window on the front and a small porch on the side. I parked right next to the awning which was on the side of the unit, and I got out of the car and went up to the front door and knocked on it.

Julian himself, or a guy I imagined was Julian, opened the door. He squinted his eyes, and looked at me. "Can I help you?"

I showed him my business card. "Hello, my name is Avery Collins. I'm representing Esme Gutierrez in her murder case. I think you might have some information for me and I need to speak with you."

He shook his head. "I'm not talking to nobody about this case. Nobody no more. Sorry, amiga, I can't say nothing. I say something, then these guys, they come back. I ain't putting my life on the line for nobody. Sorry."

My heart sunk. I had a feeling this would happen. "Mr.

Rodriguez, with all due respect, it's very important I talk to you about this. I have a hearing tomorrow, an important hearing, and I need an eyewitness. You can testify the girl killed in the Esme Gutierrez case was not Aria Whitmore at all, but an imposter. I know you have information about this and I need for you to tell me what you know."

He shook his head again. "I'm not going to testify for you. I'm not going to get involved with this at all. It's not my neck on the line. Sorry. But I will tell you this. I'll give you the name you want. The name of the girl who took Aria's place. Her name was Sophia Delgado. That's all I'm going to say. And I'm not going to testify in no court. You weren't here. You got that? You were never here. I never said a word to you. You got that?"

At that, he slammed the door in my face.

Chapter Thirty

I GOT TO THE COURT, knowing that even though I was ready to go to war, I probably would lose this one. Not only that, I had a feeling I would make a fool of myself. Nonetheless, I had to try.

"Mr. Atwood, Ms. Collins," Judge Warner greeted both of us when we walked into the courtroom at exactly the same time. "Come on up. I guess we're here on a motion to reopen the autopsy of Aria Whitmore."

"Yes, Your Honor," I said. "As you can see from my motion, during the original autopsy, there was not a valid identification of the body. The original autopsy did not include dental records, nor did it include fingerprints. And I would like for that to be done. Also a DNA analysis."

"And why, pray tell, do you want that to be done?" Judge Warner asked. "I read your motion that there were some questions you have about the identification of the body. However, this was not an issue when the original autopsy was performed. Her father and her step mother both positively identified the body as being that of Aria Whitmore. Now you're telling me it possibly wasn't her?"

"That's exactly what I'm telling you," I said. "I've received information since the autopsy has been closed and the body has been released that has led me to believe the person killed at the Whitmore home was not Aria."

Brent was standing right next to me in front of the bar. I could tell he was trying not to laugh. He was giving me the side eye, a sly grin on his face and he was shaking his head.

The judge was leaning forward, listening to me, and then he sat back in his enormous black chair. "Mr. Atwood, I read your response to her motion and I take it you're opposed to this idea of reopening the autopsy. Is that right?"

He nodded and then broke out in a huge grin. "You might say that. I mean, reopening an autopsy is highly irregular to begin with. In fact, I don't think it's ever been done. At least not in my 10 years of prosecuting cases has it ever been done. I don't know what kind of information Ms. Collins is referring to when she says she got information that led her to believe the person who died in this case was not in fact Aria Whitmore. She hasn't told me what kind of information she has."

I felt uncomfortable. "That's true. I haven't told him anything. But I have a witness who could testify that Aria died years ago. She was replaced by an imposter by the name of Sophia Delgado. Sophia is the woman who passed away in this case, not Aria."

I looked up at the judge, and I could tell he was rapidly losing patience. "Who is this witness you're talking about?" he asked.

"Aria's birth mother. Her name is Lauren Whitmore, and she's the one who told me what had happened."

"And this Lauren Whitmore could testify?" the judge asked.

I looked down at the floor. "I, um…"

Right at that moment, I got the surprise of my life.

Regina was coming through the door, and with her was a most welcome face.

Lauren Whitmore was with her.

Chapter Thirty-One

"AS A MATTER OF FACT, I do have a witness. And she's ready to testify at this hearing today." I looked over at Lauren and she smiled and nodded. I took that to mean she was feeling lucid that day.

Judge Warner looked over at Brent. "Do you have any objections to this witness testifying today?" he asked him.

"Yes, as a matter fact I do have an objection," Brent said. "This witness was just sprung upon me right now. I don't know who this witness is. I haven't had any kind of discovery related to this entire thing, and I haven't had a chance to do any kind of background review on this witness. With all due respect, Ms. Collins can't just spring a witness here to testify. Ms. Collins just filed this motion yesterday, and here we are today in a hearing already on the matter. I understand the exigent circumstances surrounding Ms. Collins' request, but I must object to her bringing in a witness before I've had the chance to prepare."

Judge Warner nodded. "Counselor makes a point. Nonetheless, as even Mr. Atwood acknowledges, time is of the essence with this situation. The longer we delay this, the more likely it will be that the body will be in such a state of decomposition that the fingerprints might not be legible any longer. Now I understand you have not had time to prepare for this hearing, but I must tell you, I'm inclined to grant Ms. Collins' request. I would like to hear from this witness and see what she has to say. I believe both sides should have a thorough examination and have all the evidence they need to go to trial. And if there is a chance the body identified as Aria Whitmore is not her, I need to know that. That's a very important part of this case. But I would like to hear this witness' testimony."

I looked over at Brent and he wasn't smiling any longer. He realized the judge took me seriously and he was probably going to lose.

He finally just shrugged. "Well, then, let's get on with it."

I took a deep breath and called Lauren to the stand.

I went through a direct examination of her, and she told the court what she told me. She admitted on the stand she was mentally ill at the time, and her memory was a bit hazy on everything, but she knew when she got out of the mental hospital and tried to go home that the girl she saw at that house was not her daughter. Her neighbors tried to tell her it was her daughter, that Aria had plastic surgery after getting into an accident in Mexico, but she knew better.

"I'm a mom. I know my daughter. And I know when somebody is trying to pretend to be my daughter. This girl, she sounded like her, she looked like her, but she wasn't her. I could tell just by looking into her eyes."

Her testimony lasted about an hour, and then it was time for the cross-examination. I knew Brent would have a field day with this one, and I was not far wrong.

"So you admitted on direct examination that you literally had just gotten out of the mental institution when you went home and saw the girl you thought was not your daughter. Is that right?" Brent demanded.

"Yes, that's right." She nodded. "I'm not going to lie about my problems. I definitely was suffering from a mental breakdown during that time. I mean, I'd gotten out of the hospital, but I still was suffering from delusions."

"So then you'll admit that there's a possibility you were having another delusion when you thought you saw a girl who wasn't your daughter. Isn't that right?"

She nodded. "Yes. There is that possibility. As I said, I'm very hazy about this entire thing. I still am. I'm still very confused about it. Who wouldn't be? It was during the worst time in my entire life. My daughter was dead. My husband claimed my son did it. And then I go home and I see a girl claiming to be my daughter. She looked like her. So yes, I was very confused. I was confused then as to what was going on and I'm confused now. I'm not going to claim otherwise."

"So what you're saying is there's the possibility your daughter never actually died back then. You testified on direct that your husband was dosing you with LSD during this time. You testified you thought that was an attempt to bring on your symptoms of schizophrenia, because he knew you were prone to it, isn't that right?"

"Yes, I'll admit that's a possibility. But I don't think so. I don't believe I imagined my daughter dying. I don't believe I imagined seeing somebody in her place. But I don't know for sure. I'll admit it."

Brent questioned her aggressively for about another half-hour before he announced he had no further questions.

She stepped down after the judge excused her.

"Okay, here's what I'm going to do," Judge Warner said. "I'm going to order the autopsy reopened. Now I understand this woman had hazy memories of her daughter dying and someone else stepping in. But if there is even a chance the victim in this case is not who we think she is, I think we need to know it."

"Thank you, Your Honor," I said.

I got what I needed. Now it was just a matter of finding out if the evidence would be good enough to be dispositive in this case. I needed it to show the victim in this case was not Aria. And then, from there, I could put together my theory of the case.

———

TWO DAYS LATER, I got the results back from the reopened autopsy. It was unsuccessful. Apparently, the body had been cremated. Just recently. Originally, Sophia's body was buried in a casket in the ground. But, just two days ago, unbeknownst to Judge Warner or Brent, the body was exhumed and cremated.

The body had been released to Jacob, so it was within his rights to do things that way. But why? Why now, after people had started digging and threatening my brother, who was getting too close to the truth? Was the timing a coincidence?

No. There were no coincidences. At least not ones this major.

Somebody was covering this up. Somebody knew I would ask to reopen the autopsy and that somebody made sure that didn't happen.

I sighed. My work would be cut out for me, that was for sure.

Chapter Thirty-Two

September 5 – The day of trial.

I WAS nervous about going to trial. Even though I had my theory on the case, and I was fairly certain about what had happened, whether or not I could prove it would be another matter entirely.

My client's life depended on it.

Literally.

What made me really nervous was that the media glare was as bright as it had ever been. I'd been watching the news and saw the reporters at the courthouse. I also saw the throngs of people lining the courthouse steps. I was nervous, because I didn't know what they would do to me. I knew there were still quite a few people using this case as a cudgel and using Esme as a scapegoat and stand-in for all immigrants south of the border. One person in particular, Grayson Wright, was really getting people riled up. He had come to my attention when Regina told me about him.

"Dude's really wacked. He's like some kind a cult leader,

like a Manson or something. He's got these people who follow him around like The Dead. I don't know, man, he's a scary cat, that Grayson. You better just be careful."

I knew what she was saying. I was still getting death threats, just not as many as there used to be.

But this Grayson character, he concerned me. He was apparently on satellite radio, had a show for three hours a day, and I listened to this show on demand. Regina was not far wrong. This guy *was* really wacked. He was hateful, bigoted, ignorant and just plain wrong. Worse, he was apparently whipping people up against me and my client.

Nonetheless, I knew what I needed to do. My client needed me. I had all the information I needed to go to trial. That was all I really knew at that time.

That morning, I packed up my plastic box filled with my files. I dressed in my gray pantsuit, black heels, and a navy blue button down. I came into the living room after taking one last look at myself, and Aidan was in the living room on the couch.

"You ready?" he asked me.

"That a trick question?" I asked him.

"No. That's not a trick question. Are you ready?"

"As I'll ever be."

I went out the front door, after saying goodbye to Aidan, and took the elevator down, all the way to my car in the basement garage. I got out my fob and clicked it to unlock the car.

I had the distinct impression someone was following me. I looked around before I got into the car. Then I got in the driver's seat and started the car up.

I looked in my rearview mirror and screamed.

There was a man back there.

He had a knife.

Chapter Thirty-Three

"WHO ARE YOU?" I demanded. I looked at his knife and I looked over at the glove compartment of my car. I had a gun in that compartment. I just had to figure out if I could reach for that gun before this guy slit my throat.

"We've been warning you," the guy said. "We've been sending you messages on your email about this case. You don't know who you're dealing with here. You have a client guilty as the day is long and you've been warned to get off her case. Now today is the day of the trial and I can't let you go in there and defend her. I can't let you go in there and present evidence she's innocent when she's clearly not. If you do that, that illegal spic will walk scot-free, and then every other illegal spic who comes over here will think they can get away with murder, too. And I can't let that happen."

I knew it would be pointless to try to argue with this guy. He obviously had it in his head that Esme was guilty no matter what. He wouldn't wait for the facts or the jury to come in. No, he was judge, jury, and executioner. So talking to him rationally, telling him he needed to wait until the trial was over to decide if she was guilty or not, wouldn't do anything.

"Listen, I have a job to do," I said. "And that's it. No more, no less than any kind of job you do. I have a client, her trial starts today, and nothing you do will prevent me from doing my job." I looked at his knife and saw his hand was shaking as he held it.

I'd been to prison, so I knew when a person was serious about threatening someone's life. You could just tell in their eyes and by their body language if they were going to do it.

This guy wouldn't do it.

His eyes got wide and his face got red. "You're going to withdraw from her case! If you don't do it, you're going to die right here, right now. Do you understand me? You're going to die, bitch."

"Do you happen to listen to a guy on the satellite radio by the name of Grayson Wright?" I asked him calmly. "Is this guy your hero by any chance?"

That was the only thing I thought to say. I would try to make some small talk with this guy and maybe bring him back to reality. I could tell just by looking in his eyes that he might've been on some kind of drug.

Then again, maybe he was just not living in reality.

Kinda like Lauren, but violent.

"What of it? Grayson Wright, he knows what he's talking about. He knows what kind of destruction those immigrants have brought to our country. They don't belong here. Neither do you. Esme needs to go back to where she came from and I think you need to go with her."

"Go? You want me to go to El Salvador? Do you know how silly that sounds? Why would I do something like that? Besides, I thought you were going to kill me. I can't very well go down to El Salvador if I'm dead."

At this point, I was positive he wouldn't hurt me.

"Please leave," I said. "Or I'm going to call the cops and tell them you're threatening me and then you'll be arrested. However, if you just leave right now, I won't call the cops. It's your choice."

He glared at me but opened the door and got out. Then he stared at me through the window, trying to look at me as menacing as possible. I just shook my head and drove off.

I thought about calling the cops about the weird guy then thought better of it. I needed to be in court at 9. I couldn't take the time to make a report about this, especially since this guy was probably long gone. I decided just to leave it alone.

That was a weird scenario, but nothing about this case had exactly been normal. It wasn't just the fact that the media was crawling all over this and people were passionate on both sides. Yes, there were plenty of people who wrote me death threat emails and really screamed about me on the air. But there were plenty of others on the other side counteracting all of that. They were supportive of Esme and supportive of me. They were immigrant's rights advocates, people who were refugees themselves, people who were just goodhearted. A lot about this case had made me lose some hope in humanity, but, mainly, a lot of the people involved in this case made me realize that the good people far outnumbered the bad.

I got to the courthouse and there were throngs of people in front of it. I parked in a parking lot across the street where I had to pay $10 to park all day. Then, when I got closer to the courthouse, I saw the people. I hoped they wouldn't recognize me, but, then again, I figured I probably stuck out like a sore thumb. After all, I was carrying my file box behind me on a wheeled cart. Not that I was the only attorney doing that, not by a long shot. On any given day, there were several different trials going on, which meant there were always quite a few attorneys who, like me, were hauling their files on a wheeled cart behind them.

But my mug had been plastered online all during this case. So I knew the people would recognize me.

Satellite trucks were lined up on the street, and I saw quite a few people talking into microphones as if they were reporters. Several reporters tried to get a statement from me but I refused to talk to any of them. And quite a few people started screaming various cuss words and vile names. I heard every word in the book and every name as well.

But the cops were down there, some of them in riot gear. They were going to keep everybody in line so I realized I probably was safe.

I got up the steps, went through the glass doors, showed my card and went through the lobby. I got to the elevators and went to the eighth floor. There, Christian was already waiting for me, with Esme.

Esme was dressed in a silk maroon shirt and black pants. She had a gold necklace on and small pearl earrings. She also had a bracelet on. Her blonde hair was tucked neatly up in a bun. She looked like a housewife. That was by design. I'd met with her many times over the past few months, going over the case and all the developments. And I made sure she was dressed in nice clothes.

She looked nervous. "Do you think he's here?" she asked. I knew who she was talking about. Jacob. She was terrified of him, especially after I told her what I found out about him. One thing I knew - Jacob would be my star witness. He was actually on both witness lists – mine and the prosecutors. I knew the prosecutors would simply ask him questions about Esme, and about finding his daughter in the guesthouse. He was their star witness as well. But, for me, the questions I would ask him were questions that would decide the fate of the case.

After I got the Ancestry.com results from Christian, I had a pretty good idea as to what happened. And some other facts had also come to light about Sophia_and what she knew. I found out some very interesting facts about her as well. Once I put everything together, I had a pretty good theory of the case - who did it and why.

The only question I had in my mind, of course, was whether or not I could prove it. Not that I had to prove anything. Obviously – the state always had the burden of proof in any trial. They had to prove their case beyond a reasonable doubt. Yet I also knew the reality of the situation. And that was that the jury would convict if they had a person in front of them unless the defense did a damned good job of showing the person didn't do it. That was my goal. That was my job. I didn't have to prove anything, but yet I did. And I knew that.

I sat down and saw that Brent Atwood and his second chair, Gina Matthews, were already in their places. The judge would go through the usual motions *in limine* and any other kind of pretrial motions we wanted to make. I had several and I knew the prosecutor did as well. It was basically just tying up loose ends. Both of us would go through our evidence and the judge would decide if there was anything that could not come into the record.

I knew my theory of the case was a novel one. To say the very least. Yet I was encouraged this judge would give me a wide berth.

The only thing that was troubling me, however, was the fact that I could not obviously use the Ancestry.com test results against Jacob. Therefore, I had to have creative ways of figuring out how to nail him to the wall. Once I found out the results of this test, it was just a matter of trying to find some kind of corroborating evidence to show what I needed to show.

Nobody was in the courtroom because the media wasn't allowed in just yet. We would go through our pretrial motions and then jury selection, and then the media would be invited in during the trial portion. But I didn't anticipate the trial would begin for another several days. Because of the intense media scrutiny of this case, we would have to choose alternate jurors.

It was going be tough enough to choose a jury of 12 who could be unbiased about this case. It seemed everybody had an opinion about Esme Gutierrez and about whether or not she was guilty. Hardly anybody on the street would say they hadn't heard about it. How could you not hear about it? It was one of those cases that permeated just about everybody's consciousness. It was like the Kardashian family – you just couldn't get away from it, no matter where you went, no matter what you did. Even if you didn't want to hear about it at all, you still knew something about it.

So the process of picking a jury would be a painstaking one, to say the least.

The judge invited both of us to come up and we both presented our pretrial motions. Brent was very specific about a few pieces of evidence he did not want to have come in, and I was just as specific about evidence I did not want to have come in. The judge would listen to both of our sides to determine what was allowed in and what wasn't.

In the end, it was a wash. Neither one of us really prevailed on the piece of evidence we were really worried about. I knew that after the whole situation with the reopening of the autopsy thing, this judge would allow as much evidence in as possible. His philosophy was that if he got appealed, he wanted to be appealed on the basis of letting too much evidence in as opposed to not enough.

"Let the jury hear it all," he said. "And sort it out. I'm all for transparency. Now I know that Ms. Collins has a unique interpretation of the facts. To say the very least. But I'm willing to let her present evidence on what she's trying to prove, even if it's unconventional. She has her theory on the case and I'm going to let her present evidence about it."

I was happy to hear that because I knew Brent was not so willing to want to give me the benefit of the doubt with what I was trying to prove. He had already called me several times before the trial, trying to get me to take one plea deal after another. And, to tell the truth, I was somewhat inclined to talk to Esme about these pleas. After all, anything short of the death penalty would be a win for us. But, at the same time, I knew I could not browbeat her into accepting a plea deal. Not when I was fairly certain she didn't do it.

There was one witness I thought would be extremely helpful for me - Arnold Garcia. Arnold was a voice coach. There was one thing that always nagged at me about this entire scenario – how could an imposter step into the role of Aria so fluidly? After all, Sophia Delgado was an immigrant from Mexico. Regina found out her background once Julian Rodriguez gave me her name. Even if Sophia spoke perfect English, I wondered how she could imitate Aria's voice well enough to fool people who knew her really well.

So I went back to see Julian. I thought he might be in a better frame of mind. When I saw him, he confirmed that Sophia spoke perfect English. She apparently had a knack for languages like Regina. And then he mentioned this

Arnold Garcia person. He explained to me that Arnold was Sophia's voice coach. Because she was a musician, she had an ear for pitch, which was probably why she got the job. That and the fact that she looked enough like Aria to pull it off. Apparently, she had the same build and coloring as Aria. Her features were reasonably close - close enough that it would not be out of the realm of possibility that she could be Aria after Aria had plastic surgery.

However, the voice would've given her away. If her voice was not the same as Aria's, there would be no amount of explanation to convince the people who knew Aria well that this was Aria and not an imposter.

That was where the voice coach came in. Apparently, Sophia worked with this voice coach for six months. That explained why Jacob wanted to make sure he drove his wife crazy enough to go into the hospital for six months. That would've given him time to work with this new girl and train her. Julian said that while Sophia spoke perfect English, she had a heavy accent when she came up. She worked with the voice coach so thoroughly that by the time she stepped into Aria's shoes, she could imitate her voice perfectly.

I managed to track this guy down, and, even though he was apprehensive about testifying – after all, he was complicit in this entire thing – he agreed to take the stand in the end. I felt that was the only way to show the woman killed in that room was not Aria, but, rather, Sophia Delgado.

After what I found out about Jacob's background, the entire murder fit in perfectly.

Brent was fighting me the entire way. He was fighting me on every motion I made to the court about what I wanted to prove. At first, I thought I would have to subpoena Arnold. He wasn't willing to talk to me at first. So when I went to court to ask for permission to subpoena him, Brent was there objecting the entire way.

Thank God the judge was willing to be liberal about this entire case, because if he wasn't, I might've been SOL.

Brent was fighting me about even making evidence about my theory of the case. He knew what questions I would be asking Jacob and he had asked the court I not go in that direction. But the judge overruled him, so I would have free rein to show what I needed to show.

So, on the day of the trial, I was ready to go. Loaded for bear. I knew just what I wanted to show and I knew just how to show it.

The only thing was – would the jury buy it?

Chapter Thirty-Four

THE JURY SELECTION went somewhat smoothly. I prepared the questions I would ask the jury on *voir dire*. I wanted to see how open-minded they were about the kind of case I would present. In particular, I wanted to know who was a buff of true crime. I wanted to know who was the kind of person who would watch documentaries on Netflix on criminals, who would watch *Dateline* episodes, who liked to read the kind of books that Ann Rule would write. Ann Rule got her start writing the definitive biography of Ted Bundy and wrote many nonfiction books about other criminals after that.

The reason why I wanted to know about this was because the true-crime buffs were usually people desensitized to the mind of a criminal. To them, this entire scenario would be much less outlandish. Truth was often stranger than fiction and avid readers of true crime nonfiction books, and avid viewers of documentaries on TV and Netflix, knew the criminal mind could be extremely devious.

In this case, I knew Jacob had something major to hide.

Something so devastating that he would literally kill to protect it and then cover that murder up. It was all part of a very carefully laid out plan. A plan that Sophia Delgado knew about, of course. She had to have known about it, because she was a participant in the cover-up. And that was bad enough for Jacob. It was bad enough knowing that there was one sane person in this world who knew what he did. And that person's name was Sophia Delgado.

So why did he kill her now? I discovered that answer over the course of my investigation as well. It wasn't just that he was freaked out that Sophia had been pulled over by a cop for suspicion of driving under the influence. She was not, however, arrested for it. The cop who pulled her over made the mistake of allowing her to make a phone call before he put her in the police car because she was recognized as Jacob Whitmore's daughter. Since Jacob was a very important person in the Coronado area, cops gave deference to his family. So Sophia was allowed to make a phone call to Jacob and tell him what was going on. Needless to say, Jacob was down at the station before the cop and Sophia even arrived there. The charges were dropped and Sophia was never fingerprinted.

That was a close call. It was a close enough call that there was the possibility that Jacob would've killed her after the incident. He had to have known that one of those days, Sophia would be arrested for drunk driving and would not be allowed to make a phone call to him before being brought into the station. And if she was ever fingerprinted, that would be it. The jig would be up and questions would be asked.

So, the near arrest might've been a catalyst for doing what he did.

Might've been.

Then again, I found out another fact that was even more devastating than that. Another reason why he would've killed Sophia.

And this particular fact, to me, was dispositive.

———

AFTER TWO DAYS of intense questioning and *voir dire*, we had our jury.

I was ready to go.

Chapter Thirty-Five

AFTER WE DID our opening statements, it was time to party.

The prosecutor's opening statement was pretty good. It laid out the facts, such as they were. It was completely ridiculous, as Regina had stated, that they would try to show that an immigrant would risk being deported by doing something as stupid as stealing from the Whitmores. Not just stealing from them, but stealing a necklace as valuable as the one she was accused of taking.

My opening statement, I believe, was better. I had a much more complicated set of facts I would have to show, therefore I had to carefully lay it all out. I had to show my argument, bit by bit. Element by element, I had to lay it out for them. I could see that when I began my opening statement, many of them looked somewhat confused. But, by the end of my statement, I could see they were with me. I saw their faces change from perplexed to *a ha* in a blink of an eye.

After opening statements, Brent was apparently ready to go.

"Counselor, call your first witness," Judge Warner said to Brent.

He called as his first witness the police who were on the scene. I wasn't too interested in them. I knew that whatever they had to say wouldn't hurt or help our case. Nevertheless, I did ask one of the officers on the scene about the interrogation.

"Officer O'Neill," I started to ask him. "I could see by the interrogation transcripts you were questioning my client for six hours. Is that right?"

He nodded his head. "Yes. That's correct."

"And during that period of time, this period of six hours, did you allow my client to have a bathroom break?"

He got closer to the microphone. "No. We did not."

"You didn't? But I don't understand. According to the transcript, you and Officer French took several breaks during this period of time. In fact, one of those breaks was for lunch. Now isn't it true you did bring lunch into my client, including a large pop?"

"Yes. That is true."

"And the pop was actually a Diet Coke, isn't that right?"

"Yes. That is correct."

"And was that pop a 32 ouncer?" I asked him.

"Yes. That's correct."

"And you still kept her for another four hours after you gave her that pop, isn't that right? In fact, you not only gave her that pop, but you also gave her three other bottled waters, isn't that right?"

"Yes. That is correct."

"Now, isn't it true you told her that if she just told you

what you wanted to hear, that she murdered Aria Whitmore in cold blood, she would be free to go?"

"I did tell her she had to tell the truth about what had happened that night. If she did tell the truth, then, yes, she would've been free to go."

"That was a lie, wasn't it? If she would've admitted to having murdered Aria Whitmore, she would've been under arrest, not free to go, isn't that right?"

"Yes, that is correct."

"So, you're admitting you lied to her," I said.

"Yes. We did lie to her about that."

"And she asked to go to the bathroom several times, didn't she?"

"Yes. But we were not going to allow her to do that until after the interrogation was through. We made that perfectly clear. It's a security risk. We did not have a female officer at that time who would have been able to escort her into the restroom. So we had no choice but to make her stay there until we were through with questioning her."

I nodded. "You didn't have a female officer available to escort her? Is that what you just said?"

"Yes. That's what I just said."

I knew that was a lie. "Oh. So Officer Monroe, a female officer with 20 years experience, was not available that evening?"

"No. She was busy with paperwork. Her shift was over."

"She was in the building, wasn't she?"

"Yes. But she was busy."

I went through a list of the other female officers who were around, and every time I mentioned it, Officer O'Neill said that particular female officer was busy during this time.

"And isn't it true that during this interrogation that my client was wearing a short sleeve shirt and a pair of shorts?"

"Yes. That's true."

"And you and Officer French were in fact wearing long sleeves and pants?"

"Yes. That's true."

"And isn't it true you deliberately put the temperature of the room down to 66° while my client was in there?"

"Ma'am, the point of an interrogation is not to make sure the suspect is comfortable."

"No, as a matter fact, the point of the interrogation is to make sure the suspect is very uncomfortable, isn't that true?"

"No. That is not true. However, we adjust the temperature of the room according to the comfort level of the officers, not the suspect. Officer French and I were comfortable with the room's temperature. That was the only thing important during this time. Not that Ms. Gutierrez was comfortable."

"And didn't you tell Ms. Gutierrez, my client, that if she just cooperated with the two of you, you would talk to the prosecutor about going easy on her?"

"Yes. I did tell her that."

"And what, exactly, would going easy on her entail in this case?"

"Just that I would tell the prosecutor that Ms. Gutierrez cooperated. The final decision, of course, is up to the prosecutor. But I would put in a good word."

"Now isn't it true that even after you and Officer French went out of your way to make sure my client was as uncomfortable as humanly possible, assuming my client was not wearing an adult diaper, which she was not, my client still did not confess to killing Aria Whitmore. Isn't that right?"

He got closer to the microphone. "Yes. That's correct."

"I have nothing further."

The state then called in the medical examiner. I had a few questions for her as well. She testified that her preliminary examination showed the victim had shown signs of blunt trauma and had been strangled. She concluded that the victim died because of strangulation, not because of the blunt force trauma.

I thought about what Lauren had told me about how the real Aria was killed and how she was killed by a large rock. The fake Aria was killed by blunt force trauma as well.

Because the medical examiner was not able to establish the victim in this case was not Aria, simply because the original autopsy was not focused on identification matters, and then the body was cremated, I would have to cross-examine her about other matters. Specifically, I asked her about the entire situation about the reopened autopsy. That was important, because I wanted the jury to understand why I couldn't definitively prove the person who died in Aria's place was not her.

"Now, Dr. Jackson," I said to her. "Isn't it true I made a motion to the court to have the autopsy reopened because I found out new information about the victim, but I found that out some six weeks after the original autopsy was performed?"

"Yes. That is true."

"Were you able to establish the victim in this case was not Aria Whitmore?"

"No. I was not."

"And why were you not able to establish that fact?"

"Because Mr. Whitmore apparently had elected to have the body of the victim cremated."

"And the body was cremated after it was buried, isn't that right?"

"Yes. That is correct."

"So, as you understand it, Jacob Whitmore had his daughter buried in a coffin. And then, two days before the body could be exhumed for the new autopsy, before anybody in this case could be notified, Mr. Whitmore had his daughter's body exhumed and cremated. Isn't that right?"

"Yes. That's correct."

I let that fact speak for itself. It was very suspicious that Jacob would do that. Why have his daughter's body exhumed and cremated unless you're trying to do a coverup?

He was a clever one, that Jacob Whitmore. But maybe not that clever. If he was, he would've had the body cremated to begin with.

I opened my mouth, intending to ask some more questions, but I realized the questions I really needed to ask were the ones I needed to ask Jacob himself. It would be a very fruitful examination when he finally took the stand.

The prosecutor had a few more witnesses, and then it was time to wrap up for the day.

I felt fairly confident I had drawn blood, so I was happy with the exchange with the medical examiner. I knew I could wrap things up in a nice neat bow when I had to.

I was looking forward to that.

Chapter Thirty-Six

AT THE END of the day, I got out on the street and saw people were still gathered in front of the courthouse. In fact, there were more people now than there were earlier. Some guy had a bullhorn and he was talking into it. He was telling the crowd about how we must not let things stand. He was saying that immigrants were the cause of all the problems in this country, and Esme was just the tip of the iceberg. I had to bite my tongue to keep from engaging with the guy. He was such a lunatic. In a way, I felt sorry for him. I felt sorry for anybody who had so much hatred in their heart.

I got home and Christian came home with me. I invited him over for dinner, as I wanted to go through the case with him. I also wanted to talk to Aidan about all of this. Aidan was no longer being as weird with me about this case as he used to be, just because there was no longer a reason to be. I had already talked to Julian Rodriguez about the situation because he was finally cooperating with me. In fact, Julian had agreed to testify in court about what he knew. So, as far as Aidan was concerned, he was in the clear with this whole situation.

However, Aidan had a surprise for me. A surprise guest.

His guest's name was Brad.

Brad Whitmore.

Chapter Thirty-Seven

"HELLO," I said to the guy who was standing in the living room with my brother. Brad was tall, about 6 foot 3, and was small framed, but had kind of a large gut. He was balding on top, which was highly unusual, considering the guy was only 20 years old.

"I'm Avery Collins," I said to him, extending my hand. He just looked at my hand and didn't shake it. "I'm representing Esme Gutierrez in the murder of your sister." I looked over at Aidan, who was looking pretty satisfied about having found this guy.

Ever since I found out there was a Brad, Brad was Aria's brother and was being blamed for the death of the original Aria, I was in hot pursuit of trying to find him. I'd asked Lauren about it but she was no help. She told me he moved without telling her where he was going, just out of the blue.

I knew Brad would be a material witness, to say the very least, but I had no idea where he was. Yet Aidan finally tracked him down. I had no idea how he found him, but I was happy he did.

The guy nodded. He looked down at the floor, refusing to make eye contact with me. He looked at Aidan furtively and I got the impression that Aidan and he had bonded in some way.

Aidan came over to me. "Brad told me he broke into the house that one night. He had the knife. He wanted me to tell you this because he's very sorry about it. He hopes you can forgive him but he really wanted you to not defend Esme Gutierrez. He wanted that because he thought he'd killed Sophia Delgado. He told me he got the incident with Sophia mixed up with the incident with Aria all those years ago, and the two things blended together in his mind. He still was convinced he had killed Aria all those years ago but now he's not so sure."

I opened my mouth and shut it again. "Brad, I would like to ask you a question."

I had a feeling this Brad was the mysterious X. I had always suspected X had known Christian was on the case with me because the person who threatened me over the email was the same person who broke into my home - there was a business card from Christian on the dining room table, asking me to call him about the case. That card was gone, presumably taken by the intruder. There was a second business card, the one I used to call Christian.

I always wondered if the person who had contacted me, X, knew Christian had been on the case because of that business card.

I felt my heart start to quicken as I realized there was a possibility that this guy, along with the possibility he could testify in court, assuming he was not in the throes of psychosis, would also have information for me about who killed Becky.

He didn't look at me. Rather, he looked at Aidan, who

nodded. "You're going to have to address the questions you have for him to me. He doesn't communicate very much with people. In fact, it took me a long time to gain his trust."

I raised an eyebrow at Brad. I wondered how long Aidan had known about this guy. I would have to talk to him later about how he found him, how long he'd known him, and why he didn't tell me about him a long time ago. I was very thorough with my witness list and had included him on it. However, I could just see the prosecutor asking the judge to exclude him because the prosecutor didn't know about his existence prior to the trial.

Once again, I found myself wanting to brain Aidan. He managed to make things much more difficult than necessary.

"Okay, here's the question I want you to ask him. Did he write me threatening emails, signing them simply X?"

Aidan turned to Brad. "My sister, Avery, wants to ask if you threatened her over email."

Brad got closer to Aidan and whispered something in his ear.

"Yes," Aidan said to me. "He wrote those threatening emails." And then he looked over at Brad, who was holding up two fingers. Brad whispered something else to him. "The two emails."

I swallowed hard. I wondered how a guy who seemed so nonfunctional could write such an intelligent and articulate email. But perhaps I didn't need to wonder that. This guy obviously was non-communicative with people in person. That didn't mean he was not highly intelligent and able to write a good email. After all, his mother said he was highly intelligent.

I took a deep breath. I didn't want to get my hopes up. I

didn't want to think this guy really had information about the murder of my best friend. But then again, I had to ask him that question. If there was even a chance he had that kind of information, I would press him on it.

"Ask Brad if he was serious when he wrote he had information about the murder of my best friend. Please ask him that."

Aidan bowed his head as he talked to Brad, and I saw Brad whispering in his ear.

"Yes. He states he does know information about that."

I shook my head. This was all so crazy. I would be getting information after all these years. Then again, I had no idea if I could trust anything this guy had to say. However, if he could possibly lead me to a place where I could tell a cop about what happened to Becky, then this guy was gold, as far as I was concerned. No, not gold. Platinum. He would be that valuable to me.

"Okay. What information does he need to tell me? Who killed her?"

I saw Brad whisper into his ear. He whispered in his ear for quite a while. I could not hear what he was saying, and that, of course, was by design.

"He has information about who knows what happened to your friend. There was a friend he knew when he was young. This was before he went into the mental institution at age 12. This friend knew your friend. The person who killed Becky was extremely wealthy and makes his own father look like a pauper. His father is a billionaire, Avery. So if the person who killed her was even richer than him - well, you can just imagine. He told me that's why the prosecutor hid evidence. Your attorney was apparently in on the whole situation. They conspired to make sure you were convicted of this crime."

What he was telling me was something I'd suspected all along. I just didn't want to believe that somebody would have that kind of power over other people's lives. That they could be so corrupt they could railroad an innocent person into prison. These people ruined my life. And they did it because, why? Money? Did he bribe them? Or maybe he blackmailed them. No, he probably just bribed them. If you dangle enough money in front of people, they will dance to your tune, no matter what your tune happened to be. If you offered the prosecutor and the public defender enough money to make sure somebody is railroaded for a crime you did, that person will get convicted, no matter what.

That person was me.

All of a sudden, I thought about the stories I had learned about in prison. I went to the library one day and found the *Count of Monte Cristo*. That was a story about an innocent boy made to pay for a murder he didn't commit. As in my case, the reason he was put in prison was because of corruption at the highest level. In the end, he managed to escape from prison and take revenge, one by one, on everybody responsible for his situation.

I wondered if I could get that same opportunity. I wondered if I could find out exactly who caused me to go to prison for something I didn't do and if I could take my revenge on them. One by one, just like in the book.

First of all, however, I would have to find out who did it. And why.

"Does he know exactly who was behind all this?" I asked him. "Can he give me a name?"

Aidan whispered into Brad's ear and he whispered back. "Yes. He can. He can tell you exactly who did it. However, he's afraid to tell you. This person is still alive and still knows Brad knows what he did. This guy's been watching him all these years. Brad's afraid that if he tells you, this guy will kill him. Also, he tells me there's not much you can really do to this person. There's no way to prove this person did anything. It was too long ago and there is no real evidence against him. So, Brad doesn't want to tell you who it is. He thinks it would cause more harm than good. He wanted you to know that you went to prison because of corruption."

I sighed. What this guy was doing was almost cruel. He knew who was responsible for me going to prison and he couldn't tell me? I could understand his reasoning – if he really felt his life was in danger, or would be in danger if he said something about this guy, then I could hardly blame him for not wanting to tell me about who it was. But to come over here and tantalize me with these hints – it was too much.

"That's good, Aidan. Listen, thank you for bringing this guy over. I appreciate it. But I'm in the middle of a trial. My client's life literally depends on my being sharp. So, I'm very sorry, but I have to go out on the balcony with Christian. We have to brainstorm about the questions I'm asking my witnesses. I'm going to present my case within the next few days so I'll have to be on my game."

I looked over at Brad. "Thank you, Brad, for coming and telling me this piece of information. If you decide to change your mind about actually giving me a name, then please don't hesitate to come back. In the meantime, I'm going to get my investigator, Regina, to look into the matter. Hopefully she can figure out something. At least we know now that the person who framed me came from the upper-crust world. I had a feeling he did and this just confirms it. So, in a way, that narrows it down for Regina."

At that, I went out my sliding glass door and sat on the

balcony with Christian. He was sitting in one of my big comfortable chairs, a Bloody Mary next to him. There was a Bloody Mary for me as well, just waiting for me to take a sip. We would go over our notes and brainstorm about the prosecutor's next witnesses. I was just going to put the visit from Brad out of my mind. I certainly couldn't have what he told me occupying my headspace. Not now and not at least for the next week or so. Not until the end of trial.

I called Regina.

"Regina, it's Avery. Listen, I need for you to start doing some digging. Brad Whitmore was just here. He's the son of Jacob, brother of Aria, and also apparently the author of the threatening X emails. Which makes sense because his mother told me he was a computer genius. That was why he could cover up his digital footprint so well that even Christian couldn't find him, let alone the FBI. Anyhow, he gave me some clues on who framed me for Becky's murder. He told me the guy behind it all was a rich guy who makes Jacob Whitmore look like a pauper. He apparently got the information from a friend before he went into the mental institution at age 12. He won't tell me anything more than that. But you've tracked down people with less information, so see what you can do."

"Will do, boss. So what will you do once you find out who's behind all that shit? You going to take it to them, Count of Monte Cristo-style? You gonna ruin their lives, one by one? 'Cause you know it wasn't just the one bastard involved with this. There's probably five or six rotten eggs in this bunch. I've a feeling that when I get going, the rot will go from the highest level down to the lowest. But yeah, I'll start shaking the trees. I'll see what rotten fruit falls out of it. Just leave it to me. I'll figure it out."

I nodded. I felt better knowing Regina was on the case.

She was right, however. Once I found out who was involved, I would take my vengeance. I was already marking my public defender and the prosecutor as part of it. I always suspected they were dirty. Now I knew they were. I just needed to get the proof to bring them down. I would burn everybody down by the time I got finished.

If I did that, maybe I could start sleeping at night.

Chapter Thirty-Eight

THE PROSECUTOR'S case wrapped up in two more days, and it was time for my side to get going. Jacob was the main witness for the prosecutor, as I knew he would be. He put on a show, crying on the stand. I had to bite my tongue to not rip into him when I cross-examined him. I knew the truth.

Colleen was another witness the prosecutor put on. She, too, put on a show. Just as much of a show as Jacob. I held her less responsible for this entire shit-show, but I still blamed her. I didn't know how much she knew about the whole Aria-to-Sophia mess. For all I knew, she could be the innocent party in all of this.

But that still didn't make her an innocent party, in general. After all, she was complicit in the whole *Handmaid's Tale* shenanigans they were doing with the domestic workers over there. She knew about it, she encouraged it, and the whole thing was just sick. And, personally, I thought it was why Sophia was killed.

The one thing I didn't do when I cross-examined Jacob, however, was ask questions about what I needed to know about his prior life. And he had a prior life. Literally. That was one thing I found out from Ancestry.com. I was anxious to ask him questions about it on the stand. However, since cross-examination questions are generally limited to topics brought up during the direct examination, I didn't want to get too far over my skis.

I reserved the right to call Jacob as my witness and I was relishing the fight.

Chapter Thirty-Nine

THE FIRST WITNESS I called for my case in chief was Arnold Garcia, Sophia Delgado's voice coach.

Arnold Garcia was around 50 years old, short and squat with a balding head. He seemed like a happy guy, however, and every time I spoke with him he was always jolly, smiling, and ready with a kind word and a good joke. He was a Mexican immigrant, although he'd been in this country for the past 40 years, being brought here when he was only 10 years old.

I was happy Arnold was willing to testify for me. After all, this entire thing threatened to bring him down as well. He was involved with covering up a murder. I wasn't sure he knew he was complicit in covering up a murder, but he had to suspect there was something amiss when Jacob asked him to coach this new imposter to sound exactly like his dead daughter.

I called him to the stand, he raised his right hand, he took the oath, and I got to work.

"Can you please state your name for the record," I said.

He got closer to the microphone. "Arnold Raul Garcia," he said.

"And Mr. Garcia, can you please explain to the court who you are and what you do for a living?"

He cleared his throat. He looked nervous but I didn't blame him. Most people were nervous, especially when they weren't used to doing something like this.

"I'm a voice coach. My practice is focused upon helping immigrants lose their accent. But I've been known to work in the past with actresses and actors from Hollywood and the stage. I've trained actors and actresses to speak in a certain accent, and I've also trained actors and actresses working on a biopic on a particular person to get the voice of that particular person correct. So, for instance, I worked with actresses and actors portraying such figures as Marilyn Monroe or JFK, helping them imitate the voice of Marilyn Monroe or JFK perfectly."

I nodded. "Were you approached by Jacob Whitmore seven years ago?"

"Yes."

"And why did he approach you?"

"He told me he had a young girl living with him, Sophia Delgado, and needed this young girl to sound exactly like his deceased daughter, Aria Whitmore."

"And did he tell you why he needed that?"

Arnold cleared his throat again and he looked nervous. "He told me he had a wife who was having a lot of problems after his daughter had passed away. He told me his wife was in a mental institution because of it and he didn't know what to do to bring his wife back to him. So he said he found a girl who looked just like his deceased daughter and wanted this new girl to sound just like his deceased daughter. He wanted the new daughter to replace the old daughter, and so he wanted the new daughter to be as similar to his deceased daughter as possible."

I knew that was the reasoning Jacob gave to Arnold and I also had a strong suspicion that Arnold knew that story was BS. I also understood that Jacob Whitmore paid him a pretty penny - six figures or more, just for working with this one client. Arnold never told me exactly the amount Jacob paid him, but I knew it had to be a lot. For that amount of money, Arnold probably decided it was in his best interest to be willfully blind. Not that I necessarily blamed him. After all, he wasn't complicit in the actual crime. He was complicit in the cover-up, but what can you do?

"He told you he had this girl named Sophia Delgado and he wanted you to work with her to make sure she sounded just like his daughter, Aria. Is that right?"

"Yes. That's right."

"And where did you work with her?" I asked him.

"She was down in Mexico. She was living in a hacienda in Tijuana, and I moved in with her for a period of six months. She told me she'd previously been in America. She came to America this time with a fellow by the name of Julian Rodriguez. But she told me Jacob owned this hacienda and wanted her to stay there while I worked with her on her voice."

"And was she a good student?" I asked him.

"A very good student. She was very musically inclined. She had perfect pitch. She could identify a note just by hearing it. So it was not difficult at all to train her to sound exactly like Aria Whitmore. It was somewhat challenging at first, just because she had a thick accent, having come from Mexico. So, I first had to work with her on losing the accent. And once I worked with her on losing her accent, I could work with her on getting just the right pitch and tone that made her sound just like Aria Whitmore."

"So you obtained voice samples for Aria, right?"

"Right. Apparently when Aria was 13, she started a video log on YouTube. You know how they do, talking to the camera about their lives. So I had about a year's worth of video logs for her. It wasn't difficult at all for Sophia to match her voice."

"How long did it take for Sophia to perfectly match Aria's voice?"

"Not long at all. After about two months, I felt she was matching Aria's voice completely. However, the contract I had with Jacob was for six months, so I just stayed on at the hacienda with Sophia for the rest of that time. I was working with her even after she perfected the voice, just for reinforcement purposes."

I knew why Jacob wanted this guy to take his time. The cover story was that Aria was in an accident in Mexico and was allegedly in a coma in a Mexican hospital. At least that was the cover story Jacob had given to Aria's teachers, their neighbors and the people who knew her well.

Jacob paid the Tijuana hospital to doctor up some medical records for his daughter. He also paid the cops in Mexico to falsify a police report showing she was in a car accident. He had all of his ducks lined up in a row and even drove his wife literally crazy so she would forget what happened to her own daughter. And even if she did remember what happened, her having a break with reality was perfect for his cover story. If she started telling people that Aria was really dead, no one would ever believe her.

It was gaslighting at its finest.

He had it all figured out. However, I was one step ahead of him. I not only had Arnold testify about how he helped cover up the murder, but also had lined up Julian Rodriguez, who knew the truth, and, of course, Lauren. Julian didn't want to testify - he was afraid of Jacob - but he was under subpoena. I thought better about calling him, however. I knew he was so afraid of Jacob that he probably might lie.

As for the motive for killing Sophia, I had Calista. She would testify, but after Lauren.

I asked Arnold a few more questions, Brent cross-examined him, and he was on his way.

Lauren was next on my list. She would testify about what she knew. And I knew the prosecutor would cross-examine her much more stringently than he did Arnold. After all, with Arnold, there wasn't really much he could ask him. But with Lauren, it would be a field day. After all, she was literally insane.

Granted, at the moment, she was lucid again. The Bridges Recovery center was all she needed to get straight. She'd been in there for the past three months and the change in her was remarkable. She'd gained back the 30 pounds she apparently had lost when she got on the streets, and her hair was back the way it should be – full and lush. She looked 20 years younger because she'd given up smoking and drinking and was on meds that were tweaked and tweaked and tweaked until the doctors found just the right combination that made her schizophrenia go into remission for the moment. She really benefited from the lifestyle at that place – the yoga, the acupuncture, the nutritious food, the exercise, all of it. I was proud to say she'd blossomed. She'd even found a job.

If she stayed on her meds, there was a possibility she could have a somewhat normal life. I wanted, more than anything, for her to have a home of her own.

Lauren took the stand. I had to admit, the way she was dressed – in a light cream suit, with a colorful top and scarf around her neck, combined with a pair of matching pumps - I could see the woman she was before all of this happened. It helped that she looked much better, with her skin and hair, and the lifestyle. But, at the moment, she had the elegant bearing I imagined she did before. She looked like a rich woman. I knew that appearance was everything, and I hoped she could make such an impression on the jury that they would believe her.

She raised her right hand, was sworn in, and I got to work.

"Please state your name for the record," I said to her.

"Lauren Whitmore."

"And you're the former wife of Jacob Whitmore, the father of the victim in this case, is that correct?"

"Yes. That is correct."

"I would like to just get this out of the way. You have had problems with mental illness, isn't that right?"

"Yes. I definitely have. I suffered from late onset schizophrenia. That means I did not have any kind of symptoms of schizophrenia until I was 35 years old. Then, at the age of 35, I had a mental breakdown. There are many reasons for that, but I spent six months in a mental institution."

"Now you stated there were reasons for your mental breakdown. Can you tell the court what those reasons were?"

"Yes. My daughter, Aria, was murdered at the age of 14. I do not know who killed her, but I know she was murdered. I found her, in her bedroom, and she had been hit on the head by a large rock. It was a rock she got from a gift shop in a museum."

243

"And after your daughter was murdered, what happened to you?"

"I couldn't handle it. My mother always had problems with her mental state. I found out when I was an adult that she was a schizophrenic. And I've since read articles about how stress can bring on serious mental illnesses that a person might always have, lurking, and not made manifest. And then, when a person suffers from extreme stress, that illness manifests. That's what my psychiatrist has told me."

For the next hour and a half, Lauren told the jury exactly what she told me. She told the jury about the LSD dosing, the stay in the hospital, the delusions about seeing her daughter every day. She told them about seeing the girl who looked like Aria, but wasn't her. She told them about how the real Aria had been killed. She covered every base in a calm and composed manner.

This was going better than I'd ever hoped.

Then she said something that made me really happy.

"I'm not living on the streets anymore," she said. "I managed to get a job. It's just a small job, working at a nursing home. But it's enough to rent a room from a nice couple in Sunset Cliffs. I don't make a lot of money, and I can't really drive Uber or Lyft or any of that because of my background, so almost every penny I make goes to rent and food. But I'm off the streets."

My heart soared when she said that. That was all I really wanted for her.

I asked her a few more questions and then it was time for Brent to cross examine.

And he immediately tore into her.

"Now, Ms. Whitmore, you admitted on direct examination that you did not really believe your eyes when you saw there was a new girl who taken the place of Aria, isn't that correct?" he demanded.

"Right. That's right. I really didn't believe there was a new girl there."

"And you admit that during that period of time you were having issues with your mental balance. Isn't that right?"

"Right. That's exactly what I said."

"Now isn't it possible you imagined the entire thing? Is it possible you imagined Aria was murdered? Maybe you had a nightmare or something like that, or maybe your schizophrenia, which you admitted was late onset, was made manifest with no triggering event, and so you lost touch with reality and only thought your daughter was murdered?"

"You mean, is it possible my schizophrenia wasn't brought about by my daughter being murdered, but that it just randomly happened, and that made me imagine my daughter was murdered?"

"Exactly. I know I worded that question awkwardly, but that's what I'm getting at. Is that possible?"

"Yes. That's possible."

"So, you admit it's possible you imagined the entire thing? You just imagined your daughter was killed by a large rock and you just imagined she was replaced by somebody new?"

"Yes. That's possible. But I don't think so. I've come across some information that made me know exactly why my husband would've killed Aria in the first place."

My ears perked up. Christian had gotten ahold of that Ancestry.com test result, so I knew why Jacob had killed Aria. I couldn't get these records on my own, however. I could not put them into evidence, because they were obtained illegally. When I asked the judge if I could subpoena the records, he refused. Which was unfortunate, because I thought that maybe he would allow me that since he was so liberal about everything else.

I was holding my breath. I wondered if she'd come across something she hadn't yet told me about.

She nodded. "I have in my possession some DNA test results that my daughter got from that organization called Ancestry.com. And it clearly shows my husband had something to hide."

Chapter Forty

WHAT? She had the test results? She never even told me that. And she didn't bring it up on direct examination, either. I knew chances were good they couldn't come into evidence but this was a possible game changer.

I thought Brent recognized the implications of her having those test results. And he wouldn't ask her about them at all. He wouldn't open the door and I could hardly blame him. In fact, he wanted to shut down questioning after she mentioned that, right away.

"I have nothing more for this witness," he said.

I stood up. "I would like to ask for a short recess, because I need to speak with my witness."

Judge Warner nodded and banged the gavel. "Actually, it's time for lunch. So this is a good time for a break, anyway. It is now 12:15. I would like to ask the jury to be back here at 1:30. Please do not be late. There are lots of great restaurants in the vicinity you can go to, but don't forget, none of you can discuss this case. I'll see everybody in a little over an hour."

I motioned to Lauren to come with me.

"Let's go to lunch, my treat."

She smiled and put her arm around my shoulder. "Avery, I owe everything to you. You got me into that wonderful place in the Pacific Palisades. It has literally meant everything to me. I mean, I'm not cured. I'll never be cured. But I've had a longer period of lucidity than I've ever had, at least since I first started coming down with the symptoms of this disease. I have hope now that maybe I can live a normal life, and it's all thanks to you."

"Well, you did the hard work. But I need to talk to you about what you just said on the stand. So let's get some lunch. Christian will come with us and I need to talk to you about this."

The three of us left the courthouse, and we shoved our way through the throngs of people.

"Where do you want to go?" I asked when we got out on the street.

"I'm game for anything," Lauren said.

"I know. There's this great little Italian place called Osteria Panevino. It's over in the Gaslamp Area, over on Fifth Street. They have gnocchi to die for, and a lot of northern Italian dishes. When it comes to Italian places, it's my favorite place to go. We could sit outside. It's a beautiful day."

Lauren smiled. "I know that place. In my former life, Jacob and I used to go there all the time. You're right, it's a great place to go. Let's go. I would say I'd like to treat you, but –"

"I wouldn't hear of it," I said to her. "It's on me."

We got to the restaurant, asked to sit outside and we ordered our food. And then Christian got right to it. I knew he was just as curious about the whole Ancestry.com thing.

If she had those results in her possession, I'd have to figure out a way to get them into evidence. Christian and I would have to brainstorm that one.

"Okay," Christian said to Lauren. "What gives? You said on the stand you had the results of the DNA test. How did you get a hold of them?"

She took a deep breath. "Well, I told you she was doing that for a school project. I always assumed Aria was killed before she got her chance to turn her test results into the teacher. Mind you, it was always voluntary. The kids didn't have to give the teacher the test results if they didn't want to. But I knew Aria wanted to. She wanted to participate in it because she was interested in finding out the history of the people who were her ancestors."

"Even after she found out what she found out about Jacob? She wanted to give the test results even then?"

"See, that's the thing. I always figured Aria never found that out. I would've been very surprised if Aria would've known something like that and not said anything to me. But here's what I found out. I found out that Aria had ordered two sets of this DNA test. She ordered one set to come to the house and one set to go directly to the teacher. I don't really know why she did that, but that's what she did. And the reason why I found that out was because I contacted her teacher. Her name is Helen Rosen. She'd never looked at the test results. But she had them in Aria's file and she gave them to me."

I started to get excited. Maybe I was being prematurely excited, because I didn't know if the judge would allow these test results to be admitted into open court. I would have to ask for an emergency motion *in limine* on the matter. I had a feeling the prosecutor would have a very good argument for keeping those DNA test results out. Namely, because it would be impossible to show the chain of custody. I would have to get the teacher to testify about how she received the test results and there was no time for that. Not only that, it would be too easy to just doctor up the document. It wasn't like I could get around the hearsay rule by saying it was part of the business records exception, unless I could call somebody from the Ancestry.com place, who had actually composed the report, who could testify it was prepared in the ordinary course of business.

It would be an impossibility to actually get the test results into evidence. I wondered if I could possibly use it in another manner. I wondered if I could use the DNA report to throw Jacob off balance by stating to him I had the test results. Probably, Brent would object even to that. I couldn't make reference to the Ancestry.com report, because I would be making reference to a piece of evidence that wouldn't be allowed.

I gamed out the possibilities but came up empty. The most I could do would be to get the evidence into open court. The judge had been liberal with my evidence so far. That would be a long shot. To say the least. And it would be an appealable error if he allowed them in.

In a way, I wished Lauren didn't actually have those test results in her possession. After all, they wouldn't do any good.

I looked at Christian. "Think about any possibility that we could get those test results into evidence," I said.

"I'm thinking, but I don't see it. It wouldn't come under the business records exception to the hearsay rule, and, let's face it, the chain of custody isn't there. But it's good to know she has the records."

The food came, and, just like I remembered, it was delicious. We chatted about how she was doing, and she told me about her new job. She said it wasn't much, and it was a lot of work, but she was happy to be doing it. She was happy to be doing any kind of job. She was thrilled she was off the streets, working an honest day's work, and had a soft place to land at night.

Chapter Forty-One

AFTER LUNCH, we made the half-mile trek back to the courthouse. I was actually looking forward to my next witness, because I felt she could shed a lot of light on what had happened with Sophia and why she was murdered.

When we got in the courtroom, the jury was just coming back in. The judge also came back in, banged his gavel, the bailiff announced him, everybody stood up, and sat back down. "Now, I hope everybody got a good lunch. We're going to be continuing with the defendant's case, and Ms. Collins, call your next witness."

"The defense calls Calista Kassis."

Calista would put Jacob and Colleen on blast to the entire world. At the moment, I was happy the media had been invited into the courtroom. Because, if nothing else, the sick part of their lives would be broadcast to the world. Jacob's even more sick secrets would also be broadcast to the world, but nobody thought Jacob was a choir boy. He was known to be ruthless and a scumbag. But Colleen's reputation was sterling.

It wouldn't be after this.

Calista approached the bench. She was dressed in a black pantsuit, with a green turtleneck underneath it. Her blonde hair was straightened and she was wearing minimal makeup. On her earlobes were a pair of dangly earrings. On her neck was a pearl necklace.

She raised her hand, was sworn in, I asked her name, she stated it, and I got right to work.

"Now, Ms. Kassis, you are, or you were, the domestic worker for Mr. and Mrs. Whitmore, is that correct?"

"Yes. Yes I was. I was up until a few months ago." I knew when I talked to that immigration judge and threatened to expose him for his corruption, so Calista was no longer in fear of being deported, she was free to quit the job and testify against them.

"Did you recently have a child?"

"Yes."

"And who is the father of that child?"

"Jacob Whitmore."

I knew the jury was waiting for this particular witness to take the stand. I knew they were aware of what she would say, because I'd covered all of that in my opening statement. But I still heard gasps behind me, which told me they were still shocked.

"Jacob Whitmore. Can you tell me how you came to have a child for Jacob Whitmore?"

She nodded. She looked ashamed as she looked down at the stand in front of her. She had tears in her eyes.

"Mr. Whitmore told me that when I came to work for him what he wanted from me. Or, actually, it was his wife, Colleen, who told me. She explained to me that she could not have children and needed me to bear children for her. I was an immigrant, a refugee from Syria, and this is a very bad time for people like me. Not many people from my country are even being allowed to come here anymore. I came here without documentation. I applied for asylum the moment I got here, but I didn't know if it would given to me. I was lucky to even come to this country at all. I was terrified of being sent back. I would do anything I possibly could to make sure I stayed in this country."

"Did Mr. Whitmore make any promises if you did this for him?"

She nodded her head. "He did. He told me he had a line with this certain immigration judge. One bad word from him and I'd be sent back. But he also said that one good word from him and I'd be guaranteed to stay. So I would do anything at all to stay."

I knew that, just like with Esme, she was forced to have abortions. "Was there anything in particular that Jacob wanted, as far as babies? Did he want a son or a daughter?"

She nodded her head. "He definitely wanted sons."

"And what would happen if you got pregnant with a daughter?"

"He would force me to have an abortion and we would start all over again. We did that four times before I finally got pregnant with a son."

Now for the piéce de rèsistance. "Did you happen to tell Aria about what was going on?"

She hesitated. "I did. But I knew Aria was not Aria. She told me one night in confidence about what had happened. She didn't tell Esme, though. She was afraid to tell even me, but she had to tell somebody. She was having a lot of problems with doing what she was doing. She told me she had to tell somebody about it."

"You mean, she told you she was actually Sophia Delgado?"

"Objection, hearsay," Brent said getting to his feet. I wondered why he didn't make an objection earlier. Maybe he wasn't paying attention.

"Sustained," Judge Warner said. "Ms. Kassis, you may tell the court what you told Aria. You may not tell the court what she said in response. Please proceed."

I was happy that at least something came in as far as what Calista knew, as far as Aria being Sophia. This would explain a little bit about why Sophia got upset enough to tell Jacob what she knew and what she would do about it.

I knew Sophia was extremely upset when she found out about the abortions Jacob forced Calista and Esme to have. She was Catholic, very religious and thought it was disgusting that these women were forced to have abortions. I knew Calista and she had spoken. She knew both women were exploited by Jacob and also knew she held the secret that would ruin him.

"So, did you tell the woman that everybody knew as Aria that you were being forced to have abortions?"

"Objection, relevance," Brent said, getting to his feet.

"Goes to motive, Your Honor. My theory of the case is that Sophia found out exactly how much Jacob and Colleen were exploiting immigrants and that led her to go to the authorities about what he was doing. And, since she had an ace in the hole, the proof she was not really his daughter, he knew she was dangerous."

The judge nodded his head. "I'll allow it. Ms. Kassis, please proceed."

"Yes." She bowed her head, and dabbed her eyes.

"Did you tell her that my client, Esme, was being forced to have abortions as well?"

"Yes."

"So the woman everybody knew as Aria knew you and my client were being exploited by the Whitmores?"

She nodded. "Yes. That's what they do. They exploit the vulnerable, the weak, the helpless. They know that if they get brown immigrants in, they can do anything at all to these immigrants. All they have to do is threaten to have them deported, and these women will do anything. And she was an immigrant too. Sophia. She was an immigrant."

"Other than being forced to have abortions and being forced to have a child for the Whitmores, did they treat you well?"

She shook her head. "No. They did not."

"What do you mean, they didn't treat you well?"

"They didn't pay me. At all. And I did a lot of work for them. Esme and me, we did all the housework around that enormous house. That was a lot of work and we also did a lot of the cooking. The laundry, cleaning their six bathrooms, vacuuming, dusting, every single day. Mopping, picking up dry cleaning, on and on and on and on. And neither Esme nor I got any money for any of that."

This direct exam was going very well. This woman was painting Jacob as the monster he was. I looked over at the jury and saw their faces were contorted in horror at what Calista was saying. A couple of them were shaking their heads with disgusted looks on their faces. I smiled, then turned back around so I could ask Calista a few more questions.

"You know my client, Esme, correct?"

"Of course. I worked with her for many months."

"To your knowledge, have the Whitmores ever accused her of stealing anything from them?"

"No. Never."

"I have nothing further for this witness."

I sat down and Brent stood up. He cross-examined her for the better part of the next half hour. But it was no use. I could tell just by looking at the jury that I had hit home with my questioning.

It was getting to be in the late afternoon. I thought long and hard about that Ancestry.com document. There was no harm in asking for a motion *in limine*. The worst that could happen would be the judge would tell me there was no way he would allow that document to come in. I wouldn't be out anything if he said that because I was expecting it.

Nothing ventured, nothing gained.

Brent had finished his cross-examination of Calista and the judge asked me to call my next witness.

"I'd like a short recess, Your Honor. I'd like a conference with Your Honor and the prosecutors. Thank you."

Judge Warner nodded his head. "It's a good time for a recess. Okay, ladies and gentlemen of the jury, stretch your legs a little bit. This court will recess for 15 minutes. Please be back by 3:45. Thank you."

The jury filed out and I could feel my heart pounding. This might be the game changer, if the judge would allow this piece of information in. If he didn't allow it in, it wouldn't change my original strategy. However, my original strategy would rely on a lot of luck, and a lot of skill in breaking down Jacob when he took the stand as my witness. It would be so much easier if I could just bring in this DNA test and show the jury exactly who Jacob was.

I went to the bench, along with Christian, Brent, and his second chair, Gina Mathews.

"Well, counselor, what did you need to have a conference about?" Judge Warner asked me.

"I have a document I'd like to enter into evidence.

However, I needed to see if I could possibly schedule a motion *in limine* on the document."

"And what, exactly, is the document in question?" Judge Warner asked me.

"I have in my possession a Ancestry.com report. This is the report that will help establish Jacob Whitmore's true identity. It's crucial to prove motive for why Jacob would've killed Sophia, Aria's imposter. Furthermore, it establishes motive for murdering Aria. Now, I understand this is not a trial regarding the murder of the original Aria, but it's very important to establish the chain of events that led to Sophia's death."

"Obviously, this report won't be admissible," Brent said. "It would be impossible to establish a chain of custody." He was pretty cocksure about himself, and probably should not have been, because I was starting to understand that this judge wanted as much information as possible to be available to the jury to establish my case. I'd never been in front of this judge before, so I had no idea if he was always this liberal with his attorneys in court, or if he really wanted to make sure this case was tried fairly.

And getting this particular report into evidence would be sensational, to say the very least. It would be something that would make headlines all over the world. That much, I knew.

"Ms. Collins, how would you go about establishing the chain of custody for this report?"

I took a deep breath. I did not have time to subpoena the teacher, Helen Rosen. Moreover, I knew she would be working tomorrow, so it would be difficult to persuade her to come to the court willingly to testify. But that would be the only way to get this report into evidence. I'd have to get her to testify about how she received the report, and that she had not actually reviewed the report, but just put it into Aria's file. She was also going to have to testify that she didn't alter the report in any way, shape, or form and she was the only one who had access to it. In short, she would have to establish a chain of custody for the report. Even then, it would be difficult to get past the hearsay objections. I knew that would be the sticking point, if there would be a sticking point on this matter.

"I could get the teacher, Helen Rosen, to testify in court in the motion *in limine* hearing. We can do it early tomorrow morning, before the jury is scheduled to report. She can testify about the chain of custody."

Brent was shaking his head. "Your Honor, an Ancestry.com report is hearsay. Plain and simple. It cannot fall under any of the hearsay exceptions, including the business records exception. Ms. Collins would have to bring in the custodian of the records, and that custodian would have to have actual knowledge of the information contained in the report. She might be able to track that person down, but not by tomorrow. And I'm not going to agree to any continuance of this case."

I decided to throw something at the wall and see if it stuck. "There is another exception to the hearsay rule. It's an exception for family records. If a record is a statement of fact about the personal or family history, including genealogy, then that record is excepted from hearsay."

Brent jumped in. "That particular exception is clearly for records involving a person's family tree. It doesn't cover something like Ancestry.com, which is not the family tree record per se, but, rather a family DNA record. That's very different than what is contemplated in that particular rule."

The judge nodded. "Ms. Collins is right. There is a rule that states that family records are excepted from the hearsay rule. While I agree with Mr. Atwood that rule probably does refer to family tree reports, the rule has not been very specific on exactly what kind of genealogy reports are allowed, and not allowed. Since this is a borderline case, I'll allow it, provided Ms. Collins is able to call Helen Rosen to the stand tomorrow morning at 8 AM, for a motion *in limine* on whether or not the report is admissible. When the jury comes in, I'll adjourn until tomorrow. However, if you, Mr. Atwood, can find case law that shows that report is not admissible, I'll consider that."

I sat down after thanking Judge Warner profusely for his ruling. I was happy I knew about that hearsay exception so well off the top of my head. Truth be told, the family records exception was not used very often. I'd never used it. But I knew that it was there, so it saved me.

However, it also put a lot of pressure on me. If I couldn't get Helen Rosen to come to court tomorrow morning at eight, without a subpoena, I was dead in the water anyway on this matter.

The jury came in, the judge excused them for the day, and it was time to go home.

But I wasn't going home.

I would call Regina and see if she could meet me. I needed her to talk to Helen Rosen, and fast.

Chapter Forty-Two

I CALLED Regina from the car on my way home from court. "Regina, you need to do something for me, and you need to do it for me as soon as you can. There's a lady by the name of Helen Rosen. She works at the Waldorf School in San Diego. I believe she's still a teacher there, anyhow. I need you to see her and do what you can to make sure she's in court tomorrow at 8 AM. Bribe her, whatever you need to do, I just need to have her in court tomorrow morning. I cannot subpoena her, there's no time for that. Thanks."

Regina and I talked for a few minutes, and I hung up. All of a sudden, getting that report into evidence was primary on my mind. I didn't even know that it was a possibility until Lauren told me what she told me, and now that was all I could think about. I would simply question Jacob about his past. And I knew he would lie about it, because why not? He would try and make me look like I was a fool, and I was prepared for that. My questions were geared for that. All I had to do was put some reasonable doubt in the jury's mind, and my job was done. But if I could just get this report into evidence, it would make my life so much easier.

I knew that if Regina wasn't able to secure Helen's cooperation by tomorrow morning at eight, I would be devastated. I hated that I felt that way. I just figured there would be no way the judge would even allow it, even if there was testimony from Helen. But when he indicated he was open to it, I suddenly knew I wanted that report to be entered into evidence. I wanted it badly.

I went home, after picking up the dogs from their daycare, and I took them to the beach. I sat on the sand, watching the waves come in and out, one dog on my right side and one dog on my left. I was leaning against a small chair in the sand, and my phone was always by my side.

I realized I needed the calming sound of the waves coming in and out because my anxiety had suddenly spiked. I felt a nagging knot in the pit of my stomach as I waited for Regina to call me. I just wanted her to give me some kind of a status update. Was she able to find Helen? Was Helen able to get off work tomorrow morning to come and testify? Was Helen *willing* to testify? These were the questions that were running through my mind as I checked my phone, again and again, making sure it worked. All the while, I sat there on the beach, listening to the waves, and feeling like things would take a turn for the worse if I couldn't get that report into evidence.

I got up and started walking the dogs. We got closer to the shore, and I let the warm water lap around my ankles. In the distance, I could see people surfing. I was halfway tempted to get my own wetsuit on and join them. I wasn't a very good surfer. Aidan was much better than me, but he had a lot more practice than I did. Surfing was something he did all the time. When he wasn't working, going to school, interning, and getting baked, he was surfing. Me, I just did it on occasion. I wasn't the most coordinated person in the entire world, that was for sure.

But I wanted something to take my mind off of the damn phone that refused to ring.

As I walked along the shore, I finally heard Regina's ring. I had programmed the phone to start playing Radiohead's song *Creep*, simply because that was mine and Regina's favorite song. I heard the opening bars and I immediately picked up.

"What's the word?" I asked her. I tried to keep the desperation out of my voice, but I knew it was there anyhow.

"I found the chick and she'll be there tomorrow morning. You just gotta give her a $500 spa gift card. She ain't doing it for free and she told me she could really use a good microbrasion facial and also wants to get her eyelashes extended. Personally, I don't think she really needs eyelash extensions, but whatever. She likes Secret Spa and Salon in La Jolla. You go get that card and she'll meet you at the court tomorrow morning at eight."

"Woo hoo!" I screamed. "I'll be driving to that spa right now. Love you, girl!"

I hung up and decided to take the dogs with me up to La Jolla. They really enjoyed driving in the car, and La Jolla was about a half-hour drive, considering traffic.

I went to that spot, got a card, and went home.

I slept a good night's sleep that night, the best sleep I've had in a long time.

Chapter Forty-Three

THE NEXT DAY, I got to the court bright and early. I got there at 7:30 in the morning because I was just too wound to sleep late. I'd called Helen on the phone and told her what I needed from her and she told me that was just fine. She was able to take off from work, and the reason why she wanted the spa gift card was because that was where she would be heading after court.

"I figured that since I'm taking the morning off, I might as well just take the entire day off and play hooky. I'm looking forward to a day of pampering. That'll be my reward for coming in and testifying for you in court."

I was nervous. I knew there was a good chance the judge would allow those DNA results to be entered into evidence. At the same time, I knew Brent was probably going to be loaded for bear. He was probably going to be coming with case law and everything else. I decided to do my own research on the matter. I didn't find a case on point, however. At least, not in the state of California. I was cheered by that, because I doubted that Brent could find on-point case law about it, either.

Sure enough, when Brent got into the courtroom, he had copies of statutes and rulebooks. "I researched the whole hearsay exception issue, and in the state of California the exception has to be a family record. As in a record that was kept by the family. I'm going to renew my objection to this entire proceeding."

"I understand that, but the federal rules are much more ambiguous as to what constitutes a family records exception," I countered. "It simply says that if there is evidence about family history contained in a family record such as a genealogy, whatever that means, that record is excepted. I believe that the Ancestry.com is a modern-day genealogy chart that a family would keep. I know the California rule is a little bit more specific, but I don't think it's necessarily a bright line either. This could be considered a family chart." I knew I was stretching the argument, but I also knew this judge was probably going to rule in my favor. He'd already decided he would hear this motion *in limine*, so that was a good sign.

Helen arrived, and it was time to go. Helen was a young and pretty brunette woman, very petite, with dark hair and big brown eyes. Her nose and lips made her look like a little pixie girl, and Regina was right - she didn't need eyelash extensions. She had full eyelashes anyway, the kind of eyelashes I'd always coveted for myself.

She smiled and I felt more at ease about her testifying.

The judge got on the bench, and the bailiff instructed us to remain seated. "Now, I understand we have a motion *in limine* hearing this morning before the jury is scheduled to arrive. This is on the matter of the admission of a Ancestry.com DNA report that was in the possession of a Ms. Helen Rosen. Counselor, you may call your witness."

At that, Brent stood up. "Your Honor, if it please the court, I would like to renew my objection to this admission. I still believe it is hearsay under the California Rules of Evidence. The rules of evidence excepts family records if they are contained in a family Bible or other family chart. This particular piece of evidence is not contained in any kind of a family chart or Bible, so I still believe it is excluded by the hearsay rule."

"I understand your objection, and it is on the record. Appeal me if you like, but I'm going to allow this record as long as Ms. Rosen here can establish a chain of custody. So, Ms. Collins, you may proceed."

I took a deep breath and the bailiff instructed Helen to take the stand. She raised her right hand, was sworn in, and I got to work.

"Please state your name for the record."

"Helen Alexandria Rosen."

"And Ms. Rosen, you have in your possession a DNA report that was given to you by a student by the name of Aria Whitmore. Is that correct?"

"Yes. That's correct."

"And why do you have that report in your possession?"

She told the jury about the extra credit assignment she gave her students, and how the Ancestry.com report fit in with it.

"And you received the DNA report for Aria Whitmore?" I asked.

"Yes. I did. I received it in the mail, as I guess Aria ordered the test. One test came to her, and one test came to me."

"And when you received that report, what did you do with it?"

"I put it in Aria's file. I didn't open it. I kept it sealed in the envelope. I put it in her file and just left it there. I was not going to open it until she did her report, and, unfortunately, she got into a car accident in Mexico and was gone for the rest of the school year, so she never got a chance to present the report. And, I confess, when she came back to school the next semester, I completely forgot about giving the report back to her. In fact, I'd completely forgotten about the report at all, until I was visited by Lauren Whitmore, who asked me for it."

"And so are you representing to the court you are the only person who has had your hands on this report?"

"Yes. That is correct."

"And did you alter this report in any way?"

"No. I did not."

"I have nothing further for this witness, Your Honor."

"Mr. Atwood, do you have any cross-examination of the witness?"

"No. However, I'd like to ensure that my objection to this report is entered into evidence, based on the hearsay rule. And that is all."

"Very well. I'll allow this DNA test report to be entered into evidence. Now, it's 8:45 AM, we'll take a short recess until 9 AM." And, at that, he left the bench and went into his chambers.

I breathed a sigh of relief.

I would nail that bastard yet.

Chapter Forty-Four

ONCE THE JURY came back in, I was instructed to call my next witness, and I called Jacob himself. Jacob was none too happy about having to testify on two different days. I could tell that. He looked at me and scowled. He gave me the stink eye so bad I felt like I would melt right into the floor. But I just stared at him right back. He wouldn't intimidate me. He wouldn't make me back down. I had what I needed to show what kind of person he was and I would bury him.

He took the stand, was informed he was still under oath, and I got right to work.

"Mr. Whitmore, do you understand the reason why you've been recalled to the stand by me?"

"No. I can't say I know why you would put me back on the stand. I gave my testimony to the prosecutor and that should've been good enough."

"I wanted to call you to the stand again because I needed to ask you some questions that were not related to the questions you answered on direct exam. Therefore, I'm calling you as my witness."

He glared at me but said nothing. He couldn't have known what I had to ask him. I wanted the element of surprise, so there was no way I would go over my questions with him beforehand. "Okay then, go ahead."

I nodded. I knew where I wanted to go with this, and I knew where I wanted to start out. "Your daughter, Aria, she wasn't adopted, was she?"

"No."

I would lay a trap for him, and that was the first part of my trap.

"Mr. Whitmore, let me ask you another question. Have you ever been known by another name?"

I could almost see his face go very pale when I asked that question. He had a fake tan. I could tell it was fake because he looked slightly orange. The only exception to the general orange tint of his face were around his eyes, which were white. It looked like he probably went into a tanning booth with goggles on. But, when I asked that question, the color left his face.

He recovered quickly enough. He sat up straighter in his chair, and looked me straight in the eye. "No. I've never been known by another name."

I nodded my head. "You've never been known by the name of William McNeil?"

He swallowed hard. "No. I've never been known by that name."

I looked over at the judge. "Permission to treat as hostile," I said to the judge.

"Permission granted. Please proceed."

"I'd like you to look at a newspaper article dated November 21, 1969. You would've been 25 years old, wouldn't you have?"

"I'd like to object to the newspaper being entered into evidence," Brent said. "It's hearsay."

"It's not hearsay, because it is not being offered to prove or disprove any element of the charged offense."

"I'll allow it," the judge said. "Please proceed."

"Yes. I would've been 25 years old in 1969. Why does that matter?"

"This newspaper article, dated November 21, 1969, indicated that members of a radical right wing group, known as the White Freedom, were accused of bombing a black church in Southern Missouri. Five people died in that blast. This newspaper article indicated the leader of this group was a man by the name of William McNeil. Age 25."

"Okay. And what does this have to do with me?" he demanded.

"I'm getting to that. William McNeil was on a fishing trip in Mexico while he was out on bail, right before he'd be facing trial for the charges of murder in the 1st° and arson in the 1st°. Both of those charges carried a sentence of life in prison, and if William McNeil was convicted of first-degree murder, he could've possibly faced the death penalty."

I could see him breathing harder. "Okay. I still don't know where you're going with this, but, by all means, proceed." He was trying to act cool but I knew he was nervous as hell.

"William McNeil disappeared during that fishing trip. His body was never found, but he was declared deceased six months later."

"And?"

"I'd like to enter into evidence the newspaper article talking about William McNeil's bombing of the black church, and another newspaper article that details William

McNeil's death in Mexico. I have marked the first news-paper article as Exhibit A, and the second newspaper article as Exhibit B."

"Any objection?"

"I'd like to preserve my objection for the record. I still believe this could possibly constitute hearsay."

"Objection overruled. The articles are entered into evidence."

"And you, Jacob Whitmore, according to your biogra-phy, went to Yale undergraduate school and then the Wharton school of business. However, you started your undergraduate career at the age of 25. Isn't that right?"

I did my homework. What I found out, or, rather, what Regina found out, was that Jacob paid a lot of money to have his former identity erased and a new identity created. He had the money, because his own father, William McNeil's father, was a very wealthy man. William McNeil's father could pay any amount of money to ensure his son's disappearance was never investigated, and he could be declared dead, and that an entire new identity could be created for him. His father had enough money to hire the best plastic surgeon down in Mexico to give his son a brand-spanking new face. His father had enough money to create an entire background for "Jacob Whitmore," which ensured he'd be admitted to Yale and Wharton. And, for good measure, his father donated millions of dollars to both schools. Just in case they didn't want to let "Jacob Whit-more" in the door.

"Yes. That's correct. I did not enter school until I was 25 years old."

"And what were you doing before the age of 25?"

"I was traveling. Seeing Europe. Seeing the world. I think I didn't focus on my future until I was in my mid-20s."

"Isn't it true you're actually William McNeil?"

He started to laugh. "What, is this a joke?"

"I'm not laughing. Isn't it true you're William McNeil, the leader of a white supremacist group that killed five people in a black church bombing, and then you faked your death with the help of your wealthy father, and again, with your father's help, you had a new identity created for you?"

"That's absurd!"

I nodded. "I'd like you to read aloud this report I'm going to give you. This is a report from Ancestry.com and it was prepared at the request of your daughter, Aria Whitmore. She requested this report when she was 14 years old, for a project she was working on in school." I cleared my throat. "You have an identical twin, isn't that right?"

"No. I don't know what you're talking about."

"I do. Your identical twin took a DNA test for Ancestry.com, unfortunately for you, which means his DNA was in the database. That means your DNA is also in the database with a few minor changes, because identical twins do not have identical DNA. So this report was able to pinpoint exactly who Aria's father was. And I'll give you a hint - the name of her father isn't Jacob Whitmore."

"I don't know what you're talking about," he said.

"Can you please tell the court the name of Aria's father, according to this DNA report?"

I could tell he was unnerved. When he picked up the DNA report, his hands were shaking. His face was getting whiter by the second. He was a cornered animal, and he knew it.

"This report is mistaken. I don't know where you got this report, and I don't know how it was prepared, but obviously something happened in the lab."

I smiled. I wondered why he didn't just feign outrage

and throw a fit, claiming that Colleen must have been sleeping with somebody else. The bitch! I guessed I threw him off-balance, so he didn't think of that angle.

"This report was prepared by Ancestry.com. This is a reputable DNA and ancestry site that millions of people have depended upon over the years. I can assure you that there's never been a report of a mixup at the lab. Your identical twin is in the database, so the site was able to pinpoint exactly who Aria's father is. Now can you please read to the court who was the father of Aria Whitmore?"

He cleared his throat. "William McNeil."

"I'd like this DNA report to be marked as Exhibit C and entered into evidence."

"Any objection?" Judge Warner asked Brent.

"I would like to object for the record, to the hearsay," Brent said.

"So noted. Objection overruled. Please proceed."

I entered the report into evidence. I then walked the report over to the jury and they passed it around. I could see on their faces they were stunned. To say the very least.

"Now, isn't it true that Aria Whitmore could find out the truth of her parentage because she ordered this test to be done and you killed her to make sure she kept quiet?"

"I did not do something like that." His face was starting to get red.

"Yes you did. You killed her at the age of 14 and then you got an imposter to take her place. The imposter's name was Sophia Delgado, an immigrant from Mexico, who had the same blonde hair and blue eyes as your daughter and looked remarkably similar to her. You killed your daughter at the age of 14 and then you told all your neighbors and her teachers and friends that she was in a car accident in Mexico, so she had to have plastic surgery, and then you passed off Sophia Delgado as your daughter, Aria. Isn't that true?"

He stood up, and shook his fist. "That's not true. That's a lie."

"Is it? Is it a lie? Is it a lie that you literally drove your wife over a cliff, mentally, by giving her LSD in large doses, while telling her that it would cure her incipient schizophrenia? Instead of curing her, it made her go into full-blown schizophrenia, which is what you wanted, because you wanted to make sure nobody would believe her when she told people that her daughter was dead and there was another girl in her place. Isn't that right?"

"I don't know what kind of lies Lauren has been telling you, but I would never do something like that."

"Oh, you wouldn't? Then why is it that's exactly what she told the court? She told the court, under the penalty of perjury, that you gave her large doses of LSD. You don't believe LSD can be used to cure schizophrenia, do you? You're an educated man, surely you know better than that?"

"Of course I know better than that. Everybody knows LSD causes hallucinations and that it's bad for somebody who's having problems with reality."

"Do you realize your wife has spent the last 7 years homeless?"

"Yes. I realize that."

"And you didn't do anything to help her, isn't that right?"

"I had a restraining order against her and that's all I know."

"Now, isn't it true you forced both my client, Esme Gutierrez, and Calista Kassis, to bear your children for you?"

He started to laugh. "That's absurd. You've gone completely outer limits with your questioning."

"And isn't it true that Sophia Delgado found out what you were doing with Esme and Calista, and found out you were forcing them to have abortion after abortion, because you're desperate to have only sons? She confronted you and told you she had enough of the charade and would go to the police and tell them exactly who she was, and she would give them a fingerprint to prove it, isn't that right? You knew she was dangerous for that reason. Isn't that true?"

By this time, he was shaking with rage. He stood up and I could see a vein popping out of his forehead. "That isn't what happened. Sophia never found out about the abortions."

And then he sat down, apparently realizing what exactly he admitted to the court.

"Okay, so you admit that Aria was not Aria, but, rather, was Sophia Delgado."

"I admitted no such thing."

"But you referred to your daughter as Sophia. Didn't you?"

"No. I didn't call my daughter Sophia."

"Then who is Sophia?"

"I don't know a Sophia."

"But you stated, and I quote, 'that isn't what happened, Sophia never found out about the abortions.' Isn't that what you just now said?"

He opened his mouth and closed it again. "I must've been confused. You kept saying the name Sophia, so it came out of my mouth as well."

"Sophia threatened you, didn't she? She was getting tired of your shenanigans, was getting tired of the way you were treating your immigrant help, because, after all, she was an immigrant as well, and she threatened you. She could've ruined you, because she knew the truth about Aria. Isn't that true?"

"No. I don't know what you're talking about."

"You knew it was only a matter of time before everybody found out Sophia replaced Aria. You knew that if she ever got arrested and had to give her fingerprint, the jig would be up right then. You knew that if she ever went into the hospital and needed a blood transfusion, you would be caught – because Sophia had a different blood type than Aria did, didn't she? There were any number of things that could've happened that would expose you for what you did to your own daughter. And you knew it. You knew it was only a matter of time before everybody found out the ruse."

"Objection, badgering."

"Overruled. Please proceed."

"Well, then I'll object to the editorializing. Where is the question?"

Judge Warner looked at me. "Sustained. Counselor, please ask your question without editorializing."

I nodded my head. "Okay, thank you, your honor." Then I turned to Jacob. "Isn't it true you knew Sophia could ruin you?"

"No."

"And isn't true you wanted to get rid of Esme because you didn't have any use for her anymore?"

"No. That's not true."

"Oh, it's not? You had Calista. She was doing all your dirty work and was agreeing to have your kids. Admit it, you hate Esme, because she's from Central America, she's an immigrant, and you feel she doesn't belong here. You wanted to be rid of her, so you killed Sophia Delgado, you planted that diamond necklace in Esme's drawer, and you framed her for the murder of Sophia. Admit it."

"I will not admit that, because that is not true."

I was undeterred. "Admit the life of my client means less than nothing to you and you would've liked nothing more than to see her rot in prison for something she didn't do. Rot in prison for something you did. After all, you are a white supremacist, you were responsible for the murder of five African-Americans, and you despise people who are not just like you. Admit that."

"I will admit nothing of the sort."

"Would you be willing to be fingerprinted?" I asked him. "After all, William McNeil was arrested for the bombing of that black church. He was fingerprinted. Would you be willing to give your fingerprints?"

He looked at the judge. "That's an invasion of my privacy. I won't stand for that."

"I take that as a no? Because you know that if you gave your fingerprints, they would match the fingerprints of William McNeil perfectly. Isn't that true?"

"No, that's not why. I simply refuse to give my fingerprints because I don't want my privacy invaded."

I started to pace the floor. "And why, exactly, would giving your fingerprint be an invasion of your privacy?"

"It just would. You'd be using it to try to incriminate me and I know my rights."

"But if you had nothing to hide, it wouldn't incriminate you, now would it?"

"I have nothing to hide."

"I would imagine the FBI's going to be talking to you after this court appearance, because this DNA test gives them probable cause to do a little background search, a little investigation. And, at some point, they're going to have enough evidence to get a court order to make you give a fingerprint. It's going to come out, one way or another. So you might as well just tell the court the truth and you won't have a perjury charge on top of everything else you're going to be facing once the FBI gets through with investigating you."

He looked like he was about to explode. "The truth? I'll tell you the truth. That little bitch, Sophia, told me she didn't like what I was doing with Esme and Calista. She told me abortion is wrong, it's a sin, and I would go to hell. She told me that because of me, Calista and Esme both would go to hell, because they were having abortions. She told me she would tell the police who she really was, and she would tell the police I killed my own daughter. She told me she had it with the lie and wouldn't go through with it anymore. So yeah. I killed her. I had to kill that bitch. She would ruin me, just like you're ruining me right now. And yeah, I am William McNeil. I'm proud to be William McNeil. I'm proud of what he stood for. Yeah, I'll give my fingerprint, gladly."

I nodded. "I have nothing further for this witness."

And I sat down.

And then all at once, the court room absolutely erupted. All the newspaper reporters who were crammed into this courtroom were suddenly all at once leaving the courtroom, I guess because they all wanted to beat each other as far as filing the story about what happened here. I almost chuckled. While all this pandemonium was breaking out, with everybody shouting at once, everybody running over each other to get out the door, the judge was banging his gavel, over and over again. He was threatening to hold everybody in contempt, but they didn't care. They had a story to write and they would make sure they beat all their competitors in writing it.

Before I knew it, the gallery had cleared out. It was just me, Jacob, Christian, Esme, the prosecutors, the jury, and the judge. The judge looked like he would blow a gasket himself.

"Mr. Atwood, do you have any questions for this witness?" he asked.

Brent shook his head. "No. And, in light of the testimony of Mr. Whitmore, or should I say Mr. McNeil, the state would like to dismiss all charges against Esmerelda Gutierrez. With prejudice."

"So noted," Judge Warner said. "Please file your dismissal as soon as possible. Ms. Gutierrez, you are free to go. I'm very sorry you had to go through this. I hope you can put this behind you and go on with your life. Court is adjourned." Then he turned to "Jacob." "Oh, and Mr. McNeil, you are excused. However, in light of your testimony, I would like the bailiffs to take you into custody." Then he nodded at the bailiffs, who came over to Jacob and put handcuffs on him.

I breathed a sigh of relief. It was over. It was really over. Thank God.

Chapter Forty-Five

LATER ON THAT NIGHT, I was having a beer on my balcony with Christian and Esme. Aidan was out on a date and the three of us were celebrating. We were laughing and joking and Esme was having the time of her life.

"Oh, Lord. That look on his face when you told him you knew he was really William McNeil. I thought he would have explosive diarrhea right there on the stand," she said, laughing.

"Who's to say he didn't?" I said. I was laughing even harder than Esme.

"You did it," said Christian. "I can't believe you pulled it off, but you did."

I shrugged. "He knew the jig was up when I asked him if he would be willing to give his fingerprint. He knew the FBI would be on his tail, and that, sooner or later, they would catch up with him and make him give his fingerprint. He couldn't worm out of it this time. Everybody's wise to his game by now. Ain't no way he'd get away with faking his death a second time. He figured he might as well just come clean."

It was then I noticed that my phone is ringing.

"Dude," Regina said. "I've been doing my investigation on who killed your friend, and you're not going to believe what I found."

Next in the Southern California Legal Thrillers Series

vinci-books.com/justice-delayed

Framed. Imprisoned. Now free and out for blood.

Avery Collins spent seven years behind bars for a murder she
didn't commit. Now she's hell-bent on exposing the truth and
making her enemies pay.

Turn the page for a free preview…

Justice Delayed: Chapter One

AVERY - MODERN DAY

I COULDN'T BELIEVE what I was hearing. Apparently, Regina had managed to track down at least some of the people responsible for putting me in prison all those years ago. Could it be true? After having spent seven years of my life on a hard cot, eating crappy food, and feeling in my heart all those years a sense of burning injustice, I would have my chance to maybe, just maybe, see that justice was done. As I spent all those years in prison, all that I could think about, day after day, was getting back at the people who did this to me.

Regina and I had made a date to meet at a restaurant in Imperial Beach, which was where Regina's condo was. SEA180 was an upscale beachfront restaurant with an enormous deck and fire pits all around. It was a cool evening, as September evenings sometimes were, especially close to the ocean. The temperature around the water tended to be about 10° cooler than the mainland as it was, and around October or November, the weather cooled off considerably. Especially at night. I remembered watching the girls in the movie *LaLa Land*, when they were going to the producer's party in little tiny dresses in the middle of December and thinking about how unrealistic that was. While the temperatures never got to a freezing point, as in other parts of the country during the wintertime, it certainly wasn't tiny dress weather.

But September tended to be a little bit warmer than it was tonight. Nevertheless, I found a seat on the deck. I made sure we had a fire pit in front of us, and I closed my eyes and listened to the water coming in. I had to calm myself a bit. What Regina was about to tell me would change my life. And, once she told me, what would I say? How would I approach it? I wanted to take everybody down, one by one. I wanted to burn each one of them at the stake. But I would have to go through this methodically. I certainly could not just pell-mell, willy-nilly stab each person in the back.

Regina met me at 8 o'clock. It was a little late for dinner, but she couldn't meet until that time. I passed the time waiting for her by sipping on a dirty martini made with Grey Goose vodka, my go-to cocktail when I was feeling out of sorts. My stomach was doing flip-flops.

She sat down across from me. "You want to get an appetizer?" she asked me. "I'm really in the mood for some raw oysters, for some reason."

I motioned to the seat right across from mine. "Oysters are fine," I said to her. "Now tell me what you found out."

Her green eyes were dancing. "Well, here's what I found. Do you know about the case of Jeffrey Epstein?" she asked.

I nodded. And when she said that name, I immediately flashed back to that day in the pool with Becky. The memory was vague, and it was something buried somewhere in my psyche. But I remembered her talking to me about a middle-aged man who was interested in her. In fact, she told me she had sex with this middle-aged man. "Yes. I do know the name of Jeffrey Epstein."

"So you know what that bastard was accused of doing, right? I mean, he's dead now, of course, but in life, do you know what he did? He was a sex trafficker. He got these young girls to service his wealthy and powerful friends." Regina shook her head, a disgusted look on her face. "It's disgusting. What that dude was doing, there should be the death penalty for that one. And you know how I feel about the death penalty."

I was surprised to hear Regina talking about the death penalty in that way. But I could see she was serious. She generally was very much against the state putting people to death because she'd witnessed an execution. Her father was shot and killed by a guy high on PCP. She saw her father's killer die by lethal injection. She told me she was against the death penalty after that point in time.

"I do know how you feel about the death penalty, and I'm surprised to hear you say something like that. What made you change your mind?"

She shook her head. "I'm just blowing off steam. But what he was doing was absolutely disgusting. Do you know Jeffrey Epstein was friends with both Bill Clinton and Donald Trump? And Prince Andrew. All of them are known dogs. So yeah, these guys were getting their freak on with young vulnerable girls."

I thought about what Regina was saying and I wondered if Becky was involved in something like that. I definitely wouldn't have been surprised if she was after what she told me by the pool that one day. "Are you saying Becky was involved in a ring like that?"

"That's what I'm saying. There's a house in Del Mar, high on a cliff, belongs to a dude named Carl Williams."

My heart started to race. I remembered Becky had talked to me about an older guy by the name of Carl. I also remembered she talked about visiting him out here in San Diego. She told me he had big parties out here and she was hoping to meet men through him who would help her break into the movie industry.

At the time, I thought it was odd that her parents allowed her to visit him out here from her home in Kansas City. But her parents were extremely permissive. Too permissive. And she did fly out and visit him just about every weekend.

What was she doing during those weekends?

"Carl Williams. Who is he? What does he do?"

"Near as I can tell, the guy don't do shit. I mean, he does, but he makes his money off other people. It's not like he's actually contributing to the country. He manages some hedge fund for a lot of other billionaires. He doesn't create anything, he doesn't employ anybody, all he does is manage a lot of investments. And, apparently, he makes quite a lot of money off his sex trafficking ring as well. He gets a lot of money from his rich friends to kiddy diddle these young girls. And, when I say young girls, I mean young girls. We're talking 14 years old, and the oldest girls apparently are 17. I have no idea why these rich fucks like to get with these young girls, but apparently they do."

I took a sip of my dirty martini as I thought about what she was telling me. This Carl guy, he must've had Becky as part of his stable of girls. I wondered if Carl himself was the person responsible for Becky dying. If he was, what could I do? I would have to get some kind of evidence against him, but that seemed impossible at this point. Becky was murdered 20 years ago. I knew there was DNA evidence and evidence that she was raped, but the DNA was never matched up with anybody. That was the problem with DNA evidence – it only works to incriminate somebody if their DNA was already on file somewhere. In this case, apparently the person who had raped Becky had not been arrested before raping her, so his DNA wasn't on file. If he had been arrested before raping her, we probably would've already had him nailed to the wall.

"And what are you going to do? Also, how did you find out about this Carl Williams guy and what he was doing?"

She smiled. "I still know my girls. The girls from the street. I'm still in touch with all of them, at least the ones who are still alive."

She looked sad when she said that last line. I knew Regina had lost quite a few friends along the way. That was the perils of the street - you don't always last very long.

"And who told you about Carl and what he was doing?"

"There's this girl, name's Jean. I don't know if that's her real name, but that's the name that she goes by. Jean. She's one of the lucky ones who got out of the game. She's working as a dental assistant. It's kind of embarrassing for her, as some of her old johns come into see her dentist from time to time, and they both kind of pretend they don't know each other. Anyhow, I've been talking to the girls on the street. I've been taking your friend's picture around to them, asking them if they know her. Listen, when you told me a rich bastard was possibly behind Becky's murder, the first thing I thought about was sex trafficking. I've known far too many rich guys who get into all kinds of kinky stuff and far too many rich guys who get into young girls. So I knew that if I talked to all the girls I know in the business or were in the business, I could figure it out. And, well, Jean knows Becky. Or she knew her."

I nodded. "How old is Jean?"

Regina shrugged her shoulders. "I don't know, but I would guess she's probably around our age. Around 35. It's kinda hard to know how old she is, but that's how old she looks. She's had a hard life, so she's a little bit beat up, but she's had work done, so she's not so bad off. Anyhow, I talked to her. She knew Becky. She told me she knew Becky through the sex ring she used to work. She told me about the parties this Carl Williams would have, she told me about the girls they used, everything. I asked her if she would ever go to the police and tell them what she knew, but she told me she would never do that."

"Why not?" I knew the answer to that, but I wondered what Jean told Regina.

"She said she was scared, but I think it was something more than that. I think she told me that Carl and all of his friends had what they call immunity from prosecution. In other words, they all think they're above the law, and maybe they are. Jean said they own the prosecutor's office and own the cops as well. Apparently, Carl has all of the prosecutor's office and the cops on his payroll."

Again, I knew what Regina was talking about. Those rich fucks do tend to be above the law because they owned too many people in law enforcement.

"Go on," I said.

Regina nodded. "Jean told me that Carl has a long list of people he can blackmail to ensure he stays out of trouble. He hides video cameras all over his place. And every time a guy comes into the place and finds a girl and bangs her, it's all captured on video. And we're talking thousands of guys over the years. All of these guys have relatives who care about them. For whatever reason. And some of the guys who partake in the festivities are prosecutors themselves. And cops. So because of this practice of videotaping everybody, he's got the goods on a lot of people in the prosecutor's office and in the police force. So, in other words, if he can't bribe them, he blackmails them. So Jean told me it was pointless to go to the cops to ask to press charges against Carl and his friends because she knew nothing would ever come of it."

"I mean, think about it," Regina continued. "This house in Del Mar has been the site of all these shenanigans for all these years, and nobody has ever heard about it. Why do you think that is? Why do you think the cops haven't busted in the door by now? It seems like this guy Carl is airtight. As Jean said, he's immune from prosecution. And not in a good way."

The waiter came around and brought Regina and me some chilled oysters on a silver platter. I took one, swallowed it with some cocktail sauce, and then took a sip of my dirty martini. "Immune from prosecution. Immune from prosecution." The term "immunity from prosecution" usually meant the person literally had some kind of recognized immunity. Like, for instance, ambassadors from other countries had diplomatic immunity. That meant they could commit a crime while on American soil, but if they committed the crime while in their role of a diplomat, they were not to be prosecuted. But most people weren't above the law.

Most people weren't. However, I knew the world we lived in, and I knew that you could get out of anything if you had enough money. Apparently, this Carl Williams also knew this.

"Do you think Carl was behind Becky's murder?"

Regina sat back in her chair and took a bite of her olive. She, like me, enjoyed her dirty martinis. "I haven't gotten that far. However, I think I'm on the right track. After all, that kid, that Brad Whitmore kid, told you the person responsible for her murder was extremely wealthy. Carl fits the bill and he was involved with Becky. He's also involved in a sex trafficking ring. He's looking pretty good for Becky's murder. Then again, I have no proof of anything. I don't even have proof he has a sex trafficking ring going on. I'm going to have to do a little bit of homework on this entire matter."

"What kind of homework?"

"Undercover work. It's something I haven't done before, but something I'd like to do. Listen, you have to remember one thing – I was a sex worker. I know the lines, I know the moves, and I know the johns. I know their psychology better than any shrink. I could possibly go to this Carl guy and hit him up for a job. I don't think he'd actually hire me to be one of the girls in his stable. Because, like I said before, they like very young girls in this ring. I'm obviously not a very young girl. But Jean told me this Carl guy was always looking for an older girl to be a mother figure for the younger ones. Carl apparently has about 10 live-in girls. He still might. Mainly, the girls don't live there with him – some of the girls he got from rich people would still be living with their parents, but they'd visit Carl and his buddies while telling their parents they're going out for the night with their girlfriends or whatever."

"So most of the girls were day players, so to speak. But he has girls who live there with him too?"

She nodded. "Yes. We're talking about the runaways. He finds girls off the streets, or, rather, he'd recruit them off the streets. And that's where I come in. Maybe. My plan is to go to this Carl person and try to find a job with him. He can hire me to maybe recruit the girls or to be the house mother, or maybe even to do both. Jean told me he has women doing both jobs a lot of the time. If I can convince Carl I'm his girl, his house mother, I'm in. Once I'm in, I know exactly how to do my investigation. I know how to talk to the girls and I know how to cover my tracks. Not only that, I can figure out what the vulnerabilities are in his security system. If I could possibly get Christian to hack into this dude's files, we're golden."

I thought about what she was saying. It made a lot of sense. And I knew she'd do a good job. I also knew one other thing – Regina was drop-dead gorgeous. Olive skin, dark hair, light green eyes that were so bright they could probably be seen in the dark. Her body was perfect – gorgeous breasts, slim waist, tight legs and butt. She wasn't anybody who would flaunt her gorgeousness. She pretty much dressed down in jeans and T-shirts, her thick dark hair usually up in a ponytail, her face usually unadorned of makeup. But I knew that if she really put her mind to it that she could easily make herself beautiful enough that this Carl person would hire her in a flash. Especially if she told him about her background and how she knew how to recruit people, how she knew how to find a vulnerable girl, and how she knew how to take care of young girls. Regina told me this was something she had some experience with, as her boyfriend/pimp, Michael, often had her do this for him. He had her go to bus stations and airports, but especially bus stations, to look for girls who looked lost and frightened and possibly were runaways. That was one thing she felt shamed about – finding young women for Michael's stable.

I wondered if it could work. And even if it could work,

who was to say Regina could find enough proof to show Carl was behind Becky's murder? It made sense that he was behind it somehow because he had the power and influence to make sure everybody involved in this case would dance to his tune. But how would we ever prove it? That was the thing.

I chewed on my bottom lip as I thought about my dilemma. Regina was telling me something a part of me already knew. I wanted her to go with her plan. I would try very hard to find some kind of proof this Carl was behind murdering Becky. But if I couldn't, maybe there would be some other way to bring him down.

In fact, I knew there would be a way to bring him down. The prosecutor's office was completely dirty, so there would be no way in hell they would ever move against this guy. The cops were also dirty, so they, too, refused to do anything against him. Even if all that was true, I could still bring this bastard to justice. It might not be perfect justice. Perfect justice, in this case, would mean Carl would end up in an orange jumpsuit for the rest of his life, and, as a sex offender, specifically a child rapist, he would definitely experience the worst kind of treatment in prison. But I knew this might not happen.

However, even if it didn't happen, there was another way I could bring him down. It involved the legal system, and it involved Regina doing her job well enough to convince at least a few of the girls to turn against Carl. If she could do that, we would be on our way. I wouldn't even need the cooperation of the prosecutors, the cops, or anybody else.

"When are you going to see this Carl, and how are you going to approach him? I mean, I'm assuming this Jean person, since she's now working in a dentist's office, probably doesn't have a line to Carl anymore. I assume Carl's activities are underground, to say the very least. He can't just trust anybody off the street. I mean, what you gonna do, just go to his house, knock on the door, and ask him for a job? That'll never work."

"Of course, that won't work. Listen, I have contacts everywhere. Not just on the street, but I have other contacts that will help me out in this situation. I've got people who can vouch for me to Carl. I'm just going to have to hit up my contacts and call in a few favors. There are quite a few people who owe me a favor. It's just a matter of finding the right person who knows Carl and has his ear."

"And who are you thinking about?"

She nodded. "Listen, I've been doing my homework on this Carl person. And I do know one thing – he doesn't just hang out with other rich dudes like him. I mean, he hangs out with other rich dudes, but some of those rich dudes who hang out with him aren't exactly managing hedge funds themselves. Some of the guys who hang out there are CEOs, politicians, athletes and actors. People with a respectable job by day, and by night, want to get their freak on with a very young girl. But I also found out that some of the rich dudes who hang out with Carl are guys in the industry, just like Carl, but not quite as savory. If you know what I mean."

I knew exactly what Regina meant. Organized crime. "Who are you talking about? Russians, Albanians, Armenians, Mexicans?" I knew the Italian Mafia wasn't very strong in Southern California. In fact, the Italian Mafia wasn't that strong west of Las Vegas. But in Southern California, other ethnic groups certainly ran rampant.

"I know a guy by the name of Sergei Popov. And I've talked to him. He's a friend of mine. I asked him about

Carl's ring and he told me he wants to meet with me tomorrow night. It sounds like he knows something about it, probably knows people involved in it. I don't know, but I'm hoping he can lead me to somebody who can get me into Carl's inner circle."

When she was talking, I started feeling a sense of hope. I felt like there was a chance to finally get some closure on everything that happened and finally get a measure of justice. It was just a matter of Regina finding out what she needed to find out and then hopefully put the pieces together.

"Listen, Regina, you be careful." While Regina was street-wise, I didn't know if she was used to infiltrating such a high-level world as what she was volunteering to do for me. I knew that people, when they go undercover, were taking their lives into their own hands. If anything happened to Regina because she was working for me, I could never forgive myself.

"Trust me, I got this. I've worked with much more dangerous people than Sergei Popov and his entire creepy clan. I'll be careful, but really, it's not necessary to say that."

I had a wrap in my purse, and I brought it out and wrapped it around my shoulders. I put my feet up on the edge of the fire ring and leaned back. It was a perfect evening for a glass of wine and relaxation. My big trial was over, Esme Gutierrez was a free woman, and there was the possibility that Regina could bring this whole thing home.

At that moment, life was good.

Tomorrow, it might be a different story. But for tonight, I was content to just listen to the sounds of the ocean rolling in and out while I sat on the patio of a luxury restaurant.

Justice Delayed: Chapter Two

REGINA

REGINA KNEW what she had to do. It wasn't anything that she looked forward to, yet she knew that if wanted into the inner circle of Carl Williams, she would have to go back to her sex worker days. She had the muscle memory for it. It would be just like riding a bike. Yet she didn't want to sell her body. And she certainly didn't want to do what she would have to, which was to go out on the streets and find young girls. Her plan was to help Avery with what the two of them had talked about at the restaurant the night before – Regina was to find these girls and use them to testify against Carl in a court of law.

Regina needed to help Avery find victims in Carl's circle, talk to them in a way only she could, and see what they could do as far as suing Carl. Avery would also do what she could about going to the prosecutor's office and the police and see if they'd be interested in prosecuting these people. But Regina and Avery both held out little hope that such a move would go anywhere. Carl was just too powerful and he had too many people in his pocket for the two of them to have any hope these people would do the right thing. So it was up to Avery to financially bring this entire thing down.

It wouldn't be just the fact that these girls would be suing this bastard, but also the media attention surrounding such a sensational lawsuit would be devastating to Carl. It was all a matter of finding enough girls willing to go against him. And also to be mindful of the statute of limitations, which was two years for sexual misconduct. The advantage in this case, however, was that the victims were minors. They would almost all be under the age of 18, which meant the statute of limitations didn't start running for them.

At the same time, Regina wasn't sure that Carl was behind Becky's murder. She only knew that he was behind exploiting her. And she had a good feeling that, no matter what, the fact that Becky was being exploited was, in the end, the cause of her being killed. She also had a strong feeling that Carl had to have been behind the murder in some way because he would've been powerful enough to have corrupted the prosecutor. She'd already gone through the records on what happened with Becky's case, and she knew exactly why her friend was convicted for her murder.

The prosecutor in that case was a guy by the name of Paul Sharpton. She already had Christian hack his bank records for the period of time when he was apparently on the take from Carl. Christian couldn't find any kind of large transfer from Carl to Paul. Christian combed through all the bank transactions and came up empty.

Regina had to figure that one out too. Why was Paul so willing to make sure that Avery was convicted for the murder of Becky if he wasn't being bribed to do so? Regina figured it was something else. She knew that when corruption happened, it usually happened for one of two reasons.

Either the corrupted person was being bribed or being blackmailed. In her experience, the second scenario was much more powerful. The first scenario was powerful for greedy people. But to be greedy enough to send an innocent girl to prison for the rest of her life, that took a special kind of sociopath. Only a person without a conscience could do such a thing for money.

But, if it was a blackmail situation, all bets were off. People had a survival instinct. If they were presented with the choice between their life, or exposure of something they did, or exposure of something that someone they loved did, and the life of another, they were going to choose self-preservation every time.

Every time.

So that was something Regina would have to figure out. Exactly why Paul Sharpton did what he did. And if she could figure that out, what his big secret was, she could expose him. And if she could expose him, that would be another way Avery could get some justice on what happened to her. Because, in the end, although Regina could understand the need to self preserve, that didn't excuse what he did. Nothing could ever excuse him withholding crucial evidence from the court in the case.

There was something else unusual about Paul Sharpton. After Avery's murder case, he moved from Kansas City to San Diego. He'd been in the San Diego County prosecutor's office for the past 20 years or so. Other than the fact that his presence in the prosecutor's office made Avery sick every time he was on the other side of one of her case's, Regina wondered if Paul's move was significant in some way.

Regina also suspected that Gloria Flores, Avery's public defender, was dirty. She'd reviewed the file carefully and if

Gloria wasn't dirty, she was spectacularly incompetent. One or the other. She suspected corruption on Gloria's part as well, however.

She would do what she could to make sure everybody went down for Avery's imprisonment. Starting with Carl.

She made a date with Sergei for that night. Sergei was a very attractive Russian man, a Boyevik in a Russian clan by the name of Ivanov. The Ivanov clan ruled Southern California. They were into trafficking, drug dealing, extortion, gun running and illegal gambling. As a Boyevik, which was the equivalent of a soldier in the Italian Mafia, Sergei was responsible for trafficking women for the Ivanov clan. He wasn't involved in Carl's circle, however, as Carl strictly dealt with underaged girls and Sergei was only into trafficking women who weren't underaged. He concentrated on women between the ages of 21 and 25, recruiting them for an underground high-class nightclub in a nondescript building by the Embarcadero, right across from where the cruise ships docked on the waterfront. Regina had visited this club, mainly because she was curious, and before she got a job as a private investigator for Avery, she thought she might end up working at just such a club.

The reason why this club was underground and not an out and proud strip club, such as the clubs that dotted boulevards all over the San Diego area, from Point Loma to Miramar, was that it was a front for a prostitution ring. Strip clubs generally had neon signs that advertised the wares within. Some of the clubs featured fully nude dancers and their websites advertised exactly that.

But the club the Ivanov family ran was a different beast altogether. This was a very exclusive club, as members paid $1000 and up per month to belong. And the reason for this was simple – the girls were providing not just a show for the gentlemen who frequented the club, but the girls on display could also be bought. The club featured a number of various rooms where men could indulge their every fantasy. For instance, for men who were into bondage and discipline, there was a room outfitted with an enormous St. Andrew's cross as well as a whipping post, chains, leather suits, anything a well-heeled gentleman would desire. There was an orgy room which was just as it sounded – it was a room where groups of people would get together and have sex. There were a variety of other rooms that attracted men just looking to have a good time but were into a more vanilla variety of a sexual experience.

The girls would dance for the men in the main part of the building, most of them completely nude, and if a man desired a more intimate encounter with any one woman, he was entitled to that. With his membership, he was entitled to one free encounter every month. After that, he had to pay by the hour. The fees ranged from $500 per hour for a vanilla encounter, all the way up to $2000 per hour for an encounter that involved humiliating and degrading the woman he chose. The girls got a certain percentage of the fees these men paid, generally 30%, and the house kept the rest.

Regina's feminist instincts were appalled by such an arrangement. As far as she was concerned, if a girl agreed to be humiliated, which sometimes involved literally getting pissed or defecated on, she was certainly entitled to more than $600 per hour, which was what she got from the house while the Ivanovs took the rest of the $2000 per hour. For something like that, Regina would certainly demand more than $600 per hour.

But she wouldn't lecture anybody about their business practices. It wasn't her affair.

Sergei found the women who worked in this particular club. The women who worked in the club ranged from women who were bored housewives who worked the day shift while the kids were in school to professionals who had been in the business for years to college students working on their master's degrees. Because every woman in this club was older than 21, Sergei didn't try to recruit undergrads unless they were in their senior year.

It was important that the girls were 21 and clean because this was the understanding the police had about this club. Regina knew that Yuri Ivanov, the Pakhan of the Ivanov clan, which meant he was the head of it, had an arrangement with the police force in the San Diego area. For this particular club, the cops got 20% of the club's gross in exchange for not raiding the place. But the private agreement between Yuri and the police force was that the girls had to be at least 21. The reason for that was pretty simple, really. Girls older than 21 knew what they were getting into and weren't being exploited.

On the other hand, if the girls were not of age, that would be a problem. Younger girls were ripe for being exploited. Regina knew that in order to find younger girls, they couldn't fish from the same pool as the Ivanov club did. They couldn't find the bored housewives, the girls working on their PhDs, the long time professionals, the models trying to make it. No. With the younger girls, the trafficking generally involved either kidnapping, nabbing runaways, or, as in Regina's case, finding girls with difficult home lives who were looking to get out.

In other words, when you go younger, it necessarily involved exploitation. And that, apparently, was a bridge too far for the police force. They didn't agree to lay off of the Ivanov club if any of the girls were under the age of 21.

Therefore, Sergei was very careful about checking their IDs and if anybody didn't check out, she wasn't offered a position there.

Regina, in a way, didn't mind what Sergei did for the Ivanov clan. She was of the mindset that when you are free, white, and 21 - so to speak, as the girls who worked these clubs were from every walk of life and every ethnic background - the girls were free to do as they pleased. They were paid well for what they did, they walked into the club with their eyes opened, nobody was forcing them, and they generally were not vulnerable to exploitation.

Sergei arrived at the restaurant. The Gaslamp Strip Club, where they agreed to meet, was a steakhouse in the Gaslamp District of San Diego. The restaurant was a perfect blend of old and new. The walls were composed of exposed brick and the ceilings were a good 30 feet high. Black leather circular booths surrounding red tables lined up along a glass wall, giving the place a retro feel, while the tables in the middle of the hard-wood floor restaurant were composed of light wood with white chairs that sported rectangular backs with a hole cut in the middle of them. The bar was a typical bar, but the chandeliers were in the shape of enormous snowflakes. The chandeliers looked almost like a mobile, with uneven spokes coming out in the middle of the chandelier, and each spoke had a small light on the end of it. The menu at this place was that of a typical steakhouse and the prices ranged from $18 for a skirt steak to $30 for a 20 ounce porterhouse steak. All sides were extra, three for $19.

This place was a tad fancy for Regina. She was a burger and fries girl - In 'n' Out was her favorite restaurant. When she couldn't get into In 'n' Out, which was often the case, as their lines were hellacious, her second favorite place was

Five Guys Burger and Fries, and when she was feeling particularly fancy, she might go to the Burger Lounge in the Hillcrest area. The fries with the ranch dressing there were to die for.

But this place - she had to dress up a little. That was one thing she didn't like to do. Just as she preferred burgers and fries to overpriced steaks, she preferred jeans and T-shirts to dresses and heels. But she also knew that Sergei, even though he was nothing but a soldier in his organization, was a classy guy. He was the kind of guy who liked dark jazz clubs instead of loud nightclubs, telling Regina that she hadn't lived until she saw Esperanza Spalding or Gregory Porter performing live. He liked his martinis dry and neat, his steaks medium rare, and his women in tiny black dresses with cleavage.

She shifted in her seat and looked around. As usual, she saw admiring glances from men around the room. Not that she cared about that because she didn't. Men weren't on her agenda and never were. After all, she'd never had a good encounter with one. From her mother's boyfriends who hit on her, one of whom raped her, to Michael, who beat and exploited her, her experiences with men hadn't been positive.

Men were people she could utilize and that was that.

Sergei finally arrived at the restaurant. Sergei was tall and fit, about 6'3", with sandy blonde hair and big blue eyes. His face was angular with a strong jaw line and a perfect Roman nose. With his bow-shaped lips and light blue eyes, he almost resembled a young Paul Newman, albeit much taller than Paul Newman. With his enormous dimples and thousand watt smile, Sergei was quite the head turner himself. If Regina was inclined to date anybody, she would probably date a guy like Sergei. Yes he was involved in some unsavory business with the Ivanov club. Yet he wasn't a sex trafficker, per se, but, rather, he was a guy who knew how to talk women into working for this club. Of all the jobs he could've done for the Ivanov family, his was the least objectionable.

He saw her and made a beeline for the table she was sitting. She stood up and gave Sergei a purposeful and sincere hug. "Sergei, dude, what's going on?" she asked him as he hugged her.

He laughed at her calling him "dude." "Well, chick, I was wondering the same thing. When you called me, I got very excited." He nodded as he looked Regina over. "You know, Regina, the girls at my club age out at the age of 25. But I could certainly make an exception for you. You've kept yourself up beautifully."As he said that, he was staring at her legs and her ass, both of which were firm from running 6 miles a day. And then he started staring at her cleavage, natural double D's perched above an enviable tiny waist.

She laughed. "No thank you. I'm out of the biz." She took a sip of her Bloody Mary, a perfect blend of Keitel One vodka, tomato juice, black pepper, Tabasco sauce and other secret ingredients she couldn't place. "But I'm in real trouble. I got gambling debts. I got a marker at a casino in Vegas, I'm not going to tell you which one, so don't ask me, but I got a marker. I got some Italian goombahs who have my number. If I want to live to see Christmas, I got to make some serious cash fast." This was the story she and Avery had cooked up to show why Regina would want to work for Carl. Sergei knew Regina was an investigator so he would naturally be suspicious if Regina asked to work for Carl. However, if she told him she had serious financial issues, so serious that she might lose her life because of them, it would almost make sense for her to work for Carl.

Sergei nodded. "Okay. So, you want to work for the Ivanov club, yes? Like I say, the girls age out at 25, but I would make an exception for a woman who looks like you. I think you may be very popular in that club."

She leaned forward, giving Sergei a good look at her large and surprisingly perky rack. She would have to seduce him in order for him to say yes. That turned her stomach because she hated manipulating men or anybody else, but it had to be done. He leaned forward as well, giving her a whiff of the cardamom, cinnamon, and absinthe in his high-dollar cologne.

"No. I don't want to work for that club," Regina said. "I'm interested in Carl Williams."

Sergei started to laugh. "Carl Williams? Regina, you could certainly pass for 25, so you could work for the Ivanov club, but, I'm sorry, with those breasts, no way you would be able to pass for under the age of 17. Nice try though."

Regina sighed. Did he really think she was going to try to pass for a child? How stupid did he think she was? She wanted to say, *no idiot, I'm talking about becoming a house mother.* But she decided to keep her calm. "No. I want to become one of the girl's house mothers. I know there's always about 20 girls living at the Williams compound and I know there is at least one house mother. Somebody who makes the girls feel comfortable, somebody they could look up to, and somebody who can gain the trust of runaway girls. I know Carl employs women for that role." It was important the house have a designated house mother, because, without one, the girls in the house tended to leave. They needed somebody to be their mother figure, because most of them didn't have a mother figure at their home, which was why they went to work for Carl in the first place. They hungered for an older woman to guide them.

Sergei shook his head. "Carl already has one of those. A house mother." Then he looked at her. "But you know, Regina, if I told Carl that you would do other services for his clientele – some of them want a real woman along with their children – he probably would hire you."

Regina sighed. Was this how it would be? Would she have to use herself as bait? She didn't know if she could go through with this. But then again, it was important that she do all she could to bring down this hell house.

She leaned back in her chair, thinking about how her feet hurt. *I can't wait to get home and get into a bathtub and take these damn shoes off.* How did women wear these shoes every day? If she lived to be 100, she would never understand why women put themselves through such agony just for fashion. She surreptitiously dangled one of the shoes off her feet and rubbed the arch.

Sergei was still watching her, an amused look on his face. "So should I tell Carl that you'll entertain his clients if he needs you to?"

Regina knew this might be the only way she could get this job. "Yeah. Tell him that." She would just have to find a way to get out of it once push came to shove because she wasn't doing it any more. Her days of being a sex worker were behind her and that was how she wanted it.

The waiter came around, refreshed both their drinks, and took their orders. Regina got the filet mignon with a baked potato and salad, while Sergei got the porterhouse with fries and the white truffle mac & cheese. Regina heard him ordering the white truffle mac & cheese, thought that sounded good, and changed her order from a salad to that. She wasn't on a diet, so why not live?

Sergei leaned forward giving her another whiff of his high-dollar cologne. "So, after this, you want to go to a smoky jazz club? Seven Grand is the place I like to hang out, but maybe you'd like to invite me to your place. Or maybe we can go to my place? My condo is on the water-front. I think you'd love it."

Regina would have to take a rain check on that. She didn't want him to get the wrong idea about what she was after. At the same time, she didn't want to insult him because she needed him. Without him serving as the link between her and Yuri, there was no way she could get a job in the Carl Williams circle. She would have to finesse it deli-cately, to say the very least.

"Let's just keep this friendly, okay? Sorry, man, I don't like to shit where I sleep."

She could tell that Sergei, being from Russia, wasn't familiar with that particular colloquialism. "What you mean, you don't like to shit where you sleep?"

"I mean I keep my business contacts strictly business, and my personal contacts strictly personal. You're a business relationship for me. Sorry, I don't want to bring sex into it."

She hoped that was good enough and he wasn't insulted by her turning him down. However, she could see in his face that wasn't the case. He looked disappointed, to say the very least. "I guess you don't want me to talk to Yuri after all, do you?"

She would have to throw something out there and hope that it did the trick. "Okay, the truth is I just don't like men." That wasn't really a lie. She didn't swing to women, although she had considered it a time or two in the past, but she also really didn't like men. At least, she didn't like men in the romantic sense. She had buddies, friends who were guys. A lot of guy friends. But that was as far as it went.

At first, Sergei looked stunned. Then he shook his head. "Oh, what a waste that is. To each his own, I guess." Then he got a wicked look on his face. "Or maybe I could watch some time?"

Don't push your luck, buddy. She decided to change the subject. That was just the easiest thing to do. "So, you seen any good movies lately?"

He got the hint. But she was still unsure that he would go to bat for her. She hoped he would but was shutting the whole romantic situation down, so she had no idea.

She just had to wait and see.

Grab your copy...
vinci-books.com/justice-delayed

About the Author

Rachel Sinclair was a criminal defense attorney for eleven years, so she doesn't scare easily. She graduated from the University of Missouri-Kansas City School of Law in 1998, and worked for the Public Defender's Office for several years before striking out on her own. She currently lives in San Diego, California, with her boyfriend, Joey, and her two fur babies, Annie and Toby. In her spare time, she likes to read, bicycle all over town, Boogie Board at the beach, and watch trashy television.